C000298799

KAREN WOODS

MANCHESTER

First published in 2016

EMPIRE PUBLICATIONS
1 Newton Street, Manchester M1 1HW
© Karen Woods 2016

ISBN: 978-1-909360-40-2

Printed in Great Britain.

In Memory of Johnny Orman, gone but not forgotten.

ACKNOWLEDGEMENTS

Thanks to all my friends and family; my children Ashley, Blake, Declan and Darcy. A big thanks to my mother Margaret, she works so hard and I'm forever thankful. A big thanks to James for all his support. Look out for my next novel called B-Wing out soon. Once again thank you so much to all my readers and followers on Facebook and twitter. You can find my website www.karenwoods.net

Big thanks to John and Ash at Empire Publications for their continued support.

Follow me on twitter – @karenwoods69

Thanks

Karen

CHAPTER ONE

ELSIE BARKER STOOD beneath the arches hidden away in the shadows. Her heart was pounding. She had to be quiet and remain completely still. The rain hammered against the pavement outside as if it was angry at her. She didn't have long before her time was up, before he was there demanding what she owed him. What the hell was she thinking, coming here alone? Everyone had told her but she wouldn't listen to them. It wasn't safe and she could have been taken out at any time. Monty had told her to be there though and she had to obey him. He was a force not to be messed with. A man with power, someone who could end her life at the drop of a hat. A black car crept past in the distance, its lights low, the driver's identity hidden behind the tinted windows. All she could hear was the sound of the engine ticking over like a rapid heartbeat in her ears. Elsie zipped her coat up tightly and banged her head against the cold brick wall behind her. Was it too late for her to change her mind and run as fast as she could and never come back here again? That's daft, he knew where she lived... He knew all her family and friends, nobody was safe. There was nothing he didn't know, nothing ever got past him. Monty wouldn't rest until he got what he wanted. Her heart leapt inside her mouth causing her windpipe to tighten and with every struggled breath she took one step forward and two steps back. This was serious, she was in danger.

The arches stank of cat piss. The strong aroma crippled her nostrils with every laboured breath she took. This was a dirty, seedy place. A hideout for people who had something to hide. Her eyes looked about the floor and she could see used condoms and needles. Big brown rats could be heard squeaking and rustling away trying to escape the bad weather. This was a hot-spot where brasses took their punters to give them what they wanted, usually anal or oral sex. The things they could never get from their wives, the guilty pleasures they would never dare ask for. It was Monty's idea to meet here, he always called the shots. He ruled her life, he always had. Elsie swallowed hard, as small droplets of sweat formed on her brow.

Holding the package tightly she closed her eyes, lips trembling. Think girl, think. Her heart was thumping inside her ribcage urging her to make a decision before time ran out. There was enough money here to change her life, to start again, to move away to another area where nobody knew her, to deal with her problem, to get rid of the child she was carrying. A new beginning, a fresh start. A life without any hassle. A life without him. But, what would she tell Monty? He didn't need the money, he just needed her. To control her, to tell her what to do, just like he'd always done. The clock was ticking, she didn't have long left. Dipping her head slowly outside, Elsie clocked his toned manly frame bouncing towards her. He was dressed in black. This was his favourite colour. It reminded him that death was only ever a whisper away. Monty kept his head low, not wanting to be spotted. Had he already seen her? Was it too late for her to get on her toes? Think girl think, a new life, a new start. No more pain, no more lies. A life without him and his sick twisted rules. Her mind was doing overtime as she heard the gravel crunching closer from outside, she could hear his struggled breathing, the rustling of his raincoat as he pounded the pavement towards her.

Looking one way and then the other she made her

choice, she had to go. Elsie had to leave here and never come back to this place ever again. This town was evil, it would destroy her in the end, break her in two and reveal the dark secrets that kept her awake most nights, sick twisted thoughts. Elsie had to do something and quick. Monty would kill her if he ever got his hands on her, stop her breathing, make her pay for the betrayal. Quickly, she shoved the package deep inside her jacket pocket and dipped into the shadows. Breathlessly, she raced from the scene and never looked back. Monty's chilling voice could be heard shouting her name in the distance. It was the voice that had ruled her life for as long as she could remember. His fierce tone sent shivers down her spine causing her stomach to churn. The hairs on the back of her neck stood on end as the rage in his voice bounced around the brickwork into her eardrums. "I'll find you Elsie Barker and when I do, your life won't be worth living."

CHAPTER TWO

JOHNNY BARKER LAY in his pad and sucked in the fresh air that was flowing inside his cell window. A gentle crisp breeze tickled his body. He'd spent so many nights in this room and he was counting the days until he was a free man again. Four and half years was a long time for any man to be without family or friends. Of course he got the odd visit from his mother and sister to start with but they were few and far between. Johnny was the apple of his mother's eye when he was younger and it broke her heart when he was sentenced. He was the man of the house and without him his family were sinking fast. Johnny's life had always been set in stone for him and from an early age he was mixed up in a life of crime and drugs in the area. It was just the way it was where he lived. Living on a council estate in North Manchester was hard enough for any child but his life was somewhat worse than any of theirs. He had to look after his family, put bread on the table. His mother Elsie did what she could to give her children a good life but something always seemed to happen to put a spanner in the works. Elsie had endless men in her life and none of them had ever stepped up to the mark to look after her and her family. Johnny had had so many uncles growing up with him that he'd just given up any hope that he would ever have a father and son bond with any man that walked through the front door.

His sister Annie was younger than him and he was her protector, well, he had been until he got locked up. Armed robbery carried a lengthy jail sentence and he knew that before he got involved but he was young and out to impress. Silly mistakes led to his arrest. Daft mistakes that could have been avoided. Johnny was violent too, he had to be to protect himself and the people he cared about. He would die for his loved ones. The scar on his left cheekbone showed everyone in this jail that he was a bit tapped in the head. Some inmates said he had a screw loose and perhaps they were right. When he saw the red mist in front of his eyes there was no stopping him, he was lethal. The jail sentence had broken him to start with but as time had gone by he learned how to cope. He trusted nobody and always kept his eye on the ball. Each convict was the same in the big house. Convicts would have you over at the blink of an eye; there was no shame, no morals, they'd do anything just to get by. This was a bad place and everyone slept with one eye open.

Johnny lay on his bed, he was edgy. He was reading the last letter from his mother. He studied every word she'd written trying to digest what she was trying to say to him. Elsie was like that, she never said things up front but always went round the houses. Usually, he would phone her after bang up but after yet another pad spin his small Nokia mobile phone had been uncovered by the screws and removed. He was gutted, the phone was his lifeline, his contact with the outside world. He got five days in the block and yet another three months added to his sentence for the phone. He didn't give a flying fuck though, it was water off a duck's back. He'd do the extra days standing on his head. And he told them that too, he was so hard-faced. What did he have to come to anyway, he'd lost it all. Johnny had been shipped out to nearly every jail across the country. No governor wanted him in their prison, he was a security risk and always up to no good. Johnny was stacking the cash in here too, he never wanted for anything. He was wise and organised the wing drops. Every parcel that come over the wall from the outside world he knew about. Nothing ever got past him and it never would. He'd fought long and hard for his name in this prison and he wasn't giving it up without a fight. Johnny had proved himself on his wing too and nobody messed with him.

Of course when new inmates landed in the jail he had to show them who was boss, new convicts were a bit wet behind their ears and often pushed his buttons. Whenever he put an order in for some extra tins of tuna everybody knew someone was getting whacked over their head. The last kid who challenged him was still nursing a broken nose and a black eye on the hospital wing. Johnny had half killed him. Just when the inmate thought he was safe, Johnny burst into his pad with four tins of tuna in a sock and pummelled him half to death with it. Everyone heard the screams and nobody budged. It was jail law now and nobody interfered when inmates had a beef with each other. Johnny had respect on his wing. And yes, he had wingmen who ran about for him but whenever the going got tough Johnny always stepped up and took control of the situation. He was the boss and nobody fucked with him. Everyone had mobile phones stashed in the jail it was just something that happened. Every arse-hole had a mobile phone shoved up it and it was a standing joke amongst the inmates. Bent screws were always out to make a quick few quid and if you had the money you could get yourself anything you wanted in the slammer. The 'circle of trust' it was called and only a few convicts knew who they could approach for the stuff they needed bringing into the jail.

Johnny scratched his head as he read the letter again. Something was going on at home that his mother wasn't telling him. He was sure of it. She'd told him she was with a man and she was happy, but the letter was badly written and he just couldn't understand it. Elsie was always like that, he would see her every weekend for months then nothing for ages, she'd just stop coming in the end and nobody knew where she was. The last he heard was that his sister Annie was living with his auntie June and his mother was on her toes again. Elsie always attracted trouble, wherever she was in life, trouble just followed her. Before he was sentenced Johnny had sorted his mother out with some money and told her to look after the family. He knew it was a big ask and knew in his heart that the money would have been spent on her nightlife and the cocaine she shoved up her nose whenever she got the chance.

Johnny checked his watch and jumped from his bed. It was nearly visiting time and he had to make sure he looked good for when his sister and Auntie came to see him. June hadn't been to see him in ages and he was sure they had something to tell him because why else would they travel all the way up to Preston from Manchester? Nothing was making sense anymore and his head was done in. That was the thing about being banged up, it gave convicts time to think, to over analyse stuff, to put two and two together and come up with five. Johnny stood in his cell and stretched his hands above his head. It was time for a quick pad workout, pump his muscles, feel the adrenalin rushing through his veins. Johnny had a look about him too; handsome with a chiselled chin and raven hair. He had the deepest blue eyes anyone had ever seen. Elsie had always told him he looked the ringer of his father but as of yet Johnny had never met him. The press-ups session began. The sweat was pumping from his lean torso, every muscle was toned and on point. Gasping, growling, he was putting his heart and soul into this session. He had so much anger trapped inside him, lots of anger that needed to come out.

June and Annie sat in the visitors centre that was a stone's throw away from the jail. June kept watching the clock on the wall and shaking her head in frustration. "Fuck me, the visit is for half past two, what the hell are they playing at?"

Annie smiled softly at her and covered her mouth with her hand hiding her amusement. "It's probably another roll call. They did this last time I were here. They count all the prisoners and if anyone is missing nobody is allowed in or out of the jail. It's on lockdown."

"Well, it's a load of shit if you ask me. How bleeding hard is it to count people. I mean, it's not rocket science is it?" Annie sniggered and shot her eyes over to the window at the back of the room. The prison looked daunting. Prison life had always intrigued her and every time she came here she always asked hundreds of questions. The thought of the bad boys inside the jail stirred an interest deep inside her. Every girl loved a bad boy and Annie Barker was just like her mother when it came to men, she loved the fear and excitement these convicts could bring to her life. She loved a guy with money too, she craved the finer things in life. Annie was seventeen years old and full of attitude. Her mother's absence had seen to that. For as long as she could remember she'd been dragged from pillar to post and never really had a place to call home. They never settled anywhere for long. Just as she got used to a new home her mother did a moonlight flit again. Annie had endless babysitters when she was growing up. It was no environment for any child to live in. She was a car crash waiting to happen. However Auntie June was the polar opposite of her sister. While she wasn't blessed with good looks like Elsie, June's guilty pleasure was food, she was a big comfort eater. If any stress came into her life her head was in the fridge looking for something to rustle up. She showed love by feeding people too, anyone who came to her house she was always cooking for them or forcing cakes and chocolate into their mouths. June was a caring person and always there to lend a helping hand, especially to her sister and her children. Over the years June had seen Elsie on her knees begging for help, she never let her down once, she never turned her away. June was a problem solver and always saw the light at the end of any tunnel.

At last Johnny's name was called out for his visit. "Johnny Barker's visitors, please make your way over to the prison. Can you all check you have no mobile phones on you or any other illegal items on your person before you enter the jail," the female screw ranted. June snarled over at her and barged her way past the other visitors. The time was ticking and she needed to see her nephew before she did anything else. Lots of people stood hovering in the visitor's centre. It was like a stampede every time an inmate's name was called. Visitors sprinted out of the doors across to the prison so they could get inside the jail first and spend as much time as possible with their loved ones. Annie was in no mood to rush today, she had the hangover from hell. Usually she would be still in bed at this time after a Friday night drinking session with her friends. Johnny never knew this though, he thought she was a good girl. She liked it that way too, she was cunning and knew if her brother got wind of it, he would put a stop to it at the drop of a hat.

"Move it then slug," June shouted behind her.

Annie blew a laboured breath and picked up speed. "There's no rush, you're as bad as this lot, just chill will you?"

"I'll bleeding chill you lady, move your arse before I move it for you!"

Annie plodded over to the jail and formed a queue behind the other people stood there. Annie clocked a woman stood in front of her and examined every inch of her. The woman was in her mid-thirties. A classy woman she was, Jimmy Choo shoes and long blonde hair that was curled neatly at the ends. Even the make-up the woman was wearing was perfect and Annie stood admiring her. It was all about the money in this life and the man you bedded. Annie knew even now at this early age that she wasn't ever going to get anywhere in life on her own. She needed a powerful man behind her, someone who could give her everything she wanted and the life she was desperate to lead. A lot of her friends were like that too. Rita who was her close friend had already bagged herself a sugar daddy. It was their secret and if anyone would have got wind of it, the man would have gone to jail for having underage sex. Rita had everything she needed and Annie was jealous. New clothes, top of the range mobile phone, Rita had it all. June dug deep in her pocket and pulled out her loose change. No notes were allowed inside the prison and only coins could be used to buy the inmates a drink and some chocolate. Annie stood reading the notices on the wall. There was a paper cutting about a woman getting three years in jail for trying to smuggle a mobile phone into the jail. Annie moved closer to it and she was fascinated by what really went on inside the jail. June walked through security and stood getting searched. She had a face like thunder and hated the rigmarole of what visitors had to go through to get inside the jail. Each and every one of them were treated like a criminal, it wasn't fair, it was degrading. Annie stood for her search and the female screw was taking longer than expected. She made Annie take her neatly clipped hair out and shake it about. June stood watching this from the side and couldn't wait to voice her opinion. This was a liberty and she was having none of it.

"Bleeding hell love, you're going a bit over the top aren't you, what do you think she's got inside her hair a pissing microwave or something?" A few people who were stood by started chuckling. This was just another day in prison life and part of the process the security team had to go through each day in their job.

"It's what we have to do. You'd be surprised what we have found in people's hair. I'm just doing my job," the warden replied.

Annie was aware that June was ready for a full blown argument and she shot her a look and clenched her teeth tightly together. June backed down and licked her lips slowly. She just couldn't walk away, she had to have the last word. "It's well over the top if you ask me." The female guard just growled at June. It had been a long day and she just wanted to finish her shift without any further bother. She always got the rotten end of the stick and sometimes she had nothing left to give by the time she clocked off, the job was draining. A case of different day, same old shit. Annie picked her clips up from the small bowl at the side of her and shoved them quickly back into her hair. Her crowning glory was the same colour as her brothers. The people who knew her had always thought that they had the same father but according to Elsie, Annie's father was a big name in Salford and she had a bit of foreign blood running through her veins. It was bullshit though, there was nothing foreign looking about Annie it was just her mother trying to create a perfect world for her daughter.

June struggled to climb the flight of stairs. She was overweight and a heavy smoker and this didn't help. Every stair she climbed she was gasping for breath. Annie was clocking the other visitors as they sat down now in the waiting room. She wondered if any of them were bringing a parcel inside the jail today. She was aware this happened and always quizzed her brother on the visit to see which table the action was happening at. Annie had seen a few nickings in this jail too. On her last visit here an inmate was dragged screaming and shouting from the visiting room. He'd been seen on CCTV stashing a parcel up his arse. It was exciting for her to watch and she hoped today's visit held some excitement too.

June was stressed, small beads of sweat started to form on her brow. This was too much for her and she couldn't wait to unload her troubles to Johnny. At last, the door opened and the visitors were allowed inside the room. Each inmate was sat at a table wearing a red bib over their own clothes. Each of them looked as happy as the next person to see their loved ones. June made her way straight to the vending machine and she made sure she got her nephew a cup of coffee and a bar of chocolate. Annie pushed her perky breasts out in front of her and spotted her brother at the far end of the room. Once he'd seen her he stood up and smiled. Annie wiggled towards him and she was aware she was being watched by a few horny inmates to the left of her. The prisoners were like dogs on heat, you could see it in their faces how desperate they were for some female attention. That's all some of them spoke about, sex, sex and more sex. Annie was stood at the side of the table.

"You alright baby girl?" Johnny whispered into her ear as he picked her up from the floor and hugged her tightly.

"I'm great, how are you?" she replied. Johnny was aware of the rules in the jail and sat almost immediately, the last thing he needed was another nicking. Annie sat down opposite him and sat smiling. She was growing up fast and looked so much older now. "Wow, check your muscles out now. You're massive," Annie sniggered.

"You better believe I am. Pure muscle, not one bit of fat on me you know," she reached over and touched his arms. He was right, not one ounce of blubber was on him. He was a lean, mean, fighting machine – a tank.

Johnny was agitated and couldn't wait to find out what

was going on. "So, what's new? Why the visit today, you don't usually come until next week?"

Annie swallowed hard and started fidgeting. There was no way she was breaking the news to him, no way on this earth. Johnny could be a loose cannon sometimes and she wasn't taking any chances. This wasn't her story to tell. "Erm... I'm not sure. I'll let June tell you."

Johnny nodded his head slowly and sat back in his chair. Annie looked around the room and noticed the classy woman from earlier sat nearby. The woman was sat holding her man's hand, kissing the end of his fingers. She looked so sad and you could see in her eye she was missing her loved one. June landed at the table and plonked the hot drinks down in front of her. "Annie, you could have helped me didn't you see me struggling, bleeding lady muck, it's you who should be getting his grub not me."

Johnny leaned over the table and hugged his auntie. He could smell the stale cigarettes on her breath. "I see you're as calm as ever then."

June sat down and wiped away the sweat from her forehead with a swift flick of the wrist. "I'm sorry love for moaning but you know me and stress don't mix well," she prodded Annie in the waist with a single finger. "And, this one doesn't help either. Bone idle she is, she doesn't do a tap."

Annie raised her eyebrows over at her brother. They both knew when she was on one, they just needed to let her calm down. Johnny took a deep breath and swallowed hard. He hated bad news and today something was going to be said that he wouldn't be happy with, he was sure of it. "So, what's up? Don't lie to me because I can tell by your faces." June wasn't ready for his question so soon into the visit. She intended to tell him when the visit was drawing to an end but he'd surprised her. June was on the spot, she sat twisting her fingers and looking around the room. "Well", Johnny urged.

Annie never took her eyes from her brother, she knew by the vein pumping at the side of his neck he was already preparing himself for the worst. June blew her breath out in front of her and reached for her cup of coffee. Her mouth was dry and the stress was getting the better of her. "It's your mam, love." Johnny closed his eyes and listened carefully. "She's been missing, nobody knows where she is. I've heard she's in deep shit this time and she's in with some bad people."

Johnny cracked his knuckles and clenched his teeth tightly together. His old queen was his world and he hated the thought of her being on her own and scared. "Who's after her? I want names, don't fucking lie to me."

June was sorry she'd said anything now. She knew how hot-headed he was. His voice was raised and he was drawing attention to them all, people were looking over. "I'm not sure Johnny. I just know she's up to her neck in it this time. I think it's something to do with Monty, you know that hard nut from down the lane."

Johnny was confused, he'd heard the name before many times but he couldn't put the face to the name. Annie jumped in, she knew she would have to refresh his memory. "You know who he is. He's the one doing all the gear on the lane. Nothing gets past him he's a right cheeky fucker; everyone's out to do him in."

Johnny tilted his head to the side. How on earth did his sister know all this information? Who the hell was she chilling with to even know bad people like this? Johnny inhaled and the side of his ears pinned back. "Fuck me, why does she always end up like this?" June's bottom lip trembled. It was something she'd asked herself for years. Elsie was the elder sister but she had always been the sensible one. Elsie always sought adventure, she was never happy with the cards life had dealt her, she always wanted more excitement in her life. June knew more than she was saying, it was written all over her face, she was hiding something. Johnny knew her of old, it was obvious she was covering up the truth. Her nose was twitching at the end and she couldn't keep still.

"So what now," Annie chirped in.

"Not a fucking lot while I'm stuck in this shit hole. Argghhh… Can you get me Worm's phone number? He'll know the crack. I'll get on the blower to him and let him fill me in." June's face was blood red and she was on the verge of breaking down. Johnny hated shouting at her but she needed to understand his side of things. Annie sat back in her seat with her arms folded tightly in front of her. She was sick of cleaning up her mother's mess. All her life had revolved around her and her problems, every bastard day it was the same.

Suddenly there was shouting in the room. A couple were arguing to the side of Johnny. They were nose to nose and ready to strike blows. The screws ran over and restrained the prisoner. "She's a cunt, a dirty lying slut."

The woman was right back at him defending her honour. "Just the same as you are! Did you think I wouldn't find out about you? I'm not a dick head you know, people talk."

This was a war zone and the security in the room got the visitor out of there as quickly as could be before she was hurt. Johnny was smiling and winked over at another inmate who was sat nearby. This was a ploy, a distraction from the parcels being passed about the room. Inmates were shuffling about in their seats and stashing the swag all over their bodies. That's how it worked in the jail, every little detail was set out nicely to make sure they were never uncovered. Everybody was involved and once the inmate was removed from the visiting room they all started to relax. The screw near Johnny knew the crack too, but he was well paid by the inmates to keep his silence. He walked past Johnny and gave him a friendly tap on his shoulder. That was enough for them to both know the job was done.

June knew a bit about jail life and she was onto it straight away. She'd met this same screw on the outside and paid him off. He was a creep and he made her stomach turn. The cheeky bleeder had even tried coming onto her. He told her he liked the full figured woman. June snarled at him and one look at her face made him move away swiftly. There was nowt down for him here, not now, not ever. Annie put on her puppy eyes and leaned over the table. "Johnny all my friends are going down the club next week. I've got nothing to wear and I'm sick to death of borrowing clothes from Rita. You know what she's like don't you?" Johnny knew a sob story when he heard one. His sister just melted his heart and he could never say no to her. He was all she had and he wanted to make sure she got the best of everything.

June sat watching her at work and the corners of her mouth started to rise. "She just wraps you around her little finger doesn't she?"

Johnny smiled and agreed with his auntie. "She knows what I'm like that's why. A soft touch I am where she's concerned. I'll get Worm to drop a ton off to you later today." It was a done deal and Annie sat back in her seat and started to relax. She was a cunning cow and knew how to get what she wanted. Johnny's mind was all over the show now. He would never admit this to his family. He had to stand tall, never show fear. He'd learned that from being behind bars for his sentence. You never let anyone see what was going on inside your head, you kept your poker face and never flinched. June had eaten most of the chocolate from the table, there was one bar left. Johnny had lost his appetite and already he was planning stuff inside his head. He needed a mobile phone as soon as possible, he needed contact with the outside world. The word needed to be out to find his mother. Somebody knew where she was and it was his job to get them talking.

Just as things went quiet Annie put her foot in it, as usual. She mentioned the taboo subject that nobody ever talked about. "I saw Natalie the other day, she looked well, she's put on a bit of weight though but I think she looks good for it." June kicked at her feet under the table, she was a right gob-shite. Natalie was Johnny's ex-girlfriend. She'd broken his heart when his prison sentence started. He thought she was the one, the girl he would love for the rest of his life but how wrong could he have been. Natalie was a tart in his eyes now and she was never going to wait for him, she had just had him over. The family never told him about the other secret they held about her though, no, some things were better left unsaid. Johnny's face drained of colour. Just hearing her name sent shivers down his spine. He owed her for the pain she'd caused him inside these walls and once he was on the out he was going to settle the score once and for all. He kept this close to his chest though, no one was knowing his plans, nobody.

The visit came to an end and Johnny was itching to get back to his pad to set the ball rolling. He still had a good circle of friends on the out and Worm would do anything he asked of him. They were brothers in arms and would die for each other. Worm had not long been released from jail too. He was Johnny's co-accused but he got a lesser sentence because he wasn't named as the main man. Don't get me wrong, this guy was hard as nails and he was lethal. People should never underestimate him. 'The

Silent Assassin' Johnny liked to call him and he was right, this guy was fucked in the head. Worm had his hand in some sick shit, he had to make money somehow and every day he was trying to earn a crust. He feared no one and his goal was to make his mark. He was deep though; dark and sly but Johnny still trusted him with his life. He was his wingman.

Johnny walked back to his pad with his head dipped. When it rained in his world, it poured down. Why was everything so hard in his life? It was so fucked up, nothing was ever straight forward. Johnny had another few weeks left on his sentence and knew his hands were tied until then. The frustration was showing and he wasn't in the mood for anybody. He stomped inside his cell and banged the door shut behind him. Sitting on the bed he picked up his pillow and sank his teeth into it, biting hard. Johnny screamed like an injured animal, suffocating the sound of his breaking heart. His mother, he needed to help her. The clock was ticking and he knew if he didn't find her soon her life would be over. Johnny needed a miracle to help him out of this shit, a big fat fucking miracle.

CHAPTER THREE

JUNE CHEWED on her fingernails. Her head was all over the place today and every noise she heard made her jumpy and on edge. She had a gut feeling that the next knock on the door would be someone bringing bad news telling her that her sister had been found dead. She'd not had a wink of sleep and the dark circles beneath her eyes suggested she would never rest until Elsie was back home safely.

Annie sat in the front room talking to Rita. She was used to her mother going missing and there was no way she was losing any sleep over her. Annie was selfish like that, she only ever thought about herself. Rita was sat there full of herself as per usual and she was displaying her latest gift from her new man. This girl had changed, she looked older and she was caked in make-up. "I didn't even ask for this he just said, 'there you go, doll I've bought you another present'." Annie lifted the gold bottle of "Gucci" perfume up out of the box and pulled the lid from it. She squirted it onto her wrist and rubbed them together. "He wants to take me out tonight. Somewhere quiet he said, why don't you come with us?"

Annie sat deep in thought, she was sick to death of the life she was leading. Nothing exciting ever happened in her life and so what if the man was older than Rita at least she was enjoying herself. Perhaps, it was time for her to get a taste of the good life too. Annie twisted a dark piece of hair hanging near her cheekbone. "I might, but who will I chat to. I'm not being a cling-on. Imagine it, me just sat there on my lonesome."

Rita sat thinking and reached for her mobile phone. "Colin has got loads of mates. I'll tell him to bring one along. He will, you know," her eyes were wide open. "He'll do anything for me." Annie watched her friend texting and smiled. She wasn't a virgin anymore and why shouldn't she have some fun anyway. It was just a bit of harmless fun.

June came into the room and sat with them. She had a fag hanging from the corner of her mouth, chugging hard on it. "Worm said he was calling today to sort stuff out. I've not slept a wink me, for days. It's killing me all this stress. I swear Elsie will be the death of me." June picked up a newspaper at the side of her and tried to read it. She just couldn't concentrate. "If she's dead, oh, I don't even want to think about it. My head's mashed up with it all."

Annie brushed her comment off. She was more concerned about her night out and the chance of bagging herself a meal ticket. "Just leave her to it. I bet she's pissed up somewhere, you know what she's like. Remember last time we all sat worrying about her and she was at scabby Sandra's off her rocker. For days we all sat worrying about her and she wasn't even arsed. She just walked back in here as if nothing had happened."

June took a deep breath and played with the cuff of her jumper. "This is different though. She's been mixed up with some sick shit lately and I've got a gut feeling she's lying in a ditch somewhere."

Annie sighed and raised her eyes. "Stop being such a drama queen, you always think the worst. Trust me, when she's skint she'll turn up just like she always does. I'll tell you what, just to put your mind at rest I'll call past scabby Sandra's later and see if she's seen anything of her."

June shook her head and made the sign of the cross across her body. "I hope your right. God knows what will happen if she's not."

Annie stood and stretched her arms high above her head. Here it was; the lies, the cover she often used when she was up to no good. "I'm going out tonight June so I may as well stay at Rita's. We're going to apply for a few college courses online so there is no point coming home." June wasn't listening, her head was away with the fairies. Annie walked over to her and placed a firm hand on her shoulder. "Are you listening to me, I said I won't be home tonight?"

June's face creased with the stress she was under and she nodded her head slowly. "Yeah love, I'm glad you're doing something with your life. Don't end up like me." June was thick as pig-shit. She'd left school with no qualifications and the one and only job she ever held was at the local school, cleaning. Two weeks she lasted, she said it wasn't for her. Annie walked to the living room door and stood for a few seconds thinking. Whatever she was going to say stayed on her tongue, she never said a word. Annie went missing for days too, a week once and nobody had a clue where she was. It was just the normal thing in her family, nobody came home and nobody was missed.

Annie was sleeping in the box-room. It was very basic with just an old bed and a wardrobe with the doors hanging off. There were a few pieces of wallpaper hung on the wall but it was old-fashioned and peeling off from the ceiling where black fungus grew. Beggars can't be choosers I suppose and Annie was glad of anywhere to stay at the moment. She'd never really had a home, a place she felt safe, somewhere she was familiar with. Her life had consisted so much of moving to different locations that she never had the time to make solid friendships or have the perfect bedroom she had always dreamed of. Rita dived on the bottom of the bed and checked her phone. She rubbed her hands together and kicked her legs up in the air. "He's replied, hold on, let me read the message and see what he's saying." Rita squeezed her eyes together and tried to read the text. Her eyesight was shocking and in fairness she should have been wearing glasses. She was as blind as a bat. "Right, yep, he's bringing his mate for you to chat to. Oh my God, your first proper man. Whoop, whoop, we're on a double date." Rita rubbed her hands together with excitement and her expression became serious. Rita walked to the bedroom door and quickly checked nobody was listening. Once she knew they were safe she kept a low tone and sat back down on the bed. "Sex is so much different with an older man you know. They know what they are doing," Rita cradled her body with her arms and shuddered. "When I first had sex with Colin he made my legs shake. And I even had an orgasm. It was the first time I've ever felt like that you know, it was amazing." Annie rolled about on the bed and wanted to know more. This was hot off the press and the first time Rita had ever gone into details about her older man and their sex life. Annie was jealous. Yes, she'd had sex, but she'd never had an orgasm. She wanted to know everything, every last detail. Rita was spilling the beans now and Annie was hanging on her every word. "He just does things to me. I can't explain it. Even when I kiss him he gives me butterflies. I think I love him you know." Annie was shocked. The word love scared her. She'd seen her own mother break down so many times with a broken heart and she promised herself she'd never let herself get hurt like that, ever.

"How can you love him when you've only just started seeing him?" Annie sarcastically replied, "You're full of shit, you need to back off. Stop being so desperate."

Rita was oblivious to her friend's worries and carried on talking. "I just love him, he gives me a bit of sniff too, it helps me relax. Sex is so much better with it. It makes me do things I would never do with a straight head."

Annie snarled at Rita. This was all news to her and she'd never disclosed this before. Annie saw her arse and gritted her teeth tightly together. "He's a dirty paedo then. What the hell are you getting into? Think about it, he's nearly forty and he's having sex with you. He's grooming you in my eyes. I know you think I'm chatting shit but why would he be interested in a young girl when there are thousands of women his own age knocking about."

Rita spat her dummy out and defended herself. She loved this man and there was no way on this earth she was having anyone disrespecting him, not even her best friend. "Why are you saying stuff like that? He's a nice man and he looks out for me. You'll see tonight when you meet him. You'll eat your words, you just watch. Stop stressing over him. It's what I want, not you."

Annie pulled the make-up bag from under her bed and raised her eyes over at Rita. She knew she'd offended her and wanted to make amends. "Come on then, let's get a bit slap on and see if I can bag myself an older man too. I'll tell you one thing for sure though," she paused and held Rita's head in her hands making the side of her lips touch together at the sides. "If he's a minger he's getting slung."

Rita pulled away and chuckled. The argument was over. "Colin doesn't have ugly mates. These men are top notch. Trust me, you will be treated like a princess and want for nothing. Anyway, get a bit of sniff up your nose and you'll be sorted." Annie chuckled and brushed the comment off. She was game for anything at this moment and the thought of some excitement in her life gave her the lift she needed to bring her out of her own sad life. The girls lay on the bed laughing, tonight was going to be an eye opener for Annie for sure.

Worm pulled up outside June's house. The music was pumping from inside his car and everyone on the estate knew he'd arrived. Worm craved attention and always wanted people talking about him. In his line of business he should have kept a low profile but it wasn't in his personality to lie low, he was a show off. There were a few other men sat in the car with him. His army he liked to call them. Men who were up and coming and ready to do anything to put their name on the map. Worm walked the walk. He looked the part too, he swaggered about like he owned the place. A Rolex dangling from his wrist, he looked the dog's bollocks as he stepped out of the car. Life had been treating him well lately and he was earning cash and lots of it. He had his finger in more than one pie and he was a shady character, he was always into something. Worm stood at June's front door and inhaled deeply. His chest was pushed out firmly and he was confident that he looked good. He tapped his car key on the window. June's head was squashed up at the window in seconds and she rushed to open the door. "Come in love. I thought you'd forgot about me. I've been shitting like a new born baby all night. I swear I've not slept a wink."

Worm stepped inside the house and followed her into the front room. He'd met June before and liked her style, she was just a normal woman with no airs or graces, just down to earth and told it how it was. He walked into the front room and his nostrils twitched slightly. The house stank of stale cigarettes and cheesy feet. Worm pulled a sour look and sat down on the edge of the chair. "Do you want a cuppa love? I'll make you one if you want. I think I've got some milk left?"

Worm shook his head slowly. If the truth was known

he would never eat or drink anything out of this shit-hole. He flicked his eyes to his wristwatch. He didn't have all day and this was just a flying visit to get Johnny off his back. All day his mate had been on the blower to him to sort things out, he never let up. "Right, Johnny has filled me in about what he knows but he tells me you know a lot more than you're saying. If you want my help you need to be straight with me. Tell me everything."

June was gobsmacked, was she that bad at hiding the truth. She sunk down in the chair and held her head in her hands. "Ok, I just need to get my head round it all first. I just knew she would come unstuck one day. I told her I did, I said Elsie you're going to end up dead if you carry on. But did she listen, did she fuck! She just carried on thinking that she was untouchable."

Worm pulled a cigarette out of his pocket and flicked his lighter. He needed to go soon and the way this was going, he would be here all night. He urged her to continue. "So, go on, fill me in."

June closed her eyes and her face creased with pain as she started to tell him the full story. "She's a good girl really, she's just been a bit lost lately. You know times have been hard for her don't you?" Worm never said a word he just stared at her waiting for her to continue. "She was doing a few nights for Monty on the lane, you know, in the brass gaff?" Worm knew exactly where she meant and nodded his head slowly. "Moonlight" was well known to everyone in the area and the residents there had been up in arms for months trying to get the brothel closed down. It was a bad place and rumour had it that Monty was using foreign girls to work there for him; girls who had come to this country in hope for a better life, to be educated and find a good job. Monty was like that, he cared for no one but himself and lining his own pockets. June twisted her fingers as she continued, she couldn't look him in the eye. "She was only helping out to start with, 'just until Monty got someone in' she said but, you know what she's like, she'd find trouble in an empty house. She always gets herself involved in other people's shit." Worm sat forward in his seat and was eager to hear more. June was kicking the arse out of this story and he just wanted her to get to the point. Taking a deep breath, he listened as the story unfolded. "Elsie was having money from the till. Just a few quid here and there that's all. You know what she's like, she's a thieving bastard. Anyway, to cut a long story short Monty found out and said she had to work it off. Well, that's what she told me. I mean, I'm not having any sister of mine showing us up working as a prostitute." Worm knew immediately what she meant and the hairs on the back of his neck stood on end. He'd had a lot of time for Johnny's mother in the past and she'd sorted him out when he was in the slammer. Nothing much, just the odd postal order here and there but she'd still looked out for him.

Worm scratched the end of his nose, he was lost for words for a few seconds. How could he ever tell his best mate that he knew more than he was letting on, he'd string him up if he knew the half of it! Johnny had enough shit on his plate without adding this to it, some things were better left unsaid. "That's some sick shit, why didn't she just tell him to do one. Elsie's never been shy of telling anyone to fuck off has she?"

"Well, that's what I said but she owed him for some blow too. She's got a raging habit, she's never off the stuff apparently. A few bumps here and there she told me, to start with just to liven her up but as time went on she was constantly sticking that shit up her nose." June's expression changed and her voice was low. "Did I tell you she was sleeping with Monty too?"

Worm smirked and dipped his head low, he sniggered slightly. Elsie was a fucker and got herself into some deep shit, nothing surprised him about this woman. "I thought Jackie was his wife, she's his girl, is that right?"

June didn't know where her head was at. She was sat fidgeting and constantly licking at her dry cracked lips. "Yeah, I'm getting to that bit if you shut up for a bleeding minute and let me speak. For Christ sake let me finish. Apparently, Jackie's found out about Elsie and she'd been gunning for her for weeks. The last I heard his Mrs said she was going to knife her. You know what she's like, she's bleeding mental."

This was getting worse by the minute. Elsie was up shit street no matter which way you looked at it. Worm shook his head slowly, how on earth could he ever sort this shit out before Johnny came home? If it had just been a quick visit to someone's house to give them a good arse kicking yes, he'd have sorted it in an instant but to tackle Monty and his crew was way above his station. This was too big for him, there was no way he was getting involved. As he cracked his knuckles, he looked over at June and tried to calm her down. There was no way he was admitting he couldn't handle it. "Right, leave this with me. I'll put the feelers out and see what's going down. If Monty is involved then it's bigger than I first thought. The guy's a crank, trust me, I know."

June was choking up, the corners of her eyes filled with tears and she was struggling to hold them back. "I just want her home safe. If he wants the money back then I'll do whatever it takes to try and get it for him but at the moment I just want to know she's still alive." Worm stood and he was going to give June a hug but he held back. He was a hard man in her eyes and he didn't want to let his guard down. "Like I said, just chill and I'll see what I can find out." June walked behind him as he made his way to the front door. Once the door was open she watched him make his way to the waiting car. June sucked in a large mouthful of fresh air, her heart was racing and she looked like she was ready to collapse.

Worm jumped back into the car. Flicking the ignition, he paused and tapped his fingers on the steering wheel. There was only one thing for it. He had to go on the lane tonight and pay the brass gaff a visit. If anyone would know where Elsie was, it would be one of the working girls there. Worm was hesitant about getting involved but his loyalty to Johnny was paramount. He had to step up and help him find Elsie.

It was nearly eight o'clock and Annie was nervous about going out on her date. Of course she'd had dates before but they were with guys her own age, not men. Rita was ready and just applying some candy pink lip gloss to her perky lips. She puckered up and blew a kiss over at Annie. "Come on then, let's go and have a great night. Colin said he would meet us near the park. He always meets me there. I've told him not to come to my house because my dad would go sick if he saw him. You know what he's like, he's so over the top where boyfriends are concerned. Imagine him if he saw me with an older guy he'd shit a brick."

Annie sprayed some perfume over her clothes and took a final glance in the mirror. She looked a lot older than she was. Her long dark hair was blown straight and she had curled the end of it to add a bit of body to it. Her outfit was sexy too. A black jumpsuit with a plunging neckline, her breasts were on show, her dress was figure hugging. The girls headed downstairs and Rita was trying to be as quiet as possible. She was stood on her tiptoes. "Just let's get out of here. If my dad sees us he will be asking twenty questions. I've told him we're going to a fashion show at the college. He's not questioned it, so just leave him with it."

Rita sniggered and crept down the stairs. Just as she thought she was safe her old man stepped into the hallway and stood with his two hands on his hips. He snarled and shot his daughter a curious look. "Where do you think you're going dressed up like that? You look a right slapper, go and get something decent on instead of walking around with your arse hanging out?"

Rita was taken by surprise and Annie was the one who addressed him. Rita was going under, she swallowed hard it was a good job Annie was there to help her out. Annie smiled at him, she was a right flirt. "We're going to the fashion show, Len. Look at the state of us, we hate getting dressed up like this but the tutors have told us to. It's all about fashion and how the models dress on the catwalk. We can't go dressed in jeans and trainers can we, we'd be a laughing stock?"

Len was a grumpy old fart and he had a face like a smacked arse. He was old school and still thought he was living in the sixties. He shook his head and shoved his hands deep into his trouser pockets. "Well, it's a load of shite if you ask me girls. Who wants to see women dressed like that? Natural beauty is what it's all about, women don't need all that shit plastered over their faces to look good, they should just be happy with what God gave them if you ask me." Rita agreed with her father for once. The old fool seemed to have bought their story and he seemed to have swallowed it. They'd pulled the wool right over his eyes and now they were free to go out without any further investigations from him. Rita shouted goodbye to her dad and left the house.

The girls walked through the estate and in the distance Rita could see her lover's car parked up. The silver BMW was one of the reasons she noticed him in the first place. A man with a nice car was much sort after in the area. Fanny magnets they were known as. Rita had met Colin on Facebook to start with. It was just a random friends add and she never really took much notice of him until he popped up one night for a chat. Rita spoke with Colin for weeks before he asked to meet her. It was just fun to start with and she never expected it to go the way it did. Colin took her out for nice things to eat and she'd even gone to Blackpool with him. He'd never laid a finger on her though, that was much later and if the truth was known, it was her who made the first move. She wanted to thank him for all he had done for her. Nobody had ever made her feel that way before and day by day she was falling head over heels in love with him. The night they first made love was something she'd always remember until her dying breath. Colin had booked them in a top hotel for the night and he'd told her that there was no pressure to have sex, he said he was just glad to spend some quality time with her. Rita bought the story and even though she thought she was on the ball she never really saw what he was doing. The room was high standard and he'd even lit scented candles around the bedroom to make it as romantic as he possibly could, soft music, massage oils, the guy was a creep. Colin had bought her sexy underwear too. A black lacy set that left nothing to the imagination, you could see her private bits through it. The drugs were just something he said would help her calm down, stop her feeling anxious he said. A few lines of sniff, just to set the mood. Colin was right too, after a few snorts she was full of confidence and she was the one making all the moves. Colin was a devious bastard and he knew exactly what he was doing. Week by week he was drawing her closer and closer to the net.

Annie flicked her hair back as they neared the car. Colin was sat in the front seat with another man sat in the passenger seat. Rita nudged her in the waist as they got closer. "I bet your arse is twitching isn't it? Just remember even if you don't like him just talk to him and make him feel special. That's what it's all about you know, making them feel special. I swear if you do that he'll be flashing the cash before the night is out." Rita opened the car door and popped her head inside. "Bloody hell, it's cold isn't it?" Talking about the weather was a brilliant ice-breaker and Rita often used it when she was nervous. She slid across the back seat followed closely by Annie.

Colin turned his head slowly and his eyes were all over this new girl. "So, this is the friend then?"

Rita sat forward in her seat and rested her hand on his shoulder. "Yep, this is Annie, she's lovely isn't she?" Colin studied her a lot longer than he should have, he was taking in every inch of her body. The other man in the passenger side now revealed himself. He was late thirties and had dark brown hair, a bit foreign looking. Annie noticed how hairy his arms were and seemed a bit anxious. She hated hairy men and this one was like a werewolf.

"Alright love," he said to her. Annie smiled back at him but she was nervous and he could tell. The man twisted his body around and placed his hand on her knee, patting it gently. "I don't bite, I'm a nice kind of guy, aren't I Colin?"

The driver sniggered and nodded his head. "Yep, Carlos is harmless, soft as shit he is really, he just looks hard."

Rita was feeling a bit unsecure. The way Colin had looked at Annie had unsettled her. She wasn't sure if he was flirting with her or not but she wasn't taking any chances. "Where are we going? I'm starving, can we go for something to eat, what about that nice Italian place you took me to last week?" Colin turned the engine on and pulled away from the street. Looking through his rear-view mirror he answered Rita. "I was thinking we could go up in the hills tonight. You know a nice country pub, open fire and soft music. Ramsbottom is lovely, have you ever been?"

Rita was impressed, this guy was so romantic. "I've never been but yeah it sounds fun." Annie was still edgy but once they set off in the car she was starting to relax. Carlos was handsome and the more she studied him the more she was starting to see the best in him. He was a well-built guy and the art work on his arms was amazing. Carlos smelt of money, his aftershave was sharp and crisp, clean smelling. The more she looked at him the more she was warming to him. There was music playing in the car and everybody was starting to loosen up.

Worm drove up Moston Lane. It was nearly midnight and things were quiet in the area. Driving down the backstreets he could see a group of lads sat on a wall chilling. This was the norm in the area and this was a hot spot for a lot of the youths to hang about it. Worm knew a lot of people. He'd met lots of lads in the jails and often kept in touch with the ones who were local to Manchester. Keeping in touch made his circle of friends bigger and in his field of work it was good to know he had people he could trust watching his back. Worm pulled up and he could see Matty sat on the wall. He was a local youth who was dealing a bit of weed in the area. As soon as he saw the car he bounced to his feet and went to see who was driving it. Worm opened the car door and casually swung one leg out, one hand still resting on the steering wheel. "What's going down bro?"

Matty clocked who he was straight away and shook

hands with him. "What's up Worm? This isn't your usual neck of the woods, what brings you on the lane?"

Worm pulled his keys from the ignition and came to join Matty on the wall. "Skin up then mate," he threw a bag of weed over at him. The other lads started to relax now. They were always tooled up and ready for action. They needed to protect their turf and more often than not there was always some new gang trying to tax them and take over their patch. Worm sat on the wall and scanned the area. In the distance he could hear music and could see the back door of the brass gaff opening and closing. Matty followed his eyes and sniggered. "You after a woman then? I'll tell you what, that place is raking it in. All night long the punters are knocking at the door, gagging for it they are. I'm going to get a suck one of these nights too, just to see what the big hype is about."

Worm nodded slowly and knew this lad could help him with his enquiries. "Who runs it then? I've heard it's Monty, is that right?"

Matty sucked hard on the joint he'd just rolled. "Yeah that cunt runs most of the graft around here. He's tried moving us from here but we told him straight, didn't we lads?" A youth sat behind them laughed out loud. He was pissed and swigging on a bottle of brandy. "We told him fuck all. The greedy bastard takes a cut from our money for doing fuck all. Liberty taker he is. As if he hasn't got enough with taxing us?"

Worm swallowed hard. So Monty was all he was made out to be, ruthless. Worm was still focused on the brothel. "What's the girls like in there, are they local or what?"

Matty passed the joint about and blew a thick cloud of grey smoke out in front of him. "Mostly foreigners I've heard; Czech, Polish, Nigerians. Fuck knows really, I'm just going by hearsay."

The lad at the side of him nudged him in the waist. "They have some proper dirty cows working there too. I went for a shag the other week and it was top. It wasn't no immigrant though it was an English woman. Pretty cute she was too, off her head though, she couldn't even speak properly."

Worm swallowed hard, there was no two ways about it he had to go and see this place for himself. Matty was quiet and he seemed scared as he spoke in a low voice. "Listen mate, I know you're my pal and all that but if anything is going down with Monty keep me well out of it. The guy is an animal and I don't need the added stress in my life. Trust me, he's bad news. The stories I've heard about him are sick. The cunt's ruthless."

Worm felt his fear and tried to comfort him. He patted the middle of his arm and smiled. "Nar, I've got no beef with Monty I was just asking that's all." Matty knew he was lying but he said nothing. The less he knew the better. Worm sat with the lads and chilled for a bit. His eyes were glued to the Moonlight brothel, he was alert and watching everything that happened there. It was eerie around the lane and only one street lamp gave off any light. Cars pulled up at the brass gaff and the men inside hid their identity as they went inside. This was a dirty place, a seedy dark place.

Rita was all over Colin as they sat next to each other in the pub. Annie was drinking vodka and coke and she was relaxing now. Carlos liked her and he was filling her glass as soon as it was empty. He wanted her pissed and he was doing a good job of it, she was well on her way. They'd ended up in Ramsbottom, a small Lancashire village in the Pennines. It was quiet and discreet, just the way the men liked it, no nosey bastards poking their nose into things that didn't concern them. Carlos moved closer to Annie and whispered into her ear. "So, do you like me then? I think you're sexy if I'm being honest."

Annie cast her eyes over to Rita and she could see her tongue stuck down the back of Colin's throat. She looked him right in the eye and smiled at him showing her perfect deck of white teeth. "I think you're alright," she replied. He wanted more than just an alright. He'd paid for this girl all night and he was making sure he got his money's worth no matter what happened. Annie sat scrolling through her messages on her phone and if the truth was known she was bored. Okay, it was a free night out but she wanted some excitement and not just to be sat in a pub in the middle of nowhere. There was no atmosphere in this boozer, it was full of farmers; sheep-shaggers talking about tractors and how well the crops were growing this year as far as she was concerned. Looking over at Rita she tried to get her attention. "Are we getting off now or what, we could go to town and go to a club, anything must be better than here. It's like being sat in God's waiting room?"

Rita gripped hold of Colin's hand and smiled at him. "Yeah, let's go and have a dance, you can show me your dance moves. You're always saying how much of a mover you are, let's see you cut some shapes." Colin sneered over at Carlos. They were trying to keep a low profile with these two girls but they were right, it was dead.

Rita draped her arms around her lover's neck and whatever she said to him made him change his mind. Colin quickly picked up his car keys from the table and slurped the last bit of his drink down. "What my Rita wants, my Rita gets. Come on then, let's go and paint the town red." At last, a chance of hearing a bit of decent music, seeing people her own age, Annie was smiling. Carlos was getting a bit heavy with her now and wanted a piece of the action. His mate was getting some so why shouldn't he? If this girl wasn't putting out tonight then he was going to find someone who would. He tested the water as soon as they got into the car park. Annie was shivering, it was freezing up here in the hills. Here was his chance to get a feel of her soft pink flesh. He walked to her side and put his arm around her. "Come here you and snuggle up to me. I don't bite." Annie didn't want to cause a scene and let him have his way with her. At the end of the day it was a cuddle, nothing more. Carlos smelt good. His aftershave was strong and musky. You could always tell a man by the way he smelt and this guy smelt of money. If Annie ever stood a chance of getting a penny from him she knew she had to start being a little friendlier. There she was snuggled deep into his chest and that was enough for her date to think he stood a chance with her, she was flirting. Rita was having the time of her life and if Annie would have fallen down a dark ditch on the way to the car she wouldn't have been missed. She was besotted by Colin. Even Annie thought he was an alright guy and he was constantly flashing the cash. He was loaded and not afraid to show a girl a good time. Carlos was a bit more reserved with the cash flow and Annie couldn't see this tight arse parting with a fart, never mind buying her any gifts. Annie shot a look over at Colin and stared at him a bit longer than she needed to. He was the prize catch here, not Carlos. Her game plan had changed and she had something up her sleeve, the cunning cow. All of a sudden she became loud and seemed to be the life and soul of the party. She was drawing attention to herself and Colin was finally taking notice of her.

At the club Rita was on the dance floor strutting her stuff. She was a mad-head and didn't care how she looked. She was in a world of her own and when the beat kicked in her eyes were wide open and she was a prisoner to the beat. She'd definitely had something - magic or ecstasy. Carlos had gone home ages ago. He was a right miserable arse. He wouldn't dance and all he was interested in was getting Annie into bed. Colin was different though, he took the time to talk to Annie and they seemed to be getting on like a house on fire. Rita was oblivious to her best friend hitting on her man and as soon as she got the chance Annie was flirting away with him. This guy had a gold debit card and anyway she could, she wanted a taste of what her best friend was getting. Annie was drunk and leaned over to Colin's ear. Her warm breath tickled his ear lobe. "Rita is having the time of her life, she really likes you." She paused and stroked her finger along his top lip slowly. "I can see why too, you're a really nice man. I wish I had someone as good looking as you."

Colin rarely missed a chance to flirt and he knew what she was getting at. He'd been in this game long enough to know when a female was interested in him. He held the piece of hair dangling near her cheekbone and kept his voice low. "You're lovely. I like Rita but you're in a class of your own. More mature."

This was music to Annie's ears, this was a chance at getting a sugar daddy of her own. So what if he was Rita's fella, all was fair in love and war. Annie had to be quick before Rita returned, she had to plant the seed in his head now. Checking her friend was still dancing she made her move. "You see me Colin, I'm what you call a classy girl. I've lost interest in lads my own age. I want somebody who knows what they are doing, someone who can show me the finer things in life."

Colin swallowed hard, he couldn't believe his luck. He'd never had much luck with women his own age and to have two young girls fighting over him was something he'd never imagined. Colin thought of himself as a player, it was there for everyone to see. Every woman that walked past him had their tongue hanging out. He was like a child in a sweet shop. But, it was the young girls he lusted after, his eyes were all over the club checking out the girls. Money talked in this life and he knew he could buy almost everything his heart desired with the money he had. Rita had never disclosed what he was into but he was wadded. Colin never mentioned it either. Perhaps he was a business man, a property manager or something like that. His money was coming from somewhere and she delved deeper to find out. "Do you work Colin?" Annie asked at last.

Colin started laughing and winked over at her. He tapped the side of his nose with a single finger and sniggered. "Ask no question and I'll tell you no lies. Just let's say I have my fingers in a few pies."

Annie liked this, she loved that he was mysterious. He could have been a millionaire for all she knew and it was just what she wanted to hear before she made her move on him. She smiled at him and licked her lips slowly. Annie glanced over at Rita and made sure the coast was clear. Here it was the betrayal, what a Judas she was.

Worm sat back in his car and drove away from the youths. He circled the brothel a few times and decided he couldn't go inside. Whatever happened behind those four walls was some sick twisted shit. Matty had filled him in about the secret chambers inside there and the stories of Monty torturing people who'd tried having him over. He wasn't ready to tackle this alone, not now, not ever. Worm was worried, something was on his mind. He checked his watch and put his foot down in the car. Wherever he was going, he was in a rush.

June lay in bed and she was restless. Picking up an old magazine she tried to read some of the stories there. Her mind was racing and none of the words were making any sense in her head. Checking the time she picked up her mobile and dialled Annie's number. She was always awake at this time, she was a night owl and didn't go to sleep until late. June just wanted to hear her voice, to see how the application for college was going, to take her mind off the dramas in her life. June held the phone to her ear and listened to the ringing tone. The call went straight to voicemail. She gasped her breath and ended the call. It was just her luck, the only night she wanted to speak to Annie and she was asleep, typical. June switched the lamp off at the side of the bed and just lay staring into the night. Her body tossed and turned, it was going to be a long night.

CHAPTER FOUR

JOHNNY BARKER HAD imagined this day in his head for months and now that it was here he wasn't sure how he felt. This was his new start, his last chance to turn his life around. If he was being true to himself his emotions were high and early that morning he'd hidden his head deep underneath the bed covers and cried his eyes out. He didn't know why he was crying, he just never thought this day would ever come. How would his life pan out now that he was a free man? He sat and thought about this for hours. Going straight, turning his life around, maybe even getting a job. Johnny knew more than anyone that finding employment was a lot harder than anyone thought, especially for an ex-convict. He'd been down this road before and always ended up banging his head against a brick wall. Crime was the easy way out, he didn't have any other options. No matter which way he looked at it he could never see a way of changing his life. Everything cost money and everything had a price. People in authority expected him to live on poxy jobseekers allowance that was barely enough to feed him, let alone clothe him. Were they for real or what? They needed to walk in his shoes to see how hard it was living on the breadline.

Johnny's ex-girlfriend Natalie had always wanted him to go straight. He never believed her when she told him that if he got involved in crime again she wouldn't stand by him. He learned the hard way. Natalie broke his heart when she sent him a "Dear John" letter early into his sentence. He never got to plead his case with her. She just cut off all ties with him. Can you blame her though, who wants to have a partner who is in and out of jail all their lives. Always waiting for that knock on the door telling her he'd been arrested. Johnny had never got over Natalie and now he had mixed feelings about her. One minute he wanted to end her life when he was a free and the next he wanted to tell her how much he loved her and how much he wanted to change. Johnny and Natalie had been together since they were kids. It was always them two, soul mates everyone said they were. He'd even thought about asking her to marry him when he was on the out. How would he feel now if she'd moved on, if she had another man in her life? He couldn't cope with that, he knew he couldn't. He still loved her. Johnny had even thought of moving away from Manchester to get her out of his head. But with all this shit going on his life at the moment he knew he had no other option than to face his demons.

Keys rattled outside his door and Johnny lurched back to reality. The cell door opened slowly and a female screw stood smiling at him. Johnny liked Louise and she'd listened to him when he was at an all-time low. Not all screws were bad and he really clicked with this one. Okay, she was one of them, but sometimes in life you have to bite the bullet and give people a chance. Louise walked inside the cell and closed the door slowly behind her. There was no way she wanted any of her work mates hearing what she had to say. She was nervous, fidgeting and refraining from any eye contact with him. Slowly, she licked her lips and found the courage to say what was on her mind. "I can't lie Johnny, I'm going to be sad to see you go. We've become close haven't we?"

He walked to her side and hugged her. She was a lot smaller than he was and she looked lost stood next to him. "I'm going to miss you too. Who am I going to speak to now when I need advice?"

Louise pulled a white piece of paper from her shirt and held it out in front of her. "I know you're going home and you will probably be glad to see the back of me but here's my number just in case you fancy catching up sometime."

Johnny was taken back, he'd just put this woman in the friends zone and never once thought that she had any feelings for him. He struggled for words and took a few seconds to reply. "Louise, I never thought of us like that. I just thought we were mates. You know, just chilling together."

Louise was beetroot and realised then that she'd put her foot in it. But, he was leaving today and she had to tell him how she felt before he walked out of that room and she would never see him again. Taking a deep breath she opened up and put her cards on the table. It was now or never. "Johnny, I know this is never supposed to happen but sometimes it does. I've fallen for you and it's taken me this long to tell you. I know it should never have happened but it did and I can't help the way I feel about you."

Louise was getting upset and he didn't want to cause a scene. He had a big heart like that. Despite what people thought about him he did have a soft side to him, a loving part to his character. He tried to calm her down. "Yeah, give me your number and we can hook up when I've sorted my head out." He paced the cell and stuck his head out through the bars on the window for the last time. "Louise, I never thought for one second that you felt like this about me. I just thought you were being friendly. It's your job to be nice isn't it? Imagine if anyone got wind of this they would have your guts for garters. You'd lose your job."

Louise dipped her head and replied in a soft voice. "Why do you think I've left it until now? I've tortured myself for months with this and I just couldn't hold it in any longer." Louise was pretty. She had short blonde cropped hair and a slightly round figure but it wasn't like that in jail was it? It was them and us and you never crossed the line.

Johnny folded the white piece of paper and slid it into the back of his jeans pocket. He stepped forward and bent his knees slightly. Slowly he held her chin in his hands and looked deeply into her eyes. "I will ring you. Just let me get me head sorted when I'm out and then I will arrange to meet you." Johnny licked his lips slowly and placed a soft warm kiss onto hers. This was enough to put a smile on her face. There was no way he was ever going to ring her, he just said that to keep her happy. Imagine it, him dating a screw, he would have been a laughing stock. Johnny turned his head slowly and walked back to the bed. He picked his belongings up and swung the bag over his shoulder. He was amused and sniggered. "Wow, the fun we could have had if you would have mentioned this earlier."

Louise covered her mouth with her hand and she was laughing too. "I know, I would have most probably lost my job too for the things I'd imagined doing to you." What a filthy cow she was! A real dark horse! Johnny opened the cell door and walked onto the landing. He twisted his head back slowly. "I will ring you." A few inmates shouted over to him from the other side of the landing. This was a big day in the jail and already the vultures were circling ready to take over as the main man on the wing. Johnny walked to the pad next door to him and handed the inmate the things he didn't need on the outside. His radio, toiletries and other bits and bobs. Johnny inhaled deeply and his chest expanded as he made his way down the stairs in the centre of the jail. He was taking in every inch of this place, he never wanted to see it again in his life. Prison was for fools and the time he'd spent behind bars had taught him that crime doesn't pay. Four years he'd lost from his life, the best part of his youth. The times when he should have been out enjoying himself, sleeping with girls, going on holiday with the lads. This was the hardest part now, starting up again. He had to face the world and all its changes. His mother was still lying heavily on his mind and he knew whatever she was involved in, it was only him who could save her. It's funny though because if Elsie had been a half decent mother Johnny's life would have been so much different. He had ideas, good ways of earning honest money. A bit of an entrepreneur he was but his life was set in stone from such an early age, he had to be streetwise, know the crack, pay for the things his mother couldn't provide.

The screws patted him on the shoulder as he walked through the main gates. Johnny never looked back. The prison was his past now and he needed to look to the future if he was ever going to make it in life. He sucked in a large mouthful of fresh air. He closed his eyes slowly and nodded his head. It was true. At last he was free man. A car honked its horn in the distance and Johnny stretched his neck to see who it was. As promised Worm was there waiting for him. Johnny zipped his grey coat up and started to jog towards him. Worm stood waiting for him with a smile on his face. As soon as he got there they both shared a moment, a big man hug. See, that's how these two worked, they didn't need a single word to show they cared about each other, it was just an unwritten rule they lived by. Worm dipped his head inside the car and pulled out a bag with a new tracksuit inside it and a pair of trainers. Now this was friendship. Johnny nodded his head as he realised what was inside. "Sorted mate. I'll get home first and then I'll get this stuff on. I can't wait for a decent bath and decent bar of soap. You know what it's like in there don't you?"

Worm smiled and got inside the car. "Yep I sure do, cardboard as arse wipe and food that has no flavour, don't fucking remind me. I'm glad to see the back of the place." They chuckled as the car pulled out from the side street. Johnny sat taking in all the surrounding area. It was daunting to him and as with any prisoner who'd just done a long sentence it was hard for him to get his head around it.

Worm headed to the motorway, his foot was flat down on the accelerator. Manchester was about forty-five minutes away from Preston and he knew sooner or later Johnny would want some answers to what was going on in the outside world. Turning the tunes up in the car he hoped it might buy him a bit of time. He wasn't that lucky though. Johnny was straight on it. "So, what's the score? Has my mam turned up yet or what?" Worm wriggled about in his seat and kept his eyes on the road. He'd kept Johnny informed over the last few days but what he hadn't told him was that his mother was on drugs and selling her body. He still wasn't sure about this as it was all just rumours. Johnny wanted answers and he wasn't backing down. He was under pressure and Worm had to fill him in. Once he'd told him, Johnny sat cracking his knuckles. There was a silence in the car and Johnny's nostrils were flaring. He turned towards Worm and gripped the middle of his arm firmly. "What, so she's a brass?" Worm tried to soften the blow but no matter which way he put it the truth was there for him to see, Elsie was on the game. Johnny was white, sweat forming on the top of his brow. Sat twisting his hot palms he opened the car window and sucked in the cool fresh air. This was too much for him to take in. He held his head in his hands and sighed. "When is this shit ever going to end, ay? What fucking chance do I have of ever getting my life back on track when I'm dealing with shit like this every bastard day!"

Worm was in the same boat as Johnny and he too had tried to have a life without crime but it never worked out. Life was so hard. Once a criminal, always a criminal. Worm's mobile started ringing. He answered the call and put the call on hands free. Johnny was alert when he heard June's voice. "Worm, is Johnny there with you?"

"Yeah, you're on speaker so he can hear you." Johnny chuckled, the technology had changed so much since he was last on the streets. He was shouting now, making sure she could hear him. "Hiya, I'm on my way home. I hope you've got me a full breakfast ready just like you promised?"

June was silent for a few seconds. Cooking was the last thing on her mind. "That sister of yours is driving me up the bleeding wall. She knows you're home today and I thought she would have at least made the effort to come and give me a hand to get things ready for you. A lazy bitch she is. I bet she's still asleep in her pit."

Johnny raised his eyes to the roof. "I'll be there soon. Just relax and stop stressing. Annie will turn up when she's ready." Johnny wasn't worried about his sister. She was a good girl and she was probably just chilling out at one of her friend's houses. Girls were like that, they'd just get a duvet and a chick flick and chill out for days. Annie had been doing this all her life, weeks away sometimes, she just came home whenever she wanted.

Worm ended the call and smiled over at Johnny. "I swear, she makes me piss laughing that woman does, I don't know how you cope with her. Some of the things she comes out with are unreal. She's cuckoo."

Johnny nodded. He'd missed June's banter and he was glad he was going to get some quality time to spend with her. At the end of the day, family was all that kept him going through his sentence. June had always been there when he needed a shoulder to cry on and without her he would have just curled up and died a long time ago. She was his rock, his normality in life. June could always make him see sense and she had the knack of always calming him down when the going got tough. She was more of a mother to him than Elsie had ever been, she was always there no matter what.

The journey seemed to fly by and Johnny was already starting to notice some of Manchester landmarks. Strangeways prison was still the way he'd remembered it and the large red brick tower was still as daunting as ever. He'd spent a few months in there at the start of his sentence and shivered as they drove past it. There were some dangerous men inside those walls, sick twisted men who were serving life sentences for their crimes. This was somewhere Johnny never wanted to go again, ever in his life. The music was throbbing in the car now as the deep bass kicked in - if the truth was known it was doing his head in. He was used to the quiet life now and this racket was too much. Boom, boom boom, that's all he could hear. Worm was singing along to the track. He sniggered over at Johnny and smiled. "I'll tell you what mate when you get out in the clubs now you'll shit a brick. It's not like it used to be. Everyone's off their heads on magic and pills. You know me, I like to party with the best of them but this shit is hard-core. I had a bit of magic the other month in a club and I swear to you on my life they had to carry me out on a stretcher. I didn't know where I was or fuck all. My head was done in for days. Nar, it's not for me that crap. I'll just stick to a few spliffs to get my buzz." Johnny examined Worm closer, he was serious about what he'd just said, you could actually see the fear in his eyes. "So, how does it feel to be a free man then, I bet you're dying for some pussy?"

Johnny chewed on his bottom lip and smiled. "It's alright I think. I just need to get my head around it all. You know more than me how much your head falls off when you finish off a sentence. And, as for women, that can wait."

Worm nodded as he flicked back to the time when he was released from jail. "Tell me about it. Two weeks I stayed in my bedroom after I got out. I thought I was losing the plot. I just couldn't get my head round it all. Once my door was closed that was me, I thought I was on bang-up."

Johnny chuckled and agreed with him. "Yeah, that's the one. I just need to chill for a few days and I'll be sorted. Once I'm back on the scene everything should just fall back into place."

The car pulled up outside June's house and they could see her peeping out through the net curtains like a sniper. Once she was sure that it was her nephew she came running out of the house screaming and shouting. "Welcome home love. I've put a few butties out and that in the house for you. It's not a party but I've invited a few of the old heads round to come and see you."

Johnny raised his eyes at Worm and they both knew it was going to be a long night. Worm locked the car and they all headed back into house. "Welcome home," they all shouted as Johnny walked inside the front room. Johnny was gobsmacked and taken back. June said she'd invited a few people round, there were more than just a few here, the house was packed. Johnny was shaking hands with all the old crew and the girls were all over him like a rash, gagging for it they were. Gill Taylor spotted Johnny and her heart skipped a beat as he walked past her. She'd always had a soft spot for Johnny and now that Natalie was out of the picture, she couldn't wait to get her claws into him. The music started and the beer began to flow. June could always throw a good party and today was no different. The alcohol was stacked high in the kitchen and the food was enough to feed them all for days. June had had a whip round amongst Johnny's friends and they all put some cash into the pot to make sure that he had a good night.

A little later, Worm was on the other side of the room chatting to some girl and Johnny was stood alone pondering his thoughts. Gill Taylor saw her chance as she hurried to his side. She was chubbier than Johnny remembered and as soon as she got in his face he was gobsmacked at her confidence. "You're look good Johnny, are you glad to be home?"

He was just about to answer her when another girl jumped into the conversation. "He's mint, Gill, introduce me to this gorgeous man."

Gill saw her arse and snarled at Kerry. "Will you piss off? God, he's only been out of jail two minutes and you're trying to get him in bed."

Kerry stood with her two hands firmly fixed on her hips and fluttered her eyelids at him. "I'm just saying that's all. Whoa, wind your neck in, chillax."

Kerry danced away across the room and Gill stood watching her making sure she got the message. She turned to face Johnny and sucked hard on her gums. "She's a slapper her, keep well away, she's a dirt bag. Everyone's had a go of her, she's a right bike. A sperm bank she is." Johnny checked Kerry out and smiled. He didn't care if she was a slapper or not. He was just after a bang, not a relationship. He was a bit gutted really because she was probably the best looking girl in here. Gill moved closer to him. "So, do you think you'll ever go back to the nick then, or is this the new you?"

Why was it when a criminal got out of jail this was the first question everybody asked them? Did they want some kind of written statement, a life story or something? Why couldn't they just take him as they found him? Johnny took a deep breath, he thought about the question carefully before he answered her. "I'm just taking each day as it comes Gill. I'm not making promises I can't keep. That way, I won't disappoint anyone will I?"

Gill blushed, this guy was hot and she was doing her best to get him interested in her, he was hard work though. He wasn't biting. Gill was just an average looking girl though and probably not the best looking girl there but she still thought she had a chance of bedding this beauty. She upped her game. At first she was struggling to make conversation with him and she could see his eyes were elsewhere in the room. She had to do something and fast. Digging in her jacket pocket she flashed him a small bag of cocaine and whispered in his ear. "Do you want to put a bit of wind in your sails, a quick pick-me-up? A nice little bump."

Johnny licked his dry cracked lips and ragged his fingers through his hair. This was not what he needed right now. He'd left that life behind and he didn't want to get mixed up with it all so soon after being released from jail. He had to think quickly, make up excuses so he didn't look soft. This was a nightmare and he wasn't prepared for any of this so soon after his release. If he was being truthful the cocaine had got a grip of him before he went to jail. He had a habit, not that he would ever admit that to anyone, but he did. Day after day he was snorting this shit and some days he couldn't function without it. He closed his eyes tightly, remembering just how it felt to be high, yes, it was a good feeling but there was dark side to the drug too, a dangerous side that few spoke about. No one ever mentioned the comedown. There were times in his life when he'd been suicidal after a weekend on this shit. He'd actually thought about ending his life. That's how bad things had got. His mind was made up, only a fool would get involved with this kind of shit again. He told her straight. "Nar, not for me right now. I'm just having a few beers and taking my time. I feel pissed already and I've only had two bottles.

Anyway, I'm a new man now, drug free."

Gill was deflated and shoved the white powder back in her pocket. What a disaster this was, she thought he was dead cert for a bit of fun. Jail had changed him for sure. He was a boring fucker now, a straight head. June was on her way over to them both and Johnny was glad to escape from the situation. She was pissed, she'd had a few drinks even before Johnny had got there. It was just to calm her nerves she said but everyone there knew she was lying. She'd necked at least a half bottle of Vodka. June tugged on Johnny's arm. She went close to his ear and whispered. "I'm sorry about your mam love. It's not what you need to hear right now, but we'll sit down and discuss it properly in the morning. But, for now, try and enjoy yourself. Come on, loosen up miserable arse." Johnny seemed distant, he was shell shocked and finding it hard to cope with all the people in the house. He would have much rather just come home and chilled in his bedroom than attend his homecoming party. Jail did that to men, isolated them, played with their heads. The world was much different on the out and it was going to take some time before he found his feet again. In jail he had constantly had one eye open, he never trusted anyone and always watched his back. It was a dog eat dog world inside and you were living on borrowed time every time you let your guard down. The only time any inmate felt safe was after bang up. Once the door was locked you could start to relax and not be worried that someone was going to do the dirty on you.

The day turned into night and Gill was trying to bag herself a fuck buddy for the night. Her jaw was swinging low and she was fully wired. She stood gawping at Johnny twisting her ponytail in her hands and walked slowly over to him. There was no beating around the bush this time and she went straight in for the kill. "Are me and you getting off or what. I bet you're dying for a leg over aren't you. Four years is a long time without any female attention isn't it?"

Johnny was pissed and he was struggling to focus. The beer goggles were well and truly on and this girl looked like a super model to him now. He smiled at her and pulled her closer to his chest. "You're right, it is a long time to go without any sex but I'm sure you can help me out can't you?"

Gill didn't need asking twice. She reached over and sank a warm wet kiss onto his lips. "Come on then, show me your bedroom. I'm here for a good time not a long time." Gill giggled and pulled him up to his feet. Worm was on the other side of the room laughing out loud. He'd slipped Gill one too when he first got out of prison, she was a dirt bag who come in handy sometimes. Especially when a man needed a quick shag. Poor Johnny, this munter was going to ruin him.

Johnny lay on his double bed, his head was spinning. Gripping the side of the duvet with a tight grip he rolled about ready to spew. Gill knew what she wanted and didn't waste a single second more. Stood facing him she slipped her dress over her head and stood looking at him wearing nothing but her bra and knickers. I wish I could say the underwear was matching and sexy but in all honesty the bra was grey and the knickers were big belly warmers, passion killers. She un-hooked her bra and rolled her sweaty briefs over her fat thighs. The room was cold and goose pimples started to show all over her skin. This girl was a lard arse, blubber hanging from every nook and cranny, she was shocking to look at. "Bleeding move over then," she hissed as she tried to get into the bed next to him. Gill snuggled close to her new man and gripped his cheeks in her fat banana like fingers. Johnny was a prized catch and now she had him in her arms she wasn't letting go. Johnny had been with Natalie for years and no one ever got near him. He hadn't cheated on her once despite the endless offers. This was a day that would go down in history in Gill's eyes, improve her street cred. She was about to bang Johnny Barker. Gill took advantage of him that night because he was dead to the world. She tried every trick in the book to get him aroused but his cock was like a wet slug, lifeless. After twenty minutes of trying her best to get him hard she finally gave up and fell back down on the bed beside him. Johnny was unconscious and within minutes he was snoring his head off. Gill stared at him. She could have got up and got ready and tried to get sex somewhere else. But no, she was staying put. Hopefully in the morning he would be raring to go and when he awoke she would be there waiting for him, ready to give him a good time.

Gill's eyes closed slowly and she never saw Worm open the door and peer inside. Once the door was open he clocked Gill straight away and smirked. The look on his face was one of relief. He knew how much his pal had doted on his ex-girlfriend and this tart was just what he needed to get her out of his mind for good. Worm closed the bedroom door and headed back downstairs to the party. There were only a handful of people left in the room now. The rest had gone on into town or headed to another party. That was the thing in this area, you could always find a party or somewhere to chill, nobody was ever left alone. It was one big happy family.

Worm lay on the sofa. He was just getting ready to go to sleep when he heard the front door closing. June had been in bed for ages and he knew it wasn't her. Sitting up he was alert and searching for his jeans. Worm always carried a blade with him, he was always tooled up. It was just the way he was and he wasn't scared of sticking it into someone either. In the past he'd nearly killed a man he had a beef with. Worm couldn't really fight, he was all mouth, but once he had a tool in his hand he was lethal. He tried to control his breathing, his eyes never left the door. Slowly the door handle moved and he held his silver blade tightly in his hand. June sold a bit of weed on the estate to make ends meet and it was well known in the area that sooner or later someone would be through your front door trying to tax it from you. The light clicked on in the room and he was blinded for a few seconds. His hand covered his eyes and he was trying to find his feet. Annie stood there and sniggered as she saw him stood there in just his boxer shorts. "Eww, cover yourself up, that's hanging," she snarled.

Worm could see her now and shook his head. "For fucks sake, I shit my pants then. I thought you was a grafter."

Annie was pissed and she was wobbling as she made her way over to a nearby chair. Once she sat down she kicked her shoes off and sat rubbing at her feet. "I was going to stay at Rita's but we ended up having a big massive row. She's a right drama queen her, sometimes. I've never really seen it until now. A proper smacked arse she is."

Worm lay back down on the sofa and dragged the dark grey blanket over his body. He looped his hands behind his head and popped a cigarette into his mouth. "So, don't tell me June thinks you've been just sat at Rita's all night. Fuck me, you're wasted. It's a good job June hasn't clocked you because you'd be up shit street if she had."

Annie sat back in her seat and pulled her legs up under her bottom. "Like I'm arsed. June knows what I do. It's just a respect thing isn't it that I have to lie to her. That way she feels better and I do."

Worm chugged hard on his fag and blew a large cloud of grey smoke out in front of him. "Your kid's home, I thought you would have been home to see him?"

"Yeah, don't worry about our Johnny, he knows what I'm like. I'll catch up with him in the morning. Where is he anyway?"

Worm nodded his head slowly and kept a low voice. "He's in feather with Gill Taylor, you know the one with the face like a bulldog chewing a wasp?"

"Ewww, no way. How the hell has that happened? The girl is a fat porker. Please tell me he was pissed, don't dare tell me he's making her his girlfriend?"

"Nar, she's just a quick shag. She was all over him all night, gagging for it she was."

Annie shot a look of disgust over at him. "I swear, as long as a fanny had a few pubes on it, you'd shag anything."

Worm nearly choked. He'd never really spoken with Annie like this, he always thought she was a bit prudish. Worm studied her a bit longer than he should have. She was mint, a proper looker but that was a boundary you never crossed, you never slept with your best friend's sister. Well, not before discussing it anyway. Annie sat thinking. "So, has he asked about Natalie yet?"

Worm blew his breath and dragged his fingers through his crop of thick dark brown hair. "No, I've been lucky. But, you know sooner or later the question will pop up. To tell you the truth I'm bricking it. I don't know, fucking women. Can't live with them and can't live without them."

Annie held a cunning look in her eye. She stood to her feet and wobbled slightly. "If June asks, I wasn't pissed okay?"

Worm made a sign of the cross across his body and winked. "Your secret's safe with me. Go on, get in bed and sleep it off. Hopefully, I'll see you in the morning."

Annie left the room and you could hear the stairs in the hallway creaking as she made her way up to bed. Tonight had been a good night and it had opened her eyes to opportunities coming her way. And, as for Rita, she didn't need her friendship. As far as she was concerned she could go and take a running jump. She was sick of her stress and her problems anyway. Who needed friends, she was fine on her own!

CHAPTER FIVE

JOHNNY TRIED LIFTING his head off the pillow. It felt like a lump of lead and any movement he made was painful. Opening his eyes slowly he could see the image of someone lying next to him. Taking his time to focus he realised it was a woman. How the hell had she got there next to him, he didn't remember a thing. Her warm stale breath hit him in the face and the smell of cow shit made him heave as he twisted his head from hers. At that moment Johnny wished he was in bed alone. This was some weird shit because he'd not had anybody in bed with him for years. He folded the blanket back slowly and nearly got the shock of his life. For crying out loud his standards had dropped. He may as well of shagged a pig. There was no curvaceous figure like the one he'd seen in his ex-girlfriend, this was just a bob lying next to him in bed. He sniggered to himself and tried rolling slowly out of the bed. He was as quiet as a mouse. There was no way he was spending a second more next to this bint. Slowly, slowly, he was nearly out of the bed. One more movement and he was safe. Suddenly he felt a warm hand on his shoulder gripping him tightly, pulling him back. The buffalo had woken up. Johnny stuttered and turned his head slowly towards her. "I was just going for a piss. I'll be back soon."

Gill stretched her body out fully and yawned. "Good job, I thought you was trying to do one. We've got unfinished business." Johnny's jaw dropped. This couldn't be happening, what the hell was he going to do? Okay, she was a minger but there was no way he wanted to hurt her feelings. With speed in his step he left the room and hurried to the bathroom. Once he got there he stood looking at himself in the mirror. He looked rough and his eyes were heavy. Right, think lad, how are you going to get out of this one? Stood above the toilet he held his cock in his hand as he emptied his bladder. It was erect now and stood to attention. Smirking to himself he shook his head. One for the team he would call Gill. Was having sex with her such a bad thing anyway. It could be weeks until he got hooked up with a decent bird anyway so perhaps things weren't that bad after all. Johnny flushed the toilet and grabbed a toothbrush from the side of the sink. He hated hanging breath. Now, he was ready to go back into the bedroom. He'd decided, she was getting it. He wasn't kissing her though, no way in this world. He was going to spin her over and give it her from behind, how bad could that be?

Johnny walked back into the bedroom and Gill had assumed the star fish position. All her growler was hanging out and this girl held no shame at all. Her lady garden was like a big fur ball that looked like a squashed hedgehog and he'd never seen anything so hairy in his life. It was like one of the fannies he'd seen in a seventies porn magazine when he was younger. You know, like the ones the young lads had found belonging to their dads in the garden sheds. Kevin Moran had been the supplier of porn back in the day and word had it that his dad had every fanny magazine under the sun. It was never proved though but whatever he brought into school, it always did the job. A fanny was a fanny in his eyes and beggars couldn't be choosers, especially when they were growing up. Johnny plonked back down onto the bed and stretched his body out fully. Gill rolled next to him and without wasting a second more she gripped his penis in her hands. This was weird, he was used to masturbating himself. Closing his eyes he imagined a vision out of the porn magazine he had when he was in the nick. Dirty Donna was mint and all the lads in the jail pulled one off to her when they were feeling horny, she was filthy. Gill was quite heavy handed and at one point he was going to tell her to leave it but he kept schtum and let her continue. She looked him straight in the eyes and smiled. "I can do a great deep throat if you want me to have a go at that, wanks are not really my thing, I'm better with my mouth?"

Whoah, was he hearing things right or what, what had happened to the world whilst he'd been in the slammer. This girl was game for anything. Johnny looked at her and she was pressing for an answer. "Yeah, crack on. I wouldn't say no to blow job." Gill disappeared under the duvet. She was right too, she was mint at giving a good crunch. Johnny's toes curled at the end of the bed and he was ready to come. He was horny now and ready for anything.

Gill popped her head from out of the duvet and crawled to the top of the bed. What the hell was she doing, he was nearly there, ready to explode. "You can go and visit my lady garden if you want. I don't do sixty nines, you need to return the favour." she opened her eyes wide and smirked. "That means, this is a boomerang session. I want one back."

Johnny's face creased at the sides. Was she for real or what? Gill grabbed his head in her hands and pushed him deep between her legs. This was some overgrown motty and Johnny was lost to start with. This was a bush-tucker trial for sure. Where the hell did he start? Opening her flaps up he dipped his tongue in slowly. It wasn't as bad as he first thought smell wise. Gill was groaning with pleasure and sinking her long talons into his back. He'd forgotten how much he like to chew on it and everything was coming back to him now, he was lost in the moment. Gill screamed out as she orgasmed, she was loud and he was panicking in case anyone in the house heard her. Climbing back up to the top of the bed he spun her over and sank her head deep into the pillow. She looked good like that, well, a bit better than she did before. Johnny was like a stallion. His body was firm and every movement he made was deep inside her. Closing his eyes slowly he gritted his teeth together and rammed it home. This was just sex, nothing more nothing less. Making love was for girls who you respected and there was no way she was getting any of his tenderness, not now, not ever. The moment eventually came and after four years of being starved of a woman's body he shot his load. His body tensed and his back arched. Gill was suffocating as he pressed her head deep into the pillow and it wasn't until he'd enjoyed the moment did he realise she was gagging for breath, he was suffocating her.

Johnny rolled off her and fell to the side of the bed, exhausted. Gill blew a breath and lay flat on her back. Her cheeks were bright red and she looked like she was going to pass out. She looked over at him and smiled. After a few seconds she rested her head onto his chest, snuggling deep into it. Johnny looked at the top of her head and snarled. Did this girl want loving or some kind of after care service? No, there was no way he was getting into that. It was what it was, sex, just pure simple sex. Gill turned her head slightly and puckered up. The cheeky cow was after a kiss. He pecked her on the forehead quickly and smiled at her. "Thanks for that, it was kind of good." She sat up in the bed and she'd seen her arse, he'd hurt her feelings. "Yeah thanks a fucking bunch. Go on, do what they all do now after they've had a shag, go on tell me I have to go." He was stuck for words. But, she was right, what was the point in hanging around any longer. The deed had been done and he didn't see himself ever seeing her again but she was onto him and he had to use his plan b. "No, I wasn't going to say that I was just thinking what time is was. You know I've got to report to probation at twelve o'clock don't you? I'd love to spend more time with you but you know how these things work, if I miss an appointment they'll just bang me back up. No messing about." Gill stroked her finger along her chin. She was thinking if he was having her over or not. She wasn't sure but at least he wasn't throwing her out. "I'll go and make us a drink. Fancy a coffee?" Gill nodded and her eyes were wide open. This was a bonus and he must have liked her otherwise why else would he be keeping her here?

Johnny left the room and headed down the stairs. He walked into the front room and clocked Worm fast asleep on the sofa. Once he'd opened the curtains he made his way to him and started shaking him by the arm roughly. "Wake up, I need help to get rid of that munter upstairs. Fuck me, how did you let me end up with her?" Worm rubbed his knuckles deep into his eyes. He was still half asleep. Johnny shook him again and he was panicking. "Come on mate, hook a brother up and help me out."

Worm stretched his face and he was aware of his surroundings now. He clocked Johnny and took a few seconds to digest what he'd just said. Sitting up straight he folded the pillow behind his head and started singing. He was winding him up. "Gill and Johnny, sitting in the tree K-I-S-S-I-N-G."

Johnny started to giggle and playfully punched him the arm. "Stop fucking about, help me out ay?"

Worm held a serious expression and folded his arms tightly in front of him. "I could have told you dropped a bollock last night, but mate," he paused and raised his eyebrows high, "you was all over her, tongue shoved down her neck and everything. You were proper up for it."

Johnny went white, he stood up and backed away

slowly. He didn't remember a thing. He held a puzzled look. "What, I was all over her? Seriously. Nar, stop lying."

"Yep, telling her you loved her and all that. I'm sure you told her you would marry her."

This wasn't real, no way in this world had he told this slapper he was wife-ing her off. From the corner of his eye he saw Worm sniggering. What a fucker he was, he was having him over. Johnny gasped and at last he could see the funny side of things. "You clown, I really believed you then. But seriously, help me out. I need her gone. Like now, like in the next few minutes."

The living room opened and Gill was stood there. She hadn't heard the previous conversation and just sat down oblivious to it all. "I'm just waiting on the kettle to boil and I'll make us a brew," Johnny said.

Gill tried straightening her hair and stuck her index finger in her mouth to wet it. Stroking it under her eyes softly she tried wiping the mascara that was there, she had panda eyes. Worm jumped up from the sofa and wrapped the blanket around his shoulders. The house was freezing and no matter how much he tried he couldn't get warm, his teeth were chattering together. He followed Johnny into the kitchen and he must have had a feather up his arse because he couldn't stop laughing. Closing the door behind him with a quick movement he burst out into fits of laughter, eyes watering, unable to speak for a few seconds. "So, how did you tackle the jungle, you know, the big hairy flange?"

Johnny nearly choked and he was finding it hard to breathe. "How do you know about that?"

Worm squeezed the sides of his nose together and stamped his feet to try and control his amusement. "Because she gripped me when I got of jail too. I swear, she's got the hairiest fanny I've ever seen in my life."

He started doing hand gestures pointing to his private region. The two lads high-fived each other and Worm went back into the front room still amused by the whole affair. Once Johnny had made the coffee he joined them. There was no way any of the lads could look at each other, they were both giddy and could have broken at any time. Gill was aware of the awkward silence and shot a look at them both. "I know what's happening here. You two have been slagging me off in the kitchen. Fucking cheeky if you ask me. Johnny, you should have said if you wanted me to leave. I'm not desperate you know."

Worm wasn't having this bint calling the shots, no way. Who did she think she was? He spoke directly to her. "Listen you, take your head from out of your arse. There is no way Johnny is ever going to make you his girlfriend. You're just one of them… erm, dirt bags."

Gill saw her arse, she was bright red. She exploded from her seat and ran at Worm poking a single finger deep into his bare chest. "Whatever. He wasn't saying that last night was he? And you can keep it shut too. I only ever done you as a favour. You were punching above your weight with me if I'm telling the truth here." Worm was gobsmacked. What a cheeky bitch she was. It was Johnny's turn to giggle now. "One for the team you were Worm, so don't flatter yourself." Gill flicked her fringe from her eyes and licked her lips over at Johnny. "You know where I am if you need me. Ring me later if you want?"

With that, Gill walked to the front door and slammed it behind her. Johnny ran to the window and pulled the net curtain back slightly. He watched her waddle down the garden path. "Thank fuck for that. I thought she was going to be here for the long-haul."

Worm was still thinking about what she'd just said and his pride had been hurt. He classed himself as a prize catch and this bitch had just knocked him down a peg or three. Johnny sat slurping at his coffee trying to get used to the life on the out. Even to have someone in the same room with him at this time of the morning was something he was finding it hard getting used to. He rolled himself a cigarette and stuck it in his mouth. "So, where the fuck do we start? June seems to think my mam is in deep shit. What do you think?"

Worm took a deep breath and sucked hard on his gums. "I think she's fine. She's a woman of the world and she'll turn up when she's ready." Johnny sat and thought about it. He was right, Elsie was always doing the missing trick and he knew in his heart she could look after herself but who was this guy Monty? And what the hell was his mother doing mixed up with him? He needed to know more, suss him out. But, for now he had more important things on his mind like attending his probation appointment. Johnny sat in deep thought and listened to Worm's phone call. He wasn't feeling himself and his heart seemed to be beating faster than normal. Once the call had ended Worm smiled over at him. "Got a bit of graft if you're up for it mate. A few grand, just for a few hours work, easy money?"

Johnny hesitated. There was no way he was ready for this. His head was in bits and he was struggling to come to terms with life on the outside. Dipping his eyes low he replied. "Nar, I'll leave this one. Let me find my feet first and I'll be back on it." Worm accepted his answer and didn't pressurize him further. There would be more grafts along the way and he knew sooner or later his best mate would be back on the crime scene. Johnny clocked the time and swigged the last mouthful of his brew. "Right, can you drop me off in Miles Platting. I've got to go to probation. You know what it's like when you first get out. The cunts are all over you."

Worm started to get ready, he slipped his trainers on. "Yep, no worries, ready when you are."

Johnny was dropped outside the probation centre. Worm was going to wait with him but he declined the offer. He fancied a bit of time on his own anyway and the walk back would do him good, clear his mind, give him time to think. Twisting his head over his shoulder he watched Worm drive off. Johnny stood looking at the building in front of him and shook his head slowly, he never thought he'd end up back here again. He was last here when he was younger and knew the script inside out. All the lads did in the area. Miles Platting was a place he was familiar with and it was only about ten minutes from where he lived in Collyhurst. Johnny walked inside the probation centre and he could see about four guys sat on the chair waiting to go in to see somebody; they were the usual type, dead-legs, druggies, plastic gangsters. He walked to the reception and told them he was here. Johnny was hot, sweating, a panic attack was setting in, his expression changed. The walls seemed to be closing in on him, suffocating him, choking. He gripped his hand around his windpipe and rubbed at it hoping to ease the anxiety. Someone was talking to him but the words were not registering. He staggered to the exit, he shoulder charged the door open. Johnny needed to breathe, get some fresh air in his lungs. The door swung opened and he hurried outside. Stood with his back pressed firmly against the cold brick wall he hammered his clenched fist into his chest. This was bad, he was hyperventilating. The wind picked up and circled his body, the front of his fringe was lifting up and down. He took long, deep breaths. Johnny was white, completely drained of any colour.

A hand from behind him landed on his shoulder and for a split second he was ready to lash out, his mind was blank and he didn't have a clue where he was. The male gripped the middle of his arm and turned him around. "Are you alright mate, do you want me to get you a drink or something." Johnny squeezed his eyes together and focused. His vision was returning and the world around him was slowing down. He sucked in large mouthfuls of air and blew it frantically from his mouth. The man could see he was in some sort of trouble and rushed back into the centre. Within minutes he was back holding a glass of water. "Go on, neck a bit of that and it will sort you out." Johnny reached for the glass and swallowed large mouthfuls of the cold liquid. "Have you just got out of chokey?" Johnny sank to the floor and brought his legs up to his chest, shivering, his teeth were chattering. Whatever had just happened to him put the fear of God up him, he was in shock. He took long deep breaths, he was calming down.

Johnny nodded his head slowly and he was glad that somebody was here with him just in case he dropped down dead on the spot. Taking a few seconds to get his head back together Johnny answered him. "Yeah, I got out yesterday."

The man sat down next to Johnny and smirked. "Yep, your head's just fell off mate. It's normal when you first get out of nick. It took me months before I got to grips with the life on the out," he raised his eyebrows and jerked his head back. "This place doesn't help either. It's a lot of pressure to come here as soon as you're out but these pricks don't give a flying fuck. It's all about filling forms out. Not one of them has a clue about an ex-convict and what we go through." Johnny was listening and the colour started returning to his cheeks. He was still a bit shaky but the worst seemed to be over. "I'm Scotty by the way. I got out after a six year stretch last month. Have you sorted your benefits out and all that yet? It takes forever. I mean, you get out of the big house and they just leave you to rot.

How the fuck do they expect you to live when you've got fuck all?" This guy was on one and he was sat trying to put the world to rights.

Johnny felt slightly embarrassed. He hated anyone seeing his vulnerable side. He stood and flicked some dust from his jacket. His voice was low and the wind had been knocked well and truly out of his sails. "Cheers for sorting me out Scotty. I just went under for no reason, fuck me, I thought my days were up."

"All part of the service, lad. Anyway, where you from?" Johnny told him a bit about himself and they both started to walk back into the centre. Scotty was tall around six foot five inches. He was thin with sunken cheeks and dark eyes. Prison does that to men, it steals their youth and leaves them looking old and frail. Johnny's name was called almost immediately as they entered back in the probation office. He made his way to the door. Just before he left he turned his head and nodded at the good Samaritan.

"So, how you finding things so far," the probation officer asked. She was only young and in her in early twenties. Pretty thing she was too, slim and the most enchanting blue eyes he'd ever seen.

"Just another day isn't it," Johnny replied.

Kelly looked him over and started to take notes. She loved her job and loved meeting different people each day. She was more than just a probation officer and she always gave her best to help the ex-convicts find a new path in life. She knew more than anyone how prison affected everyone involved. Her own father had served ten years in the nick when she was growing up and she knew a lot about prison life, more than she would like anyone to know. Kelly started to help him fill some forms out. So many of them, ticking boxes, filling out his home address, adding his national insurance number, it was an endless job.

"So, what about finding work Johnny, have you thought about what you want to do now you're a free man?"

Johnny snarled at her, was she on this planet or what, she was talking out of her arse. He couldn't help himself and told her how it was in the real world. Johnny swung back in his chair and chuckled. "If you can find me a job then I'm up for it, but come on, who will give me any work. I've just got out of jail for armed robbery. No one will ever trust me. Would you?"

Kelly got her back up and sat forward in her seat. She hated people with negative outlooks and her job was to try and change the way the offenders thought, they needed self-belief, hopes and dreams. "We work alongside companies who are willing to give ex-inmates a crack at life. It's not the best paid jobs, but it's a start."

Johnny sat playing with his hands. He smiled at her, "And, do I look like someone who will work for minimal wages. These companies takes the piss and they never keep you anyway, you're just the skivvy. The moment anything goes wrong or missing they blame you and you're out on your arse. To tell you the truth Kelly, it's early days for me. I just need to chill for bit and get used to things at the moment. I might give it a go in a few months. But at the moment I'm not ready."

Kelly backed off and started writing. Her client hadn't said no to employment and that was good enough for her. Some of the lads she worked with give her a hard time and many a night after her shift had finished she closed her office door and sobbed her heart out. Some people just didn't want to be helped and the time she'd spent in the job had taught her that. Kelly had been attacked too, yes, this job was stressful and probably not worth the money she was paid. Johnny stared around the room. It was fresh and clean. It smelt of vanilla too, sweet, fresh aromas floated through the air and tickled his nostrils. It was nearly time for his session to end and Kelly was just giving him the last few leaflets she'd got together. Johnny wasn't ever going to read them, he was just taking them from her to be polite. His next appointment was arranged and he was free to go. Leaving the room he smiled back at her. "See you next week then."

She smirked and rolled the blue biro around in her fingers slowly. "Yes, you will." The door closed and Kelly sat staring into space for a few seconds. Her client was handsome and there was something about him that she liked. She's always been a sucker for a bad boy, she loved an adventure.

Johnny Barker marched out of the probation centre. He was wearing the new clobber Worm had bought him. The jacket was big on him but he knew after a few weeks of home life he would pile on the weight and fill his clothes out. Johnny looked around the area and took everything in. Nothing had really changed, only him. He set off walking and his head was somewhat clearer now. Well, apart from the banging headache he had, he had the hangover from hell. Digging his hand deep into his pocket he pulled out a tenner. Worm had bunged him a few quid to tide him over for a few days until he'd got himself sorted. A hangover needed food to recover, dirty greasy food to help ease the way he was feeling – a full breakfast with a mountain of toast. Yes just what the doctor ordered. With speed in his step he headed back to Collyhurst to a café on Eastford Square.

The square was just how he remembered it; five shops all in a row and there was a monument in the middle of it too. It had always been a favourite landmark of his and he'd often sat on top of it when he was growing up. Behind the shops was wasteland, big steep hills with landmarks in the distance. As he walked he could see where he'd spent most of the summer months when he was growing up. "Bob's Hill" was still there and every kid who'd ever grown up in the area probably had a story to tell about their adventures there. First sexual experience, glue sniffing, playing hide and seek. Johnny's heart sank. This was the place he'd spent hours with Natalie. They had their first kiss here, their first fondle... Johnny choked up slightly and inhaled deeply causing his nostrils to flare. His eyes clouded over. Where the hell was she now? Did she still think about him like he thought about her? She couldn't just be over him, just like that. They had history - a life they'd planned to share until they were old and grey. Johnny walked into the café and sat down at a table. He knew what he wanted to eat and there was no need to read the menu.

Donna had owned the café for years and recognised him almost immediately. He had been a regular there back in the day and he had a good relationship with her. "Glad to see you home Johnny. It's been a long one this has. Please tell me you're not going back there?"

Johnny stood and hugged her. She smelt of grease and grime. There was nothing really feminine about her. She was a grafter and she rarely had any time for beauty or the way she looked. "Can't promise anything, you know me Donna, I take each day as it comes."

She smiled and shook her head. Her voice was loud as she shouted behind her to her assistant. "Sort Johnny a full breakfast out on the house, he deserves it he does. Put him extra mushrooms on too."

Johnny chuckled and smirked over at the girl behind the counter. "Cheers love, can you make sure my egg is a bit runny too and that my toast isn't burn." Johnny was a fussy eater and he had some issues about what he ate. He hated fat on his meat and if his egg wasn't cooked properly he couldn't eat it. Elsie had given up years ago trying to please him and most of the time he cooked for himself. Johnny sat staring out of the window and watched the activities in the square. Two youths were stood in the corner and it wasn't rocket science to work out they were dealing weed. Johnny had done the same graft when he was growing up. Johnny was alert as he saw a black car pulling up. The shady youths sprinted over to it. He stretched his neck trying to see what was going on.

Donna was at the table now and she followed his eyes to where the car was parked. "He's a prick that man. I hate him with a passion. He's nothing but trouble."

Johnny turned slowly to face her. "Who is it, I've not seen his face before?" Donna placed the plate down on the table and pulled up a chair. She kept her voice low and checked nobody was listening. "It's Monty, it's rare you ever see him, he usually has his chipmunks doing all his dirty work for him. I swear to you, the guy is sick in the head. He comes in here sometimes and he thinks he's royalty. No manners, he thinks the world owes him a favour."

Johnny was listening now, this man's name kept popping up all over the place. "Where does he base himself, does he go in the boozers or what?"

Donna tickled the end of her chin with a single finger. "Yeah, he's goes in Billy Green's across the road. He sits in the vault, in the corner. He's always there later on. He thinks he's the fucking don, trust me he's a horrible bastard. Stay well clear of him, honest, the guy is bad news." Johnny started to eat his food and stabbed his fork into the sausage with a firm hold. Donna was still looking out of the window and speaking to him. "Rumour has it, that he's the one behind that brass gaff on Moston Lane. It wouldn't surprise me you know. He's a power freak. I believe he gets young girls to work for him," she turned her head back and her eyes were wide open. "You know, the immigrants, girls on their arses."

Johnny chewed on his food and spoke with a full mouth. "This is all news to me, where is he from, what's his background?"

Donna became a bit defensive now, she'd said too much already and she didn't want any of this to come back to bite her on the arse. Men like Monty held power and he could have closed her business down in seconds, burned it to the ground… Donna backed off. "I'm not sure, but like I said it's all hearsay so don't take my word for it." Donna pulled a cloth from her pocket and started to wipe the table nearby. Her eyes were still on the square outside and she was still watching Monty in the distance.

Annie walked into the front room and June was sat munching on some toast. "Where's our Johnny, has he gone out already?"

She nodded head and tried eating her food faster. "Yep, he's at probation so he had to get off. Anyway, I thought you were staying at Rita's last night, what happened to that?"

Annie plonked down the sofa and pulled her t-shirt over her legs. "Yeah, I was going to but she kicked off with me for no reason. We were nearly fighting, she went to hit me too!" June shot a look over at her niece. She was devious and she knew there was more to the story than she was letting on. Rita was a good girl most of the time; kind, caring, she wasn't a trouble causer. "Well, she can do one as far as I'm concerned. I don't need friends like her, she's a crank."

June sat back in her chair and folded her arms tightly

in front of her. "So, I take it you never looked at enrolling in college then?"

Annie found the remote for the TV and flicked it on. "Wow, I've just told you what happened. What did you expect me to do, stay there with her after she'd slagged me off?"

"I'm just saying there is no smoke without fire and you're probably only telling me half the bleeding story if I know you. Don't think I'm bleeding daft, give me some credit, ay."

Annie was in a strop. She grabbed a cushion from the sofa and plonked it behind her head. She wasn't in a mood to argue and she turned the volume up on the TV. June sat looking at her longer than she needed to, she was her mother's daughter alright; deep, dark, and an out and out liar. The front room was a shit-tip and in desperate need of cleaning. A duster hadn't seen this room in months and everything was old and out of date. June sat gawping out of the window. She had a great view of any visitors that walked down the garden path and, if the police were ever raiding her she always had a few minutes start before they boomed her front door in. She loved her perch, and there wasn't much she missed. June did what she had to do to get by. She was a petty thief and sold a bit of bud to line her pockets. She'd even grown her own when times were hard. Sat biting her nails she looked over at Annie and started a conversation. She hated silence and always thought she had to make conversation. "So, what are your plans for today? I was thinking of calling around to see a few of your mam's friends, just to see if they have seen anything of her."

Annie opened her eyes wide and rolled on her side. "Good luck with that then. I hope you're not asking me to go with you. I've told you before, I'm not arsed where she is. I'm sick to death of her and her drama." Annie got a text alert on her phone and read the message. She smiled to herself and pushed her phone underneath the cushion.

June was a right nosey fucker and her neck was stretched trying to see what was going on. "Was that Rita?"

Annie never took her eyes from the TV as she answered her. "Yep, she wants to meet up to sort it all out, but she can whistle. I'm not arsed any more. I don't need friends like her. I'd rather be on my own." June shook her head and walked out of the room. Annie made sure she was gone and gripped her mobile phone, she replied to the text and a cunning smirk appeared on her face.

A little later, June was plodding down the main road with her head dipped. The weather was bad and she wasn't prepared for the cold northerly wind. This woman was so unfit and every step she took she was finding it hard to breathe. June waddled down Conran Street and made her way to the estate close to it. Joan Maylet lived here and she had always been a good friend to Elsie. If anyone would know where she was, it was her. June flung her handbag over her shoulder and every step she took she was aware she could be attacked. There had been a spate of bag snatches on this estate and she was extra vigilant today just in case somebody was eyeing her up. June knocked at Joan's front door and stood back a bit so she could see the top windows. More than likely she would have been in her bedroom at this time and unable to hear her knocking. June walked up to the front door and lifted the letterbox. She cupped her hands around her mouth and shouted. "Joan it's me June, are you in or what? Come on love, open the bleeding door, it's blowing a gale out here?" She stood back from the door again and this time when she looked up she could see the net curtain twitching. A woman now appeared and banged on the glass pane to get her attention. June looked relieved that Joan was in and leaned on the garden fence until she opened the door.

Joan Maylet was a rough looking woman. She looked hard as nails. She'd spent a few months in jail and lived off the story for months. She'd told everyone she was mixed up with some of the most notorious criminals in her spell there when in fact she spent most of her time behind her door. Joan was built like an ox. She was tall as well. She looked down at June and scratched at her head. "What fucking time is it? It only feels like I've been in bed for a few hours."

June edged closer to her and she got a strong whiff of alcohol and stale fags on her breath. This woman was a heavy drinker and the Irish blood in her let her drink for hours on end, bottles of whisky, the strong stuff. "I've just come to have a chat with you about our Elsie, have you seen anything of her?"

Joan banged her clenched fist on the door panel and growled. "Have I fuck seen her, the cheeky bitch still owes me fifty quid. You better come in. I'm not discussing my business where everyone can hear it."

Joan plodded into the house and June followed her. She instantly covered her nose and started to gag as she walked further inside. There was dog shit everywhere in the hallway, splattered up walls, dollops of it everywhere she looked. Joan never even acknowledged it she just made her way to the front room oblivious to it all. Joan plonked down on a chair and reached for her cigarettes. There was a can of special brew at her side and she swallowed a gob full of it before she lit her fag. "Your Elsie is a dead woman walking, June. She's had a lot of people over and they're all gunning for her. She was sorted at first but as time went on she started being shady and covering things up. The last time I saw her she told me she was going to pay me the money back. She said she'd landed on her feet and money wasn't a problem anymore."

June urged her to continue. She needed to see the bigger picture if she was ever going to get to the bottom of this mess. June licked her lips slowly, she needed to know the truth, no matter how much it hurt her. "Is she on the game, Joan? I've heard it a few times now and I know you will tell me straight."

Joan sniffed hard and reached over to flick the ash from her cigarette. A Staffordshire bull terrier now ran into the room and sat by her side panting and licking hard at its bollocks. Joan swung her hand back and whacked the dog on its arse. "Have you shit again you dirty bastard," she snarled over at June. "I let him out last night about two in the morning and he still waits until he's inside before he shits. He'll be getting the death needle if he carries on." Joan grabbed the dog's face and spoke to it as if it could understand every word she spoke to him. "I swear to you mutt, if you ever shit in the house again you're getting fucked off from here. Let's see how you cope then when you're in the dog's home locked in a little bastard kennel all fucking day and night."

June waited until she'd calmed down again and pressed for an answer. "Is she selling her body?"

Joan cracked her knuckles and sucked hard on her cigarette. "I wouldn't call it selling her body. She was just having a good time. So what that she got presents from guys for the time she spent with them but I wouldn't have said she was selling her body. Whatever she was doing it was paying the bills."

June was relieved. This was a weight off her mind. Night after night she'd lay in her bed twisting and turning thinking her sister was in deep trouble, she started to relax a bit. Joan stubbed her cig out in the ashtray and commanded the dog to jump up on her lap. Patting him with firm hands she looked over at June. "Elsie has done her own shit for years, she always comes up smelling of roses, so just leave her to it. She can handle herself that woman, so stop worrying about her."

"It's hard not to worry," June gasped, "You know me I've always been the worrier. It's what I do."

Joan must have been touched by the emotion because she passed June a can of lager over. She very rarely ever shared her beer. "Here, get a slurp of that down your neck. It will sort out any stress you're under, look at me. I don't give a fuck anymore. I just get pissed and blank it all out."

June wasn't really a day drinker but she did feel the need to calm herself down. She opened the can and took a large mouthful. June choked, she banged her clenched fist on her chest. Her eyes were watering and she was struggling to speak. "Fuck me Joan, that's strong, it's took the lining off my tongue. What the hell is it?"

Joan sniggered and held her head back laughing. "Hard-core lager that is, it'll put hairs on your chest. Get it supped and shut up moaning before I take it back from you." June wiped her mouth with the side of her hand and started to relax.

Joan had always led a colourful life and June loved hearing the stories about the days gone by. "So, are you keeping out of trouble now Joan. You don't want to end up back in jail do you?"

Joan felt a wave of sadness pass over her. She took a few seconds to compose herself and answered. "Jail is a God send if I was being honest with you. I'm off the beer when I'm locked up aren't I? Jail is an easy life, three meals a day, no worrying about paying bills, honest, I would go back tomorrow if I could." Was this woman for real or what? What woman in the right mind would ever want to go back to prison? The two women sat sharing stories and the vodka was now out on the table. It was going to be a long day. Once Joan got started about her life she didn't know when to shut up. The two of them sat giggling.

Johnny walked along Rochdale Road and headed home. He still couldn't believe he was a free man. The fresh northern wind hit his cheeks as he walked along the main road and he had a lovely glow about him. Taking in everything around him he failed to see the young toddler running towards him with a desperate mother sprinting after her. The child grabbed at Johnny legs and started tugging at them, hiding behind them. He smiled at first and made sure the child didn't go near the road. A shrieking voice now filled his ears. "You naughty girl what have I told you about running off. You could have got ran over?" Johnny lifted his eyes and there she was, his Natalie. The girl who was still deep in his heart. He was speechless, in total shock.

Natalie grabbed the child and at first she didn't clock Johnny. She was knelt down and speaking to the child on her level. "You could have got run over, see them cars," she pointed at the busy road. "They could have killed you." Picking the little girl up in her arms she made sure she wasn't escaping any more. "Thanks for," Natalie was gobsmacked. She knew it was him now and her face was beetroot, her jaw swinging low. "Johnny, erm, I didn't know you were out."

There was a silence and neither of them could find the words to speak. The child started talking and pulling at her mother's hair. "Mummy, can we go to the shop and get some sweeties?"

Natalie tried to calm her down but never took her eyes

from Johnny. The little girl was so cute. Dark raven hair and beautiful deep blue eyes, she looked like her mother. At that moment Johnny put two and two together and a felt a sharp stabbing pain in his heart. He looked at the child again and then at Natalie. His temper was rising and he couldn't help himself. "So, she's the reason you carted me? Why didn't you just tell me you'd found someone else. For fuck's sake Natalie, how could you do this me, to us? I loved you."

Natalie swallowed hard and her windpipe tightened. Her lips were moving and no words were coming out. She had to say something, she owed him that much at least. "I loved you too Johnny but you chose the life you wanted and it wasn't with me. You had the choice, so don't you ever blame me for the way things turned out"

"How could I have had a choice when we needed some money. We had nothing and I was trying to give us a better life that's all."

Natalie was shaking and her nerves were getting the better of her, she stuttered. "You made your choice. I'm going, thanks for saving her, she's a handful sometimes."

Johnny wanted to say so much more, but what could he say now. Natalie had a baby. Another man in her life. Any hope he had of ever winning her back was gone. He could never take on another man's kid, not now, not ever. Natalie was damaged goods. Johnny watched her leave and his heart sank. What the fuck was going on with his life? Was he ever going to be at peace? Sitting down on a nearby bench he held his head in his hands. Years of emotion exploded and he sobbed his heart out. Somewhere in his mind he always thought when he got of jail he would see Natalie and they would get back together. But how could he do that now, she had a family, another man sleeping with her every night. He cracked his knuckles and punched them deep into the wooden bench causing them to bleed. He would have carried on too if a woman walking by hadn't have asked him if he was alright. He never answered her and bolted up from the bench and started to run away. Why the hell had nobody told him? Surely, all his family knew about this? What a shower of bastards they were! And, the minute he got home he was going to tell them exactly that. His head was spinning, his world had collapsed around him. He had to face it – Natalie had moved on.

CHAPTER SIX

ANNIE SAT PAINTING her long talons. Candy pink was her favourite colour and she made sure every nail was perfect with no blemishes. She sat blowing at them and smiling at herself in the mirror as she fanned her nails out admiring them. Endless texts were coming to her phone and she was replying to them instantly. The last message she sent read "I'll be there at half past eight like we arranged, see you then." Annie dabbed some more lip gloss on and walked to her wardrobe. Opening the door she grabbed the one dress that was hanging there. It was red and looked quite new. This was a special dress, her pulling dress she called it. Slipping it on over her slim body she stood looking at herself in the mirror. The bedroom door opened slowly and Johnny was stood there staring at her. She was so pleased to see him and ran at him throwing her arms around his neck. There was no response from him, nothing, he just peeled her fingers from his shoulders and walked to the bed and sat down with a face like thunder. Annie was aware he was upset and sat next to him. "I'm sorry I wasn't here last night, you know me. I was busy studying."

Johnny sniffed up hard and looked her deep in her eyes. "Did you know too? I thought you out of everyone would have said something. Why, why didn't you tell me?"

Annie had a blank look in her eyes and sat thinking, "What do you mean, told you what?"

Johnny cleared his throat and shook his head slowly before he delivered the blow. "About Natalie having a kid and fucking moving on. None of you ever said a word."

His temper was rising and she knew not to provoke him. He gritted his teeth tightly together and dropped his head low. "This has fucked my head up big-time. I've just seen her on the road and there she was playing happy families with her little girl. What a prick I looked! I can't believe it! Honest, it's done me in."

Annie choked up. Yeah, he was right, she did know about it but June had made everyone swear they wouldn't tell Johnny while he was locked away. Annie sank her head in shame, she'd let him down and she knew it. No matter what she said he was right, she'd let him down. Annie placed her hand softly on the bottom of his back. "Johnny, nobody wanted to hurt you. Imagine how you would have taken the news while you were inside, it would have destroyed you."

He snapped and he went nose to nose with her. "I should have been the one to decide that not fucking you. It was my right to know, she was all I had. Every night I dreamt about her and I thought once I came home we could have sorted shit out and started again. But now, it's all fucked up." Annie tried to comfort him but he pushed her away. He never needed any comfort and he wasn't starting now. "So," he hissed. "Who's she with then? Who's the kids father, come on you must know, you owe me that much?"

Annie took a deep breath and answered him. "Honest I don't know. You got slammed and the next thing we all knew she was pregnant. She's a slapper, just leave her to it. You don't need her."

Johnny stood and walked to the door. He turned to face his sister and the word he spoke crippled her. "Family means fuck all to me from now on. Loyalty is all I asked from you and you couldn't even do that."

Annie was going to run after him and try to explain herself but how could she? The truth was there for him to see – she had kept a secret from her brother. He was right, she was a sell-out. Annie held her ear to the door and the room shook as Johnny slammed his bedroom door shut. There were smashing and crashing noises, he was punching the door. There was no way she was going near him when he was like this, he was a loose cannon and God help anyone who got in his way now, he was a ticking bomb waiting to explode.

Annie jumped into Colin's car at their secret meeting place. Now Rita was out of the picture it was her turn to shine. Colin said he'd told Rita it was over after they all spent the night at the club. Rita had accused Annie of causing the break up and she turned into one crazy bitch once she knew it was over. She tried scratching Annie's eyeballs out and she insisted something was going on between them. Annie denied it of course but Rita was right, the two of them had been all over each other. This was their first date together and although Annie should have been a little bit nervous, she was full of herself. She had one thing on her mind. She wanted the gifts her friend had got and she would do whatever it took to get them, absolutely anything. Colin had booked them a meal out in a countryside pub. Somewhere quiet and discreet. He'd taken Rita there a few times in the past and he had a good relationship with the landlord there. They all knew the crack where Colin was concerned and they were used to seeing him with endless young girls on his arm. He'd told the landlord there that he was recruiting the girls for a modelling agency he ran but they all knew he was lying through his teeth. The guy was a pervert and everybody in the pub knew it.

Annie sat down at the table and Colin was at her side. He opened the cocktail menu and slowly slid his index finger along it. He moistened his lips and looked her in the eye. "Would you like an orgasm, or sex on the beach?"

Annie knew his game and sneered at him. She had to play along with him and get him to dig deep in his pockets. She wanted gifts, perfume, clothes, anything she could get out of him. Flicking her hair back over her shoulder she smirked and slowly tickled her lips with her fingernail. "I've never had an orgasm before, do you think I will like it?"

Colin nearly dropped down dead. This girl was playing with him and he knew it. She was sexy and seductive. Just the kind of girl he was looking for. He stood to his feet and went straight to the bar. His cock was rock hard and he had to press it down hard in his trouser pocket. The pub had a hotel upstairs and his plan was to stay the night. He always did this and Jerry the landlord had already reserved him a room in advance. Annie applied her lipstick and sat watching Colin stood at the bar. He was fit and toned and his arse was a nice round peach shape. She pondered what he was like in bed. Rita said he was mint, he made her orgasm too so that was a start. It was true, Annie had never had an orgasm. Yes, she'd had sex with a few lads but they were never sensual with her. It was always a wham, bam thank you mam. A drunken shag, nothing more. Colin came back to the table holding the cocktails. They looked pretty - she could get used to this. Her usual was a vodka and coke, nothing as classy as this. Bringing the glass up to her lips she sipped at it slowly. She was a lady now and ready to impress. The taste of the drink tickled her taste buds – it was sweet, refreshing and cold.

Colin reached over and touched her hand. He had to say this before they continued, he needed to know she would not betray his trust. "Annie, I know you're slightly younger than me and people will start talking, so I need you to keep this to yourself. Can you do that for me, that's all I ask?"

Annie nodded. It wasn't like she was going to shout it from the rooftop that she was bedding a fossil now was it? She liked to keep it quiet too because if Rita ever found out that she'd moved in on her man, she would have killed her. The law of the land was that you never touched your friend's man. Not even after you'd carted them. This was just the way it was and up to now both girls had abided by the rules.

The night was going well and Annie had tried nearly every cocktail on the menu. She was drunk and her words were starting to slur. Colin saw his chance and struck while the iron was hot. "Shall we get a room here tonight, it would be a great way to finish our night off. Plus, I'm done in now and over the limit to drive." What a crafty old bastard he was, he knew exactly what he was doing and he'd probably planned every last step of the date. Annie hadn't expected the date to last all night. This was a first date after all and she was trying to save the sex part of it for as long as she could. She sat thinking for a few minutes. It wasn't the end of the world and he probably wasn't expecting sex so soon in the relationship anyway. Annie stood up and pulled her mobile phone from her pocket. "Okay, just let me make a call then." Annie walked outside and Colin rubbed at his crotch, he was horny and couldn't wait to get his dirty sweaty hands all over her. He loved young girls, he loved the feel of their young skin against his. He was grooming Annie for sure and this daft bitch was falling for it hook, line and sinker.

Colin made sure she'd left and picked his phone up from the table. His voice was low. He didn't want anyone to hear him. "Hello, it's me. Tell the man I should have another one for him ready soon. Just let me work my magic on her. She's easy meat and it shouldn't take that long." The call ended and Colin let out a menacing laugh. He reached over and finished his drink and left the table. Annie came walking back with a big smile all over her face. She was all set to stay the night.

Worm walked upstairs and opened Johnny's bedroom door with no care for anyone sleeping inside, he was noisy and loud. The room was dark and the curtains were closed, it was pitch black. He stood for a few seconds to get his bearings. Creeping inside the room he gripped the end of the duvet and tugged it from the bed with all his might. "Come on, fuck me you're not on bang up now. You're a free man. Get up out of your pit." Worm walked over to the light switch and flicked it on and off. "Wakey, wakey, party time."

Johnny covered his eyes and dug his head deep into his pillow. He was in no mood for visitors. "Fuck off, leave me alone, you sell out."

Worm stood looking puzzled and scratched at his head. This was a bit harsh and way over the top. He smiled and ran over to the bed and jumped on it lying next to Johnny. "Come on mate, we've got a party lined up - plenty of women for us to ruin."

Johnny didn't reply and Worm was starting to lose his patience. He sat up and poked a single finger deep into Johnny's chest. "What's up with you, are you staying in bed or what? I've got some decent snatch lined up so I've got no time to be waiting around for you to sort your shit out."

Johnny bolted from the bed. His bare chest was showing, his eyes popping out from his sockets. It was going off big-time. "You're a lying cunt! Why didn't you tell me about Natalie having a bin-lid?"

Whoa, Worm wasn't expecting this. It took him

completely by surprise. He blew a laboured breath and his face creased at the sides. He knew this moment would come but he wasn't prepared for it. The shit had hit the fan and it was time to put his cards on the table, this wasn't going to be easy. Worm sat and played with his fingers. His eyes closing slowly he began his defence. "I was going to tell you. I swear down I was. But, you was in jail and I know how hard that would have been for you to deal with. You've seen guys strung up in jail over things like this and I just wanted to wait until you were home before I told you." He shook his head and sighed. "What does it matter when you were told anyway, what's done is done. It's not like you can turn back time is it?"

Johnny snapped and he was lucky he didn't chin him. "It matters to me because I've been lay in my pad for years planning a life for us both, you prick. What fucking planet are you on? You know how I felt about her. I've fucking told you enough times."

Worm wasn't being spoken to like this, no way. This wasn't his fault and there was no way he was taking the blame. He answered him back and fought his corner. "Planning a life with a girl who told you it was over. How do you make that out? She never came to see you, she never wrote you a single letter either. So how can you plan a life with a girl like that? I know it hurts but it's over, she's moved on. You're going to have to deal with it. It's life and you have to face it." Worm stood up and his nose was twitching, he was getting brave. "Anyway, don't be having a go at me. You fucked it up, nobody else."

Johnny was fuming, he dived up from his bed and his ears pinned back. He stood there facing Worm in just his boxer shorts and was raging. "Fuck you, you know I would have had your back if it was the other way around. What is it, out of sight out of mind?"

This was a war zone and Worm was preparing to go to blows. He walked over to where Johnny stood and looked him straight in his eyes. He was aware he could strike a blow at any second and he was ready for him. "Listen, I'll say it as it is. I got out of jail and I found out Natalie had a baby. What did you want me to do go around to her house and beat the living daylights out of her?"

"I wanted to know, is that too much to fucking ask? Fuck me, I saw her today and worked it out for myself. What a twat I looked. Honest, it's done me in."

Worm paced the room, his own loyalty was at question now and he had to pull something out of the bag to make things right between them. He stood facing the window and ragged his fingers through his hair. "Right, yep. I should have told you. But I didn't. I just couldn't stand to see you go under when you was in jail. I cared about your feelings that's all. So, if that's betraying you then fine. I can't change it can I."

Johnny was calming down and his breathing was returning to normal. Sometimes the truth needed to be said and now he'd heard it, he knew where Worm was coming from. Johnny stomped over to the bed and dropped his head into his hands. Worm stood watching unsure of what to do next. He inhaled deeply and through caution to the wind. "It is what it is Johnny. If I could change it I would. Anyway, they say what makes you ill makes you better. So, get your clobber on and let's get you back in the game. Natalie is not the only girl around here you know. Women are ten a penny!"

Johnny lifted his eyes and sucked hard on his lips. "Perhaps you're right but it just knocked me for six. It's done my head in, stressed me out."

"It will do but fuck her and move on. You've wasted enough tears on that slapper she doesn't deserve you anyway."

Johnny was going to fight Natalie's corner but what good would that have done. She'd moved on and he had to deal with it. Worm checked his wristwatch and started to stress. "Come on then, get dressed and we can get out of here. It's going to be a wild one tonight so I hope you're ready?" He walked to the bedroom door and twisted the handle slowly. "I'll wait downstairs for you. Hurry up!"

The door closed behind him and Johnny was alone. His chest was tight and a wave of emotion took over his body. A panic attack was returning. He blew his breath slowly and closed his eyes. There was no way this was getting the better of him he had to get through it. Sweat trickled down his forehead, he was boiling hot. Johnny stood and took deep breaths, he was in control now and seemed to be settling down. He walked into the bathroom and filled the sink with cold water. Dipping his head low he splashed his face. These attacks were doing his head in and he wanted them to leave him alone.

Worm walked into the front room and June was sat in her chair singing to herself. She was pissed and ready for falling asleep. "He's going to blow at you too," he stuttered over at her. She smiled at him and didn't have a clue what he was going on about, she didn't care either. She was in a peaceful place. Worm sat down near her and he was edgy. Anytime now Johnny could come into the room and declare war with him. He was like that Johnny, just when you thought it was safe and the beef was over he would strike. He'd seen him do it in jail a hundred times before and he wasn't resting until this was sorted out. He was on his guard. June sat singing to herself. Her eyes were closed and she seemed to be drifting off to sleep. Worm sat texting on his mobile and tried to take his mind off all the stress. Feet stomping down the stairs caused June and Worm to look at each other. It sounded like a herd of elephants.

The living room door swung open and Johnny marched inside. He was fresh now, clean shaven and dressed in a pair of jeans and a fitted black t-shirt. June smiled at him and waved her hands above her head still singing. Johnny smiled at her and came to sit on the side of her chair. "You look smart, where you off to?"

"I'm going to find myself a wife auntie June. There is no point in waiting around for Natalie anymore is there. Thanks for telling me about her by the way." Johnny stood up and nodded his head at Worm. "Are you right then, let's see if these girls are as pretty as you say."

June's jaw was swinging low. Had he really just said that to her or was she hearing things. She was going to say something but Worm growled at her and held a single finger up to his lips. June never said a word. The front door slammed shut and there was an eerie silence in the room. There was no TV on, nothing, not a single sound. The secret was out, Johnny finally knew Natalie had a baby.

Worm dived in the driver's side and Johnny was riding shot gun. Johnny could drive too but he had had to re-sit his driving test due to some reckless driving he was charged with previous years before. He was showing off really, doing a few wheel spins for the kids on the estate and before he knew it the police swarmed him and he had to take off. Fifteen minutes later he was ambushed and twisted up by the law. They knew his face and a lot of the local officers couldn't wait to put him behind bars. It had always been like that with Johnny, everybody knew him and he was always up to no good. As a kid he never had a dad and he just took it for granted that he would do his own thing. He went out when he wanted and some nights he didn't even bother coming home. Elsie never said a word to him either, she just let him rule the roost and do whatever he wanted.

Elsie's life was a car crash. A long line of failed relationships and a temper she couldn't hold. She was never a mother figure and she never would be in the future either. She was never cut out for motherhood. Worm could still sense a bit of atmosphere between them and tried to smooth things over. "Get a bit of whiff down you. It will help loosen you up."

He threw a small bag of white powder on Johnny's lap. Here it was, the test. Would he go back to his old lifestyle or had prison taught him a lesson he would never forget? Johnny held the small bag between his index finger and his thumb. He sat glancing at it and flicked it about slowly "Maybe later, not in the mood for anything yet. I'm still finding my feet." Worm was sulking, it was shit sniffing on his own and he wanted his pal to be on the same wavelength as him. Johnny opened the car window and sucked in large mouthfuls of the night air. It was cold and the winter was well and truly kicking in. The leaves were circling in the distance and each tree he looked at was nearly bare. Johnny loved trees. There was one right outside his cell window in Lancaster. Every day he would sit at the bars watching any activity that went on inside its many branches. There was a pair of wood pigeons nesting in the tree and one of the inmates had told him once these birds pair up, they stay together for life. Johnny didn't know if it was bullshit or not but he secretly loved the romance of the tale and named the two birds Johnny and Natalie. He never told anyone this of course, he had a reputation to uphold inside the slammer and if word would have got out about this the inmates would have thought he'd gone soft. Johnny cared for the birds every day. He fed them and when he could he dug a few worms up and left them on his windowsill for them. There was a bond there now between man and bird and he loved listening to them bicker and sing in the tree.

He was sure they had a nest of chicks but he could never be sure. One morning they just left, they never returned and his heart was empty. It was funny how much a small thing could have given him so much pleasure. But once they vanished, he was alone again staring at his four walls with his heart empty, nobody left to love or care about.

The music in the car was loud and if he was being honest the racket was doing his head in. He was used to quiet, calm, being chilled out, not deep baseline vibrations drilling through his ears, pounding inside his head. Was he older now, set in his ways, had prison destroyed his soul? Whatever happened to the old Johnny Barker everybody once knew? This man was nowhere near the same guy. He'd lost himself. The car drove along the busy main road. Worm had to call to the shop to pick up some beer and cigs for the party. There was no way he was going there empty handed like some scrotes did. Yes, that's right, some people just turned up to the party and drank everyone else's beer. They had no shame, just walked into the party and grabbed a bottle of beer as if they'd brought it with them. "I'll go on the lane, there's loads of shops up there and plus I can park without getting a ticket."

Johnny remembered the lane from when he was younger but as Worm drove up it he realised just how much things had changed. A lot of the shops were so different, foreign foods, shoe shops, African barbers. He looked over at Worm and hunched his shoulders. "What the fuck has happened here then? Where have all the other shops gone?"

Worm sniggered and shot his eyes about the lane. "A lot's changed hasn't it? But ay, check out that shop there, it sells goat curry and all that. To tell you the truth I was the same as you at first but these shops open nearly all fucking night now. They never close."

Johnny gazed through a shop window and all he could

see were Africans stood about chatting. For good or bad, the lane seemed to have been taken over by every colour under the sun. Worm pulled up near the bank and left the car running. Johnny sat taking everything in and watched a building near him. A black car pulled up and a big guy got out wearing black. The man was thick set and the tinted sunglasses he wore hid his identity. He'd seen this guy somewhere before, but where? There were young girls with him too, at least three. They looked foreign. These females were dressed to the nines, hair done, make-up the lot. Johnny could hear them speaking from where he was and realised they were Eastern European, Czech maybe. The man nodded at the girls and they followed him like obedient children. Johnny was interested now and got out of the car to see what was happening. Standing near a lamppost he lit a cigarette and sucked hard onto it. Gazing over at the black car he checked the wheels on it. This was the dog's bollocks; silver alloys, leather trim inside, it was worth a few quid. A girl came walking past him and she seemed in a hurry. He looked her over and tried to get her attention. "Excuse me love, what is that place there?"

The girl shot her eyes to the building and turned to face him, she was innocent looking and could have only been around sixteen. "Who wants to know?" she asked in a foreign accent.

Johnny sucked hard on his lip and edged closer to her. "I'm just asking that's all. I'm new to the area."

The girl smiled and twisted a honey blonde piece of hair dangling at the side of her face. She checked nobody was listening and kept her voice low. "It's where I work. It's a man's place for them to spend special time with the girls."

Johnny digested what she'd just said and he was blushing. Derrr... was he that green or what? Surely, he could have worked it out. Nodding his head slowly he smiled at her and acted like he already knew. He had to say something now, take the pressure off him. "I might call in then. Especially if you're working there."

The young girl fluttered her eyelashes and licked her lips slowly. "That would be nice, just ask for Martina." The man from earlier came out of the brothel now and he spotted talking. He clicked his fingers in the air and whistled over to her. Martina knew she was in trouble, her face dropped and her eyes were wide open. Johnny took a good look at this guy and he wanted to know more about him. Who the hell was he? The girl was petrified of him. You could tell that just the sound of his voice sent shivers down her spine. Johnny watched Martina go inside the building and he flicked his cigarette butt casually. His eyes were all over the man now, watching his every move.

Worm was back now and beeping the horn in the car. Johnny ran back over the road to him. He jumped in the passenger side and kept his eyes on the man across the road. "Who's that big cunt, and since when was there a brass gaff on the lane?"

Worm looked out of his window and twisted his head back quickly. He was panicking and aware the man was watching him. Flicking the engine over he pulled out from the lay-by and kept his eyes on the road. Checking in his rear view mirror he spoke. "That's Marcus Mannings. They call him Monty. I'll tell you what, you don't want fuck all to do with him he's one crazy cunt. That's the man your mam was involved with, he's a shady character, trust me."

Johnny wanted to know more and turned in his seat to face him. "So, what does he do, how does he earn a crust?"

You could tell Worm didn't want to get into a long conversation and he brushed him off. He was hiding something for sure. "Oh, he's into everything, I don't really know a lot about him. I've just heard stories."

Johnny dipped his head to look through the wing mirror, he could still see Monty in the distance. "Well, he might know where my mam is then. I'll put the feelers out about him and we can go and pay him a visit."

Worm nearly choked. "You'll be going on your own pal. Trust me, the guy is bad news, enough said." Johnny checked Worm over and he was actually scared, he could see it in his eyes. Something wasn't adding up here, Worm was scared of nobody or if he was he never showed it.

The party was booming when they pulled up outside the house. It was like a nightclub; there was loud music, girls dancing on furniture and drugs being passed about. This was just a normal council house and to look at it the distance you would have thought someone professional had organised this event. It was a top night by anyone's standards. The disco lights were all colours of the rainbow; red, yellow, pink, green. They flashed around the garden in sync with the music. There was beer there too and plenty of it, stacked high in the corner of the garden. Worm inhaled deeply and got out of the car. Johnny walked behind him but he was nowhere near as confident, his head was low and he refrained from eye contact with the people there. Worm greeted the birthday girl and pecked her on the side of the cheek. She was all over him and happy he could make it. Quite a looker she was too, top notch. Johnny was now introduced to her. He looked a right prick just stood there, he was out of his comfort zone. Worm told the birthday girl that he'd just got out of the nick too. Johnny could have fell down right there and died on the spot. How embarrassing was this? She edged closer to him and her warm sweet breath circled his ears. "Hi, I'm Kelsey, get yourself a drink and we can catch up later, you're pretty cute." Whoa, girls had changed so much since he was last on the street. They were so forward these days and seemed up for anything.

From the corner of the garden a shrieking voice was shouting Johnny's name. He squeezed his eyes together tightly and tried to make out who it was. His jaw dropped low and his mouth became dry. There she was, the biggest mouth in the whole of Manchester, Diane Seldon. She was motoring over to him. Diane was Natalie's best mate and since he was a child she'd always been in the picture. A right cocky cow she was, she never knew when to keep it shut. There she was stood right in front of him with her hands placed firmly on her hips. "I heard you were out, when was you coming to see me. I thought me and you were close?"

Diane had everyone's attention and they were all looking at Johnny waiting on his answer. He should have kept his trap firmly shut and let sleeping dogs lie but he couldn't just do it for one second. Many a night he'd been lay in his pad thinking about all of his so called friends and how they'd sold him out. Not one letter from any of them, no postal order. No kiss my arse or anything. He snarled at her and licked the corner of his mouth. "Close friend?" he rolled his eyes and sneered at her, "Are you having a laugh or what? You never came to jail to see me once, or wrote me a letter, so you can stick your friendship right up your arse"

Diane was fuming, how dare he disrespect her like this when all she was doing was trying to be friendly. Diane was never one to take things lying down and she gritted her pearly white teeth tightly together and replied to him. "Oi, it's not my fault that Natalie carted you is it? She told me it was over with you so there was no way I could betray her trust is there," she moved in and touched the middle of his arm, her voice low. "Me and you were close, don't you think it hurt me too. I was gutted if I'm telling the truth here. But she made me swear on my mam's life that I would cut all ties with you."

Worm could see Johnny was about to blow and he had to diffuse the situation before things got out of hand. He stepped in front of them and separated them. His arms held out wide. "Let's agree to disagree ay? We should all just move on. We're at a party for fucks sake. You two can sort this out another time." Diane rolled her eyes and hissed as she shot a look at him. He'd publically humiliated her, shot her down. She had to have the last word. "It's not me with the problem Worm, talk to angry boy over there. He's the one causing the problems here." This was going to go on forever, the both of them had locked horns and no one was backing down.

Worm grabbed Johnny's arm and pulled him away. He whispered in his ear. "Fuck her mate, don't let her spoil your night. You know what she's like when she's got a bee in her bonnet." Johnny grabbed a bottle of beer from the table and found himself somewhere to sit. She'd wound him up and he was raging inside. Who the hell did she think she was just coming over to him as if nothing had happened?

The party was in full swing and everyone was twisted. There was one near Johnny and he was just lying on his stomach eating grass. Whatever he'd taken had knocked him for six, he wasn't on this planet, what a weirdo! Johnny sat watching the guests at the party. Is this the way he lived his life before he went to jail? This lot had no shame, no morals, they were wild animals. There was another girl sat near him and she seemed just as bored as him. He smiled over at her and gave her a cheeky wink. The girl picked her drink up from the table and came to join him. "Are you alright, I'm a right bore aren't I? I just don't do this sort of stuff that's all." Johnny sniggered.

"Me neither, well, I used to back in the day but I suppose I've grown up and all that now," he took a slurp from his bottle of beer. "I'm Johnny by the way, what's your name?"

The girl was blushing and he could see she'd not had a lot of male attention in the past. He liked that about her, she was innocent looking. "Sandy," she replied.

Johnny sniggered and he knew it was cheesy but he just couldn't help himself. "You mean like Sandy from the film Grease," he started serenading her. "Oh Sandy, can't you see I'm in misery," he was actually singing the words to the song and holding his hand out to her.

She chuckled. "Yep, like the song. Why does everyone compare me to that film?"

Johnny was on a roll now, his confidence back and his old sense of humour returning. "I can be your John Travolta if you want." This was proper cheesy but he seemed to know what he was doing, she was sucked in by his charm.

The two of them sat nattering for what seemed like hours and Worm had already got off with some chick he'd met earlier. He didn't tell Johnny he was leaving either he just got on his toes, no goodbye or anything. Johnny checked his wristwatch. "Do you fancy getting off, it's nearly dead in here now anyway?"

Sandy looked around the garden and he was right, the guests had nearly all gone home. It was nearly two in the morning and although there were a few people left inside the gaff, the majority had moved on to other parties or gone home. Sandy was more than happy to go with him. She was drunk and needed to get some fresh air. Johnny was on foreign ground now. Usually he just went back to Natalie's and they both got their heads down there but that was then and this was now. The whole dating scene was new to him and once they started walking down the street he wasn't sure of his next move. He was fidgeting and struggling to hold down a conversation. Sandy was just walking along and following his lead. He took a deep breath and threw caution to the wind, he couldn't even look at her as he spoke. "Do you want to come back to my house to chill for a bit?"

Sandy linked his arm and rested her head on his shoulder. Looking up slowly into his eyes she nodded. "Yes, but I'm not a dirt bag. If you're just after sex then you're wasting your time. I'm just not like that."

"Nar, I never thought about sex. I just like your company and thought it would be nice for us to get to know each other better."

Sandy stroked the side of his cheek, "Well, that's fine then, as long as you know." Johnny kissed her hand and they walked along. His head was banging and if the truth was known having sex was the last thing on his mind. The two of them walked along the dark streets until they hit Rochdale road. The wind was picking up and he could see she was cold. Pulling his jacket off he placed it around her shoulders and made sure she was covered. He was good like that, he was a proper gentleman when it suited him. Even when he was with Natalie he would do things to show he cared. Little love notes left on her pillow each morning before he left, he'd even composed some poetry for her back in the day. But that was then, he would never let a girl get inside his head ever again. Once bitten twice shy or so they say. Love was just a distant memory for him and under no circumstances was he ever putting his heart on the line again.

The house was in complete darkness as they walked up the garden path. Johnny held his finger up to his lips as he slowly slid his key into the lock. The last thing he needed at the moment was June and other family members getting up to join them. He loved June but she couldn't half waffle on sometimes, chat shit and go on and on about nothing of importance. He'd nicknamed her glass eye in the past saying she could talk a glass eye to sleep. He was right too, she never shut up, boring. Johnny flicked the light switch and made his way into the front room. It was pretty tidy for a change, just a few bits and bobs scattered about. This was foreign territory to him. So, what was next, he'd got a woman back to his house and she'd already told him there was nothing down for a shag, so he had to think quickly. Johnny walked over to the radio and turned it on low. Smooth FM was on and even though the songs were quite old he secretly liked listening to the radio station. All the lads listened to the radio when they were banged up and all through the night you could hear inmates blasting out some love songs they'd heard playing. Smooth FM helped him cope when Natalie carted him. For hours he'd sob his heart out listening to the words of songs. Each tune had a message in it and when you're heartbroken the lyrics mean so much more. Michael Bolton was one of his favourite artists. He'd never tell anyone that though, it was his guilty pleasure. He loved the song "When I'm Back On My Feet Again." Every time he heard it playing he'd sing along to it with so much passion inside his voice, so much pain.

The mood was set. Barry White was playing softly in the background. This house was freezing and he went to snuggle up next to Sandy. "I think my auntie has ran out of gas, she always does it."

He was slightly embarrassed but she soon made him feel better. "Oh, don't worry about it, shit happens." Johnny looked at her a little bit longer than he needed to. His lips went to meet hers and she responded. This was a result, he still had his magic touch. The two of them were lay down entwined in each other's bodies and things were about to get steamy. Sandy pushed him away, and swept her hair back over her shoulder. "I just need a breath of air, you do remember we're not having sex don't you?"

Johnny looked puzzled and his head tilted to the side. "I know, we're only kissing. I've not touched you."

Sandy blew a laboured breath and smirked at him. "I know, but I just need a break because you're turning me on so much and I don't want to spoil things."

Oh, Johnny was back in the building for sure. His self confidence was sky high, he could still turn a woman on, make her want him. Sniggering to himself he gripped her cheeks in both his hands and kissed her again.

There was a text alert on Johnny's phone and he paused to read it. "It's Diane - we need to speak. There are things you should know." Johnny placed his mobile phone back down on the floor and held a sour expression. He moved Sandy onto his chest and stroked her hair softly. Looking at the time on the clock nearby he realised just how late it was. There was no way he was dealing with this now, Diane could take a run and jump if she thought he was running to hear what she had to say. His eyes closed slowly, he had a lot on his mind and more than anything he wanted to know more about this Monty guy. He was the one who held the answers to what he was searching for. He needed to know that his mother was safe and he was going to make this man talk no matter what.

CHAPTER SEVEN

ANNIE WAITED for Rita. She'd been on the phone all night to her and wanted to sort this whole mess out once and for all. It was three weeks now since they'd been fallen out and there was no way in this world that she was making the first move to make friends. Annie was a right stubborn cow and once she seen her arse she would sulk forever. Rita had said some nasty things about her. She'd slagged her off to everyone who would listen and there was no way she was forgiving her, she owed her a big apology. Annie was dolled up, hair neatly blown and her make-up was spot on. She sat on the wall waiting for her friend and played on her new mobile phone. Annie had already made her mind up about this and she was only here to draw a line under it. She didn't need Rita in her life anymore, she had Colin now and he was all she cared about. He gave her everything she wanted and he was even talking about taking her on holiday when he'd sorted a few things out. Annie was in love, she never thought she would say that to anyone but she was smitten for the guy, head over heels in love with him. He rocked her world.

Rita was here, heading towards her at speed. She had a face like a smacked arse. She marched over to where she was and sat down next to her. Annie stood up and made sure if there was any trouble that she could defend herself. Rita was like that, she was a right snidey cow and she would often throw a punch when her opponent least expected it. "I didn't think you would come," Rita hissed. "I'm just here to see what you have to say, so don't hold your breath!" she growled, she always made things so hard.

Rita stood with one hand on her hip, her mouth moving rapidly as she chewed on her gums. "I've heard you're seeing Colin, come on, don't be a shit-bag and just tell me how it is." Annie held a cocky look in her eyes. She wasn't scared. What did she have to lose here anyway? Friendship meant nothing to her. Taking her time, she didn't answer straight away, she was playing with her. Rita came and sat back down and looked her in the eyes. "Well, has the cat got your tongue or what, just tell me the truth?"

"It's none of your business who I'm seeing. I've heard all the stuff you've been saying about me too, to a few of the girls on the estate. Bang out of order you are. I thought we were friends?"

Rita nearly choked on the spot. This girl had more front than Blackpool. "I told everyone the truth. You were all over my man. Go on, deny it if you dare. I wasn't imagining it."

"You're talking out of your arse as per usual. You're just jealous of me, you always have been."

Rita was white, the vein in the side of neck was pumping with rage. she sat cracking her knuckles and her temper was going to blow any minute now. She laughed sarcastically. "I'm jealous of you! Are you having a laugh or what? What the hell do you have that I want? It's you who borrows my clothes and you who is always on your arse scrounging from me. Fucking scruff."

Annie didn't have to listen to this bullshit. She had an ace up her sleeve and she was going to shut her up once and for all. "Well, not any more. I have everything that I need. Colin has seen to that."

You could have cut the atmosphere with a knife. Rita's breathing was rapid and her nostrils were flaring, did she hear her right, she had to be sure. "Say that again, did you say Colin?"

Annie prepared herself for war. She knew the moment she answered the next question she was going to feel a bunch of fives right on the end of her nose but she had to get this out in the open, she had nothing to hide. Here it was, the confession. "Yeah, I'm seeing Colin. It's not like I cheated on you because you two were over before," she didn't even get chance to finish her sentence. Rita was already swinging punches and ragging at her hair. Annie had to fight back, get a few digs in. With all her might she twisted her body in different directions and finally got free. Rita was ready to go at her again and this time she had to stop her any way she could. There was an empty beer bottle near where she was stood and her eyes shot straight to it. Leaping forward she gripped it tightly in her hands and smashed the end of it on the wall. The bottle now had jagged edges and it was a lethal weapon that could kill somebody, slash them up.

Rita backed off slowly, never taking her eyes from her attacker. "Go on, do you think that scares me?" The girls were drawing attention to themselves and a crowd of people were hurrying over to see what was going on. Annie stepped forward and wafted the bottle about, she was ready to gouge her eyes out with it, scar her for life. Their eyes locked and none of them were backing down.

An older man ran in between them and he was distraught. "Turn it in you two. Put that bottle down before you do some damage with it. You're bleeding girls, why you acting like this?"

Annie stepped back and growled at the passerby. "Tell her, she's the one who started it."

Rita was being held back by two other people who'd come to help with the situation. If she would have got her hands on her she would have killed her stone dead. She was shrieking at the top of her voice, she wanted everyone to hear what she had to say. "Go on, tell everyone about the old man you've been banging for money, you dirty slag – I'm going to make sure everyone knows about it. Trust me, everyone will know about you when I've finished with you."

Annie was panicking, she swallowed hard. Colin had told her to keep this on the low, if word got out about this affair he could be ruined, put in jail, she had to fight back, shut her up. "Don't you mean you was the one sleeping with an older guy, he bought you them shoes you're wearing, go on admit it. Stop trying to turn it on me."

Rita was chomping at the bit. The strangers were holding her back by both her arms, she was livid and ready to scratch her eyeballs out. "Yeah, he was mine first and then you decided you would make a move on him. Sloppy seconds will all you'll ever be."

Annie was nursing a busted lip and straightening her hair. She tied her hair back and flung the glass bottle on a grass verge nearby. "Whatever you slapper, you know where I am if you've got anymore bullshit to say about me." There was screaming and shouting behind her as she walked away. Annie knew now she would have to watch her back in the future. Rita would hunt her down and at the first opportunity she would strike. Blood dribbled down her lip onto her chin. Annie picked up speed and headed home. She needed to clean herself up before she saw Colin. There was no way she was going to tell him she had been brawling over him.

Johnny lay next to Sandy and it was mid-afternoon. They'd been seeing each other for a few weeks now. They'd been awake for ages but they were just lay there chilling watching a few DVD's. June was awake too and she was sat munching some crisps on the chair facing them. "What time did you two get in? I was dead to the world last night, I didn't hear a thing. I could have been robbed and still I wouldn't have woken up. I must have needed a good night's sleep."

Johnny cut her short before she started going onto something else. "I'm not sure, we just came home and got our heads down."

June looked over at Sandy, she was a pretty thing and she was sure she'd seen her somewhere before but just couldn't put her finger on it. She was well groomed this girl, well spoken and well looked after. June sat staring at her and held a puzzled look in her eye. Sandy checked the time on the clock and sat up quickly. "I've got to leave. I need to be home before my dad knows I'm missing. He's corny like that, he still thinks I'm a kid. He does my head in."

Johnny sat up and stretched his hands above his head. "Just let me swill my face and I'll get changed and walk you home."

Sandy seemed edgy and sat chewing the side of her fingernails. She had never let him walk her home before and always got a taxi. She was shifty and eager to leave. "You don't have to do that. I can make my own way home."

Johnny was already standing and he was having none of it. "No, I'll walk you home. Don't worry, I won't come right to the front door. I know you're ashamed of me."

Johnny sniggered and left the room. June watched Sandy, she delved deeper. "Whereabouts do you live honey because your face is familiar to me?"

Sandy sat forward and started to put her shoes on, she kept her eyes low refraining from any eye contact. "I live in Blackley, near Polefield Road."

June digested what she'd just said and sat back in her

seat tickling the end of her chin. The address where the girl had just given her was a posh area, big houses, the people who lived there had a bit of money, June thought them toffee-nosed. "What's your mam and dad called, perhaps I might know them. I know a lot of people from that area?"

Sandy was stuttering and Johnny saved her bacon as he walked back into the room ready to go. He looked smart in a clean pair of jeans and a white fitted top that showed off his bulging biceps. He'd piled some timber on now and looked a lot healthier. "Ready when you are," he said.

Sandy stood up and smiled at June, relieved that she was off the hook. "I'll probably see you later. We're off to the pictures tonight."

June's mouth was moving but no words were coming out. She was gutted her nephew had stopped the conversation dead just before she'd got the answer she wanted. Johnny and Sandy left and June was straight to her feet heading for the window. She peered from behind the net curtains and watched them walk down the garden path. Johnny seemed happy with this girl, as if she had taken all his pain away. Maybe even filled the gap in his heart where Natalie used to be. He was alive again, smiling and seemed at peace with himself. Johnny walked down the street and Diane Sheldon was ringing him again. She'd been on the blower constantly trying to speak to him for a fortnight but he'd just blanked her, she had nothing to say that he wanted to hear.

The couple reached the end of the road where Sandy lived and they were enjoying a final kiss before he let her go home. She pulled away from him and shouted him to join her in some bushes. Sandy was panicking and her eyes were wide open. She peeped out from their hide out. "It's my dad, like I said he hates me having boyfriends he just goes over the top."

Johnny watched the black car going passed. His heart was in his mouth. It was the black car, the one he'd seen the man in, the one with the wheel trims. He'd know this car anywhere. It was Monty. Johnny's jaw dropped, now this was a whole new ball game. They hid away until the car had passed and once it had Johnny stepped out onto the road sucking in a large mouthful of fresh air. He wanted to know more about Sandy's dad. "So, your old man is Monty?"

Sandy was gobsmacked. "Yes, do you know him?"

He watched the back end of the car driving up the street and nodded his head slowly. "I've heard of him but as of yet I don't know him. He's a bit of a gangster isn't he?"

Sandy hesitated, she was always told never to speak about her father's business. It was law in her house and she knew if she was ever discovered speaking about his private affairs her life wouldn't have been worth living. "I'd rather not speak about it to tell you the truth. My dad does whatever he does and he doesn't tell me a thing."

He knew she was lying, her eyelids were flicking rapidly and she couldn't look him in the eye. Johnny walked a few paces forward and pecked her cheek with a kiss. "Go on, daddy's girl. You better hurry up home before he grounds you."

Sandy smiled and started to peg it up the road. She was sprinting and never looked back. Johnny watched her cunningly and rubbed his hands together. Reaching inside his pocket he pulled out his mobile phone and dialled Worm's number. "Yo, come and pick me up bro. I'm just at the bottom of Blackley Road. Hurry up, I've got us a job lined up."

Johnny waited on a nearby wall and pulled a cigarette from his packet. He popped one into his mouth and flicked his lighter slowly. This was a result he wasn't expecting and the job of finding his mother now seemed to be easier than he first thought. He just had to get into Sandy's family, get to know Monty's every move. Worm pulled up about ten minutes later. The car screeched to his side and the music was pumping. Johnny jumped inside and opened the window. There was a strong smell of weed in the car and as soon as he sat he was choking on the smell. Worm had been smoking some strong cannabis that blew your brains out. He looked rough, he'd met some new chick at a party and since then he'd been partying hard and the cocktail of drugs and late nights told on his face. He looked thinner and he was finding it hard to concentrate. The car pulled off and joined the traffic. Johnny turned the music down and poked him in the arm. "I think I'm going to find out where my mam is. Guess who Sandy's old man is, go on, have a guess, you'll never believe it in a million years?" Worm shrugged his shoulders, he really wasn't interested in the conversation. Johnny didn't wait for him to answer he just blurted it out. "It's Monty, she told me, how weird is that?"

Worm was listening now and his hands gripped the steering wheel tighter. "Keep well away mate, that guy is nothing but trouble, ask anyone if you don't believe me."

Johnny sat back and put his feet on the dashboard. "I'm not arsed who he is. Let's just say I'm going to get to the bottom of this prick and hit him where it hurts. Imagine it, taking over his patch, it will be like taking candy from a baby."

Worm rolled his eyes, it was obvious he'd not done his homework on this guy otherwise he would have taken a step back. It wasn't as easy as that, otherwise Monty would have been knocked on his arse years ago. Worm was not having any part of this, no way in this world. "It's up to you pal but count me out. I thought the same as you a while back but I've seen what he's done to men who have crossed him so there is no way I'm putting my neck on the line just to earn a few quid."

Johnny saw his arse and smashed his clenched fist into the side of the passenger door. "Since when have you given a fuck about anything? You've gone soft you have. I'm sick of doing little jobs and getting pennies for them. We need to think big and strike while the iron is hot! We're up and coming we are! We can have the world at our feet if we play our cards right. We need to get the firm together, we need to plan this and make sure we have the back up. The first thing I need to do though is learn how to get into that brass gaff on the lane. I met a girl a few weeks back and I just know half an hour with her and she will tell me all I need to know." Johnny was on another planet, this was complete shit he was talking, his head was away with the fairies.

Worm was quiet, his eyes were fixed on the road and he wasn't concentrating. The lights were on red and he just missed being killed by a wagon travelling on the other side of the road. Johnny grabbed the steering wheel and moved them to safety just in time, the car skidding to the side of the road. "For fucks sake, that was a red light you daft bastard. Didn't you see it coming, you could of killed us both you muppet!"

Worm was shell- shocked. His head resting on the steering wheel and he was shaking from head to toe. Johnny jumped out of the passenger side and ran around the car. He opened the door with speed and pulled Worm out by his arm. "Fuck me, get in the other side, I'll drive. Quick, hurry up before the dibble get wind of this."

The wagon on the other side of the road had smashed into a bollard. The driver was still alive and he was getting ready to come over to the car. Johnny turned the ignition over and reversed with speed. He put his foot down and headed in another direction. He could see the driver of the wagon shaking his fist in his rear view mirror. This was a close call and could have ended with them both being arrested, or dead, they'd had a lucky escape. Worm sat was his head in his hands, he was white, like he'd seen a ghost. Reaching over he patted Johnny's arm. "Sorry about that, my head's all over the place at the minute. I'm on a come down. It's all the drugs fucking with my head."

Johnny carried on driving and headed to Worm's house. Once he got there he parked the car up out of sight and got out. Worm followed him with his head hung low. "Right, go home and get your head down. I'm taking the keys with me so don't even think about going out." He shook his head and held Worm's shoulder tightly. "Mate, whatever it is you're tanning you need to ease off it. You look shocking, honest, you look like a smackhead."

Spice was the new drug everyone was dabbling in and even though he took a cocktail of substances each night, Worm knew that it was spice that was having the worst effect on him. It just sent him under if he was being honest with himself, made him feel suicidal. No words were spoken between the two. Johnny watched from a distance as his mate staggered down the garden path towards his front door. Once he was inside he shoved the car keys into his pocket and headed off on foot down the street.

Johnny had been walking for at least five minutes when he found himself on Natalie's street. It was too late to change direction now and she'd already seen him. Natalie was standing at her garden gate smoking a cigarette. Johnny stood tall and put a bounce in his step. He was no longer the underdog and he had his self-confidence back. He was near her now, her eyes were all over him looking him up and down. "Are you alright Nat, you look a bit tired?"

How could he still do that to her? Even after all these years she still gave a shit what he thought about her. But, he was right though, she'd been tossing and turning all night long, unable to sleep. Natalie had been like this for the last few weeks. She gasped and tried to answer him back. "Tell me about it, stress isn't it?"

Johnny stopped dead in his track and made his way to the garden gate. He stood facing her and their eyes met. "What stress have you got? I thought you were sorted, all loved up and that?"

Natalie was gobsmacked, her jaw swung low. "Loved up, me, are you for real?"

Johnny pulled back and tried to make a joke out of it. He didn't want to know about her private affairs anymore, he'd moved on. It was none of his business. "Sorry, I was only joking with you, you're private life is nothing to do with me anymore. Life goes on doesn't it?"

Natalie had something to say but the words seemed glued to her tongue. Her daughter now came to her side and started tugging at her legs. "Mummy, can I have a biscuit, I'm hungry." Johnny looked down at the kid and smiled. In his heart he knew now he could never go back to her now that she'd had a baby with someone else. This was their dream once and she'd ruined it. With a cocky smile on his face he started to whistle as he backed off. "Nice to see you Nat, see you around maybe and," he sniggered, "get some sleep."

Johnny was gone now and Natalie picked up her daughter and held her tightly as they watched him head up the street. She turned to her child and moved her fringe from her eyes. "I love you sweetheart, more than you will ever know."

★

It was late and Johnny was all set to go into the brothel. This was it, the start of it all. He'd been sat nearby for hours and once he saw Monty's car leave the premises he headed across the road towards the brass gaff. Johnny had never been to see a prostitute before. All his mates had but he'd always been in a relationship with Natalie and he never felt the need to see other women. Johnny pressed the small intercom button and waited until he heard the door buzz open. Walking inside he made his way up the stairs before him. His heart was beating ten to the dozen and he wasn't sure he'd made the right choice by coming here but it was too late now he was inside. Opening the door he was met by an older woman. She didn't look like she was a working girl, she just looked like a normal everyday woman. Johnny smiled at her and waited for her to invite him to sit down. A few working girls came into the room and they were all eyeing him up hoping he would pick them for business. A young stallion was a nice change from the old perverted punters they usually got - a guy who could actually get a hard on and fuck their brains out would make a change.

The older woman took control of the situation and spoke to the punter. Her voice was sweet and similar to a teacher talking to a small child. "Is it a full service you want?"

Johnny licked his lips slowly and nodded his head. "Yeah, I'm after Martina who works here. A few of my friends have recommended her."

The woman was shocked and shrugged her shoulders over to the other girls in the room. "Well, that's a first, but it's each to their own I suppose," she clicked her fingers above her head to get the girls attention. "Shout Martina for me, tell her when she's finished with her client she's got another lined up."

Johnny sat fidgeting and looked around the room.

It wasn't seedy like he'd imagined, it just looked like somebody's front room. There were two red leather sofas against the back wall and a glass table situated in front of it. The decor was quite classy too, lots of mirrors all over the wall and some nice art work. Another man came through the door and he was a lot older than Johnny. He looked like a businessman and not the sort of bloke you would usually see in a dive like this. The guy sat down next to Johnny and he could smell his strong aftershave within seconds. It was a sweet fragrance; musky, oriental. The woman who was sorting everything out was flustered and started to speak in a posh tone. "Would you like a drink Tony? Your lady will be with you soon."

He crossed his legs and chuckled loudly. "Yes please Mandy, can I have a scotch on the rocks."

Mandy was running around after this guy as if he was royalty. He shouted over to her as she poured his drink out. "So, when are these new girls ready? You said last week there was going to be more to choose from soon. Variety is the spice of life you know?"

Mandy was a bit taken back by his question and once she'd passed him his drink she sat on the side of the sofa talking to him. "As far as I know they're at the farm at the moment having all their hair done. You know the boss won't have any slackers working for us. He likes his girls to look in tip-top condition. This takes times."

Johnny was alert, did he hear her right, girls at a farm? The door opened and Martina walked in wearing a red silk dressing gown. "Maddy said someone's asked for me personally, is that right?"

Johnny stood up, he didn't want to get into a conversation in front of everyone there. He wanted to wait until they were alone. "That will be thirty pounds lovey," Mandy said. Johnny pushed his hand deep into his pocket and pulled out three ten pound notes.

Taking Martina's hand he let her lead the way. You could see by her expression that she was wary of him and she wasn't quite sure why he wanted to see her. Martina led Johnny to a room on the left at the end of the corridor. She opened the bedroom and let him go inside first. Martina looked happy and the thought of someone asking for her at the reception pushed her self-confidence sky high. She wasn't that pretty, her teeth were crooked and she was all skin and bones – there were no curves, just a flat chest, really she was nothing to write home about. Martina closed the door behind her and slipped a red dressing gown from her shoulders slowly. The poor thing was so thin, you could see her ribcage underneath her pale white skin.

Johnny patted the bed next to him and smiled softly over at her. His voice was low. "I don't want sex with you I just want to ask you a few questions." Martina's eyes were wide open and she wasn't sure if he was joking or not. "You see one of my family is missing and I think this place is something to do with it. Does anyone called Elsie work here?"

Martina's English was basic and she wasn't sure if she'd heard him right, everyone who came into this room with her wanted some kind of a sexual service and she was shocked that this lad didn't. She ignored his previous question and edged closer to him. "Let me get this right, you don't want sex or me to suck you off?"

Johnny smiled and shook his head. "No, I just want to speak with you."

Martina smiled and jumped onto the side of the bed. She liked him already and now she didn't have to perform a sexual act she started to relax. "I don't know much about this place or the girls who work here. I keep myself to myself really. I can leave when I pay back what I owe them. Most of the girls are like that here. You see, I'm from another country, an immigrant."

Johnny was listening now, he was interested. "So, how does it all work then, how did you get to England?"

Martina lay on the bed and stared up at the ceiling. Tears started to form in the corner of her eyes and she was getting upset. "I needed to leave my country, there is no life there for me and lots of girls my age do it too. I wanted to have a good job and a husband. My country could never offer that to me." Johnny placed a comforting hand on her thigh and patted it softly. "I will tell you all I know. You seem like a nice man, are you the same man who I met a few weeks ago outside this place?"

Johnny nodded. He was surprised she remembered him. "Yes, that was me."

Martina smiled and closed her eyes as she started to tell her story. "I was kind of at a low point in my life. My home life was bad and we were struggling to eat every day. My friend told me about this guy she'd met and what he said he could do for us." Johnny was on the edge of the bed and he was watching the door making sure nobody was listening to their conversation.

"Go on," he whispered.

Martina bummed a cigarette from him and lay making smoke rings from her mouth as she spoke. "They let you think they're doing you a favour, making your life easier. I should have known something was wrong the moment he changed the plan to get here. They told us for the airfare we would have to work in a factory until the debt was paid off. Martin told me I would be working in the fashion industry, you know, designing clothes. He was so believable, I never questioned him." She folded her arms tightly in front of her and goose bumps started to appear on her skin as she continued. "They took us to the farm house first and that's when I got a real feel of what really was happening. Annabel, the girl I was travelling with, was treated horrifically. They beat her and gave her drugs to quieten her down. Martin, the guy I trusted, turned into an ugly monster, he was just as bad as the others. The boss man came to the house and made our lives a misery. Each night he brought men into our bedroom and we were forced to have sex with them, not just once, nearly every night. I asked him constantly about the deal we had and he said the job he'd planned for us had fallen through so we had to repay the money we owed another way. Becoming a prostitute was what he meant. We had no other choice.

"My friend Annabel is still at the farm and I don't see her ever coming here with me. When I asked about her I was told she was sent back to my country but I know she's still there at the farm, I just know they are lying to me. One day I hope I've earned enough money to take us both away from all this but each time I ask if I've paid the money back yet they say I owe more money than I do. It's an endless cycle, it's never going to end."

Johnny bit on his fist, surely this wasn't happening. He'd heard about stuff like this on the news but for it to be happening in Manchester right under his nose, he just couldn't believe it. "Tell me more about this farm, how many girls are there, is there an older woman with bright red hair there, Elsie she's called?" Martina seemed to be quieter than she was before, this had really affected her and he could see she was in a no-win battle. He had to help her, give her hope of some kind of end to her torment. "I can help you get out of here, even get your friend back, but you need to help me first. I need to know where this farm house is and the name of the men who are working there."

Martina sat up quickly and drew her knees close up to her chest. Her heart was beating faster than normal and she was scared. "I'm not sure. It was dark when they took me there."

"Think, just try and think of where about it was," Johnny urged.

"It's near a place called Ramsbottom. I remember the name because when I read the signpost it made me smile. Martin and his men guard this place like the crown jewels. Nobody gets in or out without them saying so. There are other men who work with them too. They groom young girls like me and let them think they're safe. They buy them gifts and before they know it they kidnap them. There are English girls at the farm. I've seen them with my own eyes."

Johnny held her hands and looked straight into her eyes. "And, Elsie, do you remember her being there."

Martina sat thinking, her cheeks creased as she tried to remember. All of a sudden she looked surprised. "Yes, yes, I do. She's the boss's special woman. She has her own room at the other end of the farm the girls say. Nobody is allowed down there, only the boss man. She eats alone and nobody gets to see her."

Johnny's blood was boiling. He just knew his mother was something to do with this place. Martina held a single finger to her mouth and held her ear towards the door, she lay on her back and pulled Johnny on top of her. "Somebody's listening outside, say something, make some noise."

Johnny pretended he was having sex with Martina and lay on top of her. The door opened and a woman stood there. "Oh, I'm so sorry. I thought this room was empty," she said in an anxious voice. Johnny turned his head and growled at her. "Fuck me, close the door will you."

"Sorry, sorry," she whispered as she left the room. The door slammed shut and Martina was trembling. She kept Johnny on top of her and spoke in a quiet voice. "That's how they are here, they check you every few minutes to make sure you're not talking to anyone."

Johnny rested his head on hers and he closed his eyes slowly. "Thanks for telling me about this. I promise you that I won't forget about you. Once I find the farm I will help all the girls who are there too."

Martina gripped her fingers deep into his shoulders and sobbed. "I never ever thought anyone would care about me. Many times I have thought about going to the police station and reporting it all but they've told me they will kill Annabel and all my family if I do."

Johnny was eager to leave. This was some fucked up shit and for him to ever tackle the big man, he knew he needed strength in numbers. He needed a team, men who were as ruthless as he was, men who were willing to die if need be. One thing was for sure, blood was going to be spilled, heads were going to roll, it was just a matter of time. Johnny kissed Martina on her cheek before he left the room. Slowly he turned the door handle and walked straight back up the corridor where he was met by Mandy. "Was everything alright?" Johnny nodded his head and made his way down the stairs. He had so much planning to do now, the clock was ticking.

June sat watching the clock, she was sick of being alone every night. She thought when Johnny came home things would change, that he would spend some time with her, hours of just them two just talking about the old days. Her heart was low and she missed the years gone by, the years when her sister was by her side and they went out to the pub together. Those days would always be close to her heart, they were the best days of her life. Of course June had men in her life but that was years ago. They all promised her the life she deserved but when it came to the crunch they were all the same, full of shit. Every woman deserved a Prince Charming in their life and she was a woman who still believed they existed. She was a hopeless romantic and it was in her nature to see the good in every man she met. Perhaps she tried too hard, maybe she should have been more of a player but she hated lying to them. What was the point of pretending she wasn't in love when she was? June loved all the men she met. It didn't take much to make her fall head over heels in love either. It was the simple things that mattered to her, things like opening the door for her, making her a cup of tea, just small things to show they cared.

Barry was her last lover and he had left her half dead. He was the nicest man you could ever meet but once he had a few beers down his neck he turned into a monster. Poor June never stood a chance with him once he'd had a few scoops. They both came home after a night out and she knew he was in a foul mood with her. He always went quiet when something had niggled him, little things like her not wearing her hair right or her skirt being too short. June was all set to go to bed and the bastard pulled a hammer on her, completely out of the blue. Twelve times he sunk the silver claw hammer into her body and if one of her neighbours hadn't heard her chilling screams she would have been six foot under. June was left in a bad way, eighteen stitches she had all over her body and she spent two months in hospital recovering from this horrific attack. He scarred her for life, the memory always fresh in her mind. Elsie was always by her side at her time of need and she promised herself that from that day onward she would never have a relationship with a man again. She changed after this, her confidence was low and she very rarely ever got into a conversation with a man that she didn't know. Johnny wanted Barry wiping out when he heard what he'd done to his auntie but June would have none of it. She'd forgiven him straight away and wished him no harm. What a lovely person she was, so kind and forgiving. It was a shame she couldn't meet anyone who deserved her love because she would have made someone a lovely wife.

June opened the cupboard and pulled out the family photo album. She loved looking at the days gone by. Pulling out a snap of her sister she kissed it and held it close to her heart. "Just come home Elsie, I know you want to, just come home." June sat staring into space, her mind wandering. Her body froze, there was someone at the front door. She checked the wall clock, it was nearly midnight and nobody ever came here at this time unless it was the police. June stood up and tiptoed towards the window. Her heart was racing and her breathing was struggled. Holding her body still she dipped her head to a position where she could see who it was. June held a confused look and walked to the front door scratching her head. "What the hell do you want at this time of night?"

Rita was drunk and June could smell the alcohol on her breath from where she stood. Rita tried to focus and her words were slow and hard to understand. "Is the tart in? I want a word with her. Do you know what she's done to me?"

June stood tall. Of course she knew what had gone on, Annie had told her all about it. This was just two young girls arguing over boys. Rita was wobbling about and had to hold the wall with one hand to steady herself. She was pissed as a fart and how she made it the house was anyone's guess. June watched her carefully. She was worried that she might fall over and bang her head. Rita was all over the place. June couldn't stand it any longer, she reached over and gripped the middle of her arm. "Rita, just go home will you. Mates fall out all the time over lads. I'm sure it will pass over. Just go home."

The young girl lifted her head up slowly and her eyes were rolling about. Her speech was slurred and she had the hiccups. "Lads," she chuckled, "don't you mean men?"

June screwed her face up and shook her head slowly. "Yes, a lad from college she told me. Rita, I'm not being funny but if he fancied our Annie more than you, then what can she do about it really. It's all fair in love and war?"

Rita sneered and licked her lips slowly, what the hell was she hearing here, is this what the lying slut had told her auntie to cover her tracks. There was no way she was having this, the truth needed to be told. "June, Colin is a man not a boy. He's nearly forty years old. I was seeing him first and then your dirty skanky knickers niece thought she'd have a go on him."

June held her hand over her heart. Her mouth was wide open and she was ready to beat the living daylights out of this lying tramp. How dare she come here bad mouthing her niece like this? June gripped her by the scruff of the neck and started to frog march her down the garden path. "Rita, just go home before I knock ten tons of shit out of you. Our Annie's not that daft to get mixed up with an older man, so stop spreading rumours about her before you feel my foot right up your arse. What a cheeky cow you are, go on, piss off back home."

Rita was wriggling and trying to break free. She was falling all over the place. She turned to face June and pleaded, there were tears now. "June, on my life, it's all true. I'm not making this up. Why would I lie over something like this?" She stood up against a brick wall nearby and closed her eyes as she spoke. Where is she tonight, go on answer that? I'm sure he's bought her a new iphone too because that's what he does to get you interested. He lets you think he's in love with you."

June swung her arm back and slapped Rita right across her face. Family meant everything to her and there was no way in this world she was having anyone disrespect them like this, no way in this world. June went nose to nose with her. "I said fuck off home before I knock your bleeding block off. Annie told me how much of a bitch you are and I thought she was lying," June spat near Rita's feet. "Well not anymore, she was bang on. You're a shit stirring bitch and I don't believe a word that comes out of your evil mouth after this."

Rita started to walk off slowly, she was swaying and moaning under her breath. June was going to run after her and rag her about but what would that have solved? June stood at the front door looking out across the street. There were only a few lights on in nearby houses and everybody seemed to be sleeping. She backed off slowly inside the house and closed the door. June stood looking up into the hallway and slowly started to climb the stairs. Each step she took she gripped the rail tighter, knuckles turning white. When she reached the top she stood staring at Annie's bedroom. Was she being daft even thinking there was any truth in Rita's story? As if her legs were leading her she gripped the handle on the bedroom door. With caution she entered the room. What was she even looking for, she didn't know, she just needed to go inside. June looked at the small wardrobe. After a few seconds she opened the doors. Everything just looked the same as always, nothing had changed, just a few clothes hanging on the rail and a pair of gold shoes at the bottom of the wardrobe and...

June froze, her eyes shot to a shoe box hidden at the back. Was it really hidden away or was she imagining it? She yanked the red box out and walked over to the bed with it. Sitting down she stroked her fingers along the top of the lid. This was private stuff, something Annie didn't want anyone to see, was she crossing the line even contemplating looking inside it? June sucked on her bottom lip, her fingers twitching as they hovered over the box. She was fighting with her thoughts and her head was twisting from side to side. It was all too much for her, she had to ease her mind and put this to bed once and for all. With speed she pulled the lid from the box and scattered all its contents onto the bed. June picked up a silver heart necklace and dangled it in front of her eyes. It was silver she was sure of it and not really that expensive, costume jewellery. There was a matching ring too. June slipped it onto her fat finger and held it away from her face admiring it. From the corner of her eye she spotted something else and quickly pulled the ring from her finger. Her face was bright red and her teeth gritted tightly together. She'd spotted a packet of condoms. This was bad, her niece was having sex for sure. Rummaging through the rest of the belongings the story started to unfold, a dirty dark story she never wanted to be part of. The box held so many secrets about what Annie had been up too. Hotel booking slips, small empty bags of white powder that obviously once contained cocaine. The shit was going to hit the fan now. After all this she had to admit to herself that Rita was telling the truth. June examined all the bits and bobs in the box. There was a phone number there too with the name Colin written on it in pink lip-liner. June packed the box back up and stormed out off the bedroom. Running back down the stairs she ran into the front room searching for her mobile phone. Once she found it she dialled Annie's number. The call just went to voicemail. She launched her phone at the sofa and stood ragging her fingers through her hair. June stamped her feet and screamed at the top of her voice. "When it rains in this house, it fucking pours, arghhh…"

CHAPTER EIGHT

ANNIE LAY NEXT to her lover. Last night had been wild and they'd both only had a few hours sleep. Colin was still out of it and as she looked at him a warmth circled her heart. He'd told her he loved her last night. In the height of passion he'd looked down at her and gripped her slender cheeks in his hands and said the magic words every girl wanted to hear. Today was her first day as a loved woman. Rita was right, he was hot in the bedroom. He touched her in places she'd never been touched before, she'd been to heaven and back. Colin was adventurous too, she wasn't just lying on her back like she'd done in the past with other lovers. No, he had her all over the place, it was a good job she was flexible. Leaning over him she blew a sweet breath over his forehead. His eyes started to twitch and he was waking up. "Morning," she whispered.

Colin stretched his arms above his head and yawned. He pulled her closer and rested her head on his chest. "I don't want to let you go home. I wish we could stay like this forever, just me and you."

Annie snuggled her head deeper into his chest and she slowly run her fingers up and down the side of his body. "Me too, I hate leaving you."

Colin licked his lips slowly and let out a laboured breath, he swallowed hard and coughed to clear his throat. "What if we go to my friend's? We can stay there for a few nights, just phone home and tell them you're staying with a friend. It's a lovely house in the countryside where we can just relax." He squeezed her tightly and planted small kisses on top of her forehead.

Annie wanted this more than anything. This guy had told her he loved her and she never wanted to be apart from him again. "But, I've got no clothes here with me. I need to go home and get what I need first."

Colin sat up, he was agitated. "No, I'll buy you what you need. We need to make the most of the time we have together. I'll ring my mate now and tell him we're coming over to see him. Honest, don't worry, I'll buy you everything you need."

Annie smiled at him and fluttered her eyelashes. He was so kind to her and what set off as just a money making idea had turned into something really special. Of course she still loved the gifts he was buying her but now she'd fallen in love with him it was a whole new ball game. Annie looked at her phone. The battery was dead and she didn't have her charger with her. She decided to ring June later when they arrived at their new love nest. There was no rush, nobody would be worried about her anyway. She'd stayed out for days on end in the past and no one seemed to bother. So, it was decided, the two of them were going to spend a few days together. Perhaps, this was a trial to see if she was the one for him in the long run, the woman he would marry and nurture for the rest of his days.

Colin jumped out of bed and stood naked looking at her. "Come on then, let's make a move. The sooner we get there, the sooner the fun starts." Colin walked inside the bathroom in the hotel room and locked the door behind him. Annie rolled on the bed and punched her clenched fist into the air. She was in love, living the dream, her life was changing.

Sandy sat in her front room waiting for Johnny to come to meet her. It was nearly time and her heart was racing. They'd stayed in a hotel together last night and things were stepping up between them. He'd made so much of a fuss about meeting her parents that she had no other alternative than to arrange a meeting with them. She'd never ever invited anyone to meet her family and her heart was in her mouth every time she thought about her dad sitting down with Johnny. He was an arrogant bastard and thought he knew it all. Even with his wife his word was gospel. There was no give in him, he always thought he was right. Sandy was an only child and he had always made sure she was kept out of the limelight. The world he lived in was dangerous and if anyone got a whiff that he had a daughter she would have been targeted. No, Monty would never tell anyone about his home life.

This house was something else too. It looked like a home straight from "OK" magazine. Everything was tip-top and the place stank of money. The curtains were tailored to the window and the cream drapes added a touch of class to the room. Even the cream leather sofa was spotless, not a single mark on it, no sticky fingers, no blemishes, it looked brand new. Everything was neatly placed and not one bit of clutter was visible. Sandy sat on the edge of the sofa as her mother came inside the front room. Jackie was forty-two years old and you could tell she looked after herself. She had long dark chestnut brown hair and big brown eyes like conkers. Her figure was slender and her tits were definitely fake, nobody had perfect breasts like that unless they'd had a boob job, they were something any woman would have been proud of. Jackie smiled with her brilliant white teeth at her daughter. "Relax, I've had a word with your dad and he's been told to go easy on the lad." Jackie sat down and placed a comforting hand around her daughter's shoulder. Jackie was so emotional these days and she cried at anything. "You must think a lot about this guy if you're letting us meet him."

Sandy lifted her eyes and nodded her head. "He's lovely mam, not like the others, he just gets me if you know what I mean?"

Jackie sat back in her seat and sadness filled her eyes. She sat twiddling her hair. "I remember when we were like that. Your dad only had eyes for me once you know?" The corners of her eyes started to well up. Jackie was emotionally unstable and Sandy knew what was coming next. It was always the same when she spoke about her father. "He thinks I don't know about all the other women he's bedded, but I do." She closed her eyes slightly and you could see the pain in her eyes as she continued. "I can smell them on him when he comes home at night. He denies it all of course, but I know, deep down I've always known."

Sandy tried to console her. They'd had some terrible nights together lately. Jackie was just drinking all the time and crying herself to sleep most nights. What could Sandy do though, it was her father who was making her mother upset like this and she had no control over it whatsoever. This was something between man and wife, she had to stay right out of it, never get involved. Jackie wafted her hand in front of her face. She was blowing a breath now trying to calm down. "I'm sorry love, here's you just starting out with your new love and here's me putting a dampener on it. Not all men are like your dad love, some do actually stay faithful."

Sandy looked over at the clock and let out a laboured breath. Monty was upstairs and as soon as Johnny came to the house he would make his entrance into the room like he was the Lord of the Manor. He liked to intimidate people, make them feel weak. It's just the way he was. I suppose in his line of work he had just become accustomed to it. Monty had no respect for nobody. The family knew what he was up to in his line of work and Jackie had been to the brothel a few times over the years. She hated that her husband was involved in the sex trade and pleaded with him to get out of it but he never did. Jackie was intrigued by the girls who worked at "Moonlight" they all had a story to tell. There were a few women who she got quite close too but one minute they were there and the next they were gone. She'd asked Monty about them but he said they'd moved on to another city. She knew he was lying because none of the other girls would speak about it, something wasn't right and she could smell a rat. Jackie had met Elsie there too. She knew from the minute she set eyes on her that she was nothing but trouble. Monty had taken a shine to her and she had her suspicions that he was sleeping with her but what could she do? The bastard would never admit it. He'd swear black and blue that he wasn't cheating, he always covered his tracks and said she was going loopy and imagining things. Jackie was just stuck in this relationship now and she was falling deeper and deeper into a dark hole that she could never get out of. She thought she'd solved her biggest problem a while back but as one problem ended, another began.

Sandy jumped from her seat as she heard someone knocking at the front door. Jackie stood up and pulled her back by her arm. "Just relax, bloody hell, you're going to have a heart attack if you keep on like this," she chuckled, "and, I thought it was me who was the worrier." Sandy stood for a few seconds and composed herself, sucking in large mouthfuls of air. She was ready now, she left the room. Jackie headed straight to a bottle of gin on the table at the back of the room. She gripped a glass and quickly filled it before anyone clocked her. This woman could drink, she necked it in one and started to pour herself another one with trembling hands. Sandy stood at the front door and gave Johnny the once over. She ran her fingers through his hair and flicked the invisible dust from the top of his shoulder. She stood back and smiled. Now, he was ready to meet her old man. "Bloody hell, you're late. My dad is pretty fussy about timekeeping. Come on, hurry up and come into the front room before he comes downstairs."

Johnny's eyes were all over the place. This gaff was mint and nothing like he'd ever seen before. Okay, he'd seen some nice homes in his time but none of them were on par with this place. He swallowed hard. Johnny had already done some homework on this guy and all the reports were the same; Monty was a crank and he needed to be watched like a hawk. Jackie stood up and walked over to Johnny. She placed her arms around his neck and kissed him on the cheek. Johnny was a bit taken back as she spoke "It's lovely to meet you at last. Sandy has told me so much about you."

Her daughter was shocked and held a puzzled look. Yes, she'd mentioned her boyfriend but she'd never gone into any detail about him. She would never open up to her mother, some things were best kept private and Johnny was one of them. Jackie sat facing Johnny. He was a good looking lad and she could see why her daughter was head over heels in love with him. Even the way he spoke was something that set him aside from the others. He was a cheeky northerner, full of confidence and he had a way with words. Jackie liked him already. "Sandy, get Johnny a drink and get me a top up while you're there will you," she held her empty glass up in the air. "What do you want, lager, scotch, brandy, we've got it all?"

Johnny sat licking his dry lips. A drink was just what he needed, something to calm his nerves. Everyone thought he was so confident in the room but inside he was bricking it. Sandy was over the other side of the room and held a can of lager up at him, he nodded his head and smiled. Jackie was sat waiting eagerly on her drink, usually by this time of night she was well on her way to being pissed, she was slacking. Johnny sat chatting with the two of them. Suddenly all three of them raised their eyes to the ceiling as they heard the floorboards overhead creaking. It was showtime, time to face the music, time to meet the main man. There were noises from outside the room, coughing. Johnny had a lump in his throat and his breathing increased but he had to remain calm though, show no fear. His palms were sweating, his heart was pounding inside his ribcage. This was a nightmare. The door handle rattled and slowly moved, everyone was on edge. Here he was at last.

Johnny stood up and edged closer towards him, he held his hand out in front of him. "Nice to meet you mate, I'm Johnny." There was an awkward silence and Sandy cringed. Nobody spoke to her dad like this, they never called him mate. This was so bad.

Monty walked away from the handshake and sat down next to Jackie. Johnny was still stood there like a prized prick. He backed away slowly and sat down looking rather embarrassed. Monty nodded his head at his wife. "Get me a drink, put some ice in it too."

Jackie obeyed him. Johnny was on tenterhooks, should he make conversation or keep schtum until this bloke spoke to him first. He didn't know what to do for the best. Monty reached his hand up to take the drink from his wife. She sat back down next to him and snarled as she watched him drink it. Sandy edged closer to Johnny and tried to make him feel comfortable. Here it was, the main man was ready to speak. "By the way lad, when you speak to me in future, I'm not your mate. Let's get this sorted before we go any further. Do you understand me?"

Johnny was raging inside and if he had met this man in any other circumstances he would have knocked the cocky cunt out. Sandy shot a look at him, he had to calm down, eat humble pie, do as he asked him. Sandy nudged him in the waist and darted her eyes at him for him to reply. "Sorry, I was just a bit nervous that's all."

Monty let out a menacing laugh and slurped a mouthful of his drink. "You have every right to be too. I like that people fear me."

Jackie sneered at her husband. He was an out and out prick. Who the hell did he think he was talking to people like this? He wasn't royalty, he was just some guy who made his name by taking a few guys down that's all. Jackie hissed over at him, he was getting what was coming to him alright and she for one would laugh her head off when he got his comeuppance. "Oh, lighten up Monty. Johnny is a nice lad, give him a chance for crying out loud. This is family here, not business, he can call you by whatever name he wants."

Monty reached over and dug his hand deep into Jackie's knee. He was pressing his knuckles into her skin and causing her pain. "Just keep it shut. I'll tell him what he can call me," he leaned over and sniffed near her. "Have you been drinking again?" he reached over and inhaled near her mouth holding her head still with a tight grip. Flinging her to the other side of the sofa he went bright red. "Sort it out, I've told you about being a lush. If it carries on I'm going to sort it out. One more chance you've got, so sort it." Monty growled at her and she knew he meant business.

Sandy was nearly in tears, what a start to them meeting her new man! She shrugged her shoulders at Johnny and tried to change the conversation. "Dad, Johnny is looking for work. I said you might be able to help him out until he finds his feet?"

Monty turned his head slowly back to them. "What kind of work are you looking for, why haven't you got a job?" For crying out loud could this get any worse? What was he going to say now? Should he be upfront with him or just blatantly lie?

Johnny had to think quickly. Monty was a wise head and if he lied he would have found him out. "I've been inside. It's not something I'm proud of but I kind of got mixed up in some heavy shit and landed myself an eight years sentence. I did four and a half out of it." Monty inhaled hard and ground his teeth tightly together.

Sandy piped in from the side of him. "He's going straight now though dad. Everyone makes mistakes don't they?"

She never got chance to finish what she was about to say. Jackie flicked her hair back over her shoulder and she was at it again. "Some people just carry on making mistakes though and they never learn, do they Monty?" She was having a right pop at her husband and she was pushing his buttons now. He just brushed her comments off. He was used to her being sarcastic. It was water off a duck's back. He studied Johnny for a while. This kid could be someone he could work with, he scanned him up and down, thinking. "We'll speak later about work, but for now I want to know your intentions with my daughter. I'll be straight with you," Monty sat forward in his seat and cupped his hands tightly together as he spoke. "I won't stand for any shit where she is concerned. You fuck her about then it's me you'll be dealing with."

Jackie couldn't resist, she just couldn't keep her big trap shut. "It's a shame my father didn't say the same thing to you isn't it? I'm somebody's daughter too you know. Perhaps, you should reap what you sow."

Monty completely ignored her. He was sick of her

bullshit and the moment this meeting was over he was heading out with the lads. He hated her droning voice every minute of the day, he hated the woman she'd become. Johnny was growing more confident around Monty. He sat examining him. He was a tall man and he had thick black hair. He was trim and toned, this guy looked after himself. Monty was dressed in black as always, he never bought any other colour, it's just the way it was. Johnny tried making small talk with Sandy's parents but he was aware Monty was getting ready to go out. Jackie never took her eyes from him as he searched the table for his car keys. "Listen Johnny, come and see me tomorrow at the Thatched House pub. I'm in there about three each day, so call in and I'll see what I can do for you."

Johnny was buzzing with and his eyes lit up. "Thanks for that. And, don't you worry about Sandy I will look after her."

Monty turned his head back as he was walking towards the door with his jacket slung over his shoulder. "You better had lad, otherwise I'll come looking for you."

Monty left the room and Sandy gasped with relief. "Wow, how bad was that, I thought he was going to snap at you at first. He's not that bad really, he just puts on a big show."

Jackie was up at the large bay window and she was knocking back the last of the gin. She seemed like she was in a world of her own and she was unaware of her surroundings as she spoke to herself. "Look at you, you smarmy bastard. Do you think you can treat me like this and I'll just let you destroy me?" She let out a menacing laugh, "Over my dead body!"

Sandy walked over to her side and brought her back to the real world. "I'm going out now. Are you going to be alright, we can stay here with you for a bit if you want?"

Jackie sniffed and shook her head slowly. "No love, you go out. You don't have to babysit me. I'm used to being on my own."

Here it was, the guilt trip she always put her on. Usually, she would just stay in with her but tonight she'd made plans. This was her time and she was going to enjoy every minute of it. "Johnny, just let me get my coat. I won't be a minute."

Sandy left the room in a hurry and Johnny was left with Jackie. He wasn't one for words but he could sense this woman's pain. She was heartbroken and just crying out for help. He needed to say something to her, just a few words to show he cared. "Jackie, whatever is going on you will get through it. I've seen this before with my family and they pulled through. Time's a good healer."

Johnny smiled at her. He was impressed with his choice of words. He could pull it out of the bag when he wanted to and he stood tall feeling proud of himself. Jackie turned to face him. She licked her lips slowly. Her eyes shot to the door and she made sure they were alone. With a single finger she stroked a long talon down the side of his cheek. She was thinking for a split second and then she spoke. "You're a good looking lad, if I was a bit younger I'd be jumping into bed with you." She held her finger up to her mouth and sniggered. "Don't tell our Sandy though, our secret ay?"

Johnny was blushing, what on earth had she just said, was she coming onto him or what? Johnny was in a panic, what would he do if she stuck the lips on him, what if she groped his manhood? Whoa, this was some fucked up shit. Jackie was attractive but this kind of things only ever really happened in the movies. He was tempted alright and if things had been different he wouldn't have thought twice about slipping her one. He would have been like a rat up a drain pipe. Was this for real or what? Maybe she was just flirting with him, he must have read it wrong. Jackie sat down and crossed her legs. Her index finger slowly stroked around the rim of the glass, she was well up for it, he was sure of it.

Sandy came back into the room and put her coat on. "Are we ready then?"

Johnny was still in shock and nodded his head with an open mouth. "Yeah, ready when you are."

Sandy kissed her mother on the side of her cheek. "Don't be drinking anymore tonight mam. Try and get an early night. It will do you good."

Jackie smiled and swigged the last bit of her drink. "I might just do that, princess. Maybe in a bit though, not just yet."

Sandy raised her eyes over at Johnny. "Bye Jackie, nice to meet you, have a nice night."

Jackie gave him a cheeky wink as he left the room. His temperature was sky high and he needed some fresh air as soon as possible, he was going to burst. Her family was more fucked up than his. Yes, his family had problems but these guys were on a different level. Johnny stepped outside and sucked in a large mouthful of air. The slight breeze lifted his fringe at the front and he was starting to cool down. Sandy linked his arm as they started walking down the road and rested her head on his arm. "Crazy aren't they?"

"Not really, just like mine in a way I suppose. Your dad wasn't that bad either was he? And, that was nice of him to offer to meet me to talk about working for him wasn't it?"

Sandy cringed as he turned his body to face hers. "Don't be getting involved in any dodgy stuff with him. You know what he does right?"

Johnny had to crack on daft and held an absent look on

his face. "A bit of this and that, I think. Anything to keep his head above water."

Sandy looked away from him and folded her arms tightly in front of her. She had to get this off her chest it had been bugging her for weeks now. "My dad is mixed up in loads of mad stuff. He has a brothel, I've heard them arguing about it. They think I don't know, but I do."

Johnny acted shocked. He couldn't admit to being familiar with prostitutes. "What an actual biff bank," he sniggered to himself and forgot who he was talking too. The lads always called places like this one by different names and he just had a slip of the tongue. Sandy cringed when she heard what he said and he had to backtrack. "Sorry about that, I never meant it to come out like that. So, he runs one of them places does he?"

"Yes, it's on Moston Lane. I've heard him talk about it on the phone. Apparently, he gets young girls working there for him, you know foreigners and all that?"

Johnny was alert and as they started walking again he encouraged her to continue. "And, how do you feel about it all. It's pretty twisted that he's into all that kind of stuff. A bit weird if you ask me."

"It's where the money is I suppose," Sandy gasped, "anyway, let's change the subject now. It makes my stomach churn when I think about it all. I just thought you needed to know that's all."

Johnny was gutted, he wanted to know more about this place and she was the key to finding his mother. He squeezed her closer as they walked along the road. "So, does your dad cheat on your mam?"

Sandy's voice changed and she used a dull tone. "What do you think? You've heard her going on, why do you think she drinks all the time? She was never like that years ago, he's just destroying her. I've told her to leave him but she would never do that, she said she sticking by him."

"Does she know who the other women are?"

Sandy raised her eyes to the night sky and sucked hard on her lips. This was something that hurt her deeply, her eyes started to well up. "Some of them she knows about. He had one he was pretty fond of too because I've heard him on the phone to her in the past. I don't know what happened to her though she just seems to have fizzled out. The phone used to ring nearly every night when my dad was at home and if I answered the caller would put it down. She doesn't ring anymore though so he must have finished with her by the sound of things."

Johnny knew this had to be his mother, it had her stamp written all over it. She was like that Elsie and she wouldn't have thought twice about grassing a married man up to his wife if she had to. She was hard faced and never had any morals. Johnny smiled at Sandy. He didn't love her and he had no intention of wifeing her off either, she was just there, I suppose. He was fresh out of jail and he was keeping his options open for now. Sandy was a good girl, a bit too posh for his liking. He'd not even banged her yet and if there was no joy tonight he was going to tell her straight. He was a man with needs after all and if she didn't start spreading her legs soon he was going to start looking somewhere else.

June had been crying all night long. Annie's phone was just going to voice mail every time she called it. She was thinking about ringing the police but she reasoned that she was probably at a friend's house and she would look like a right plonker if the police put a search party out for her. No, she couldn't involve the dibble. June sat thinking for a few minutes. She couldn't tell Johnny about this either, he would go mad and probably go over the top. No, she was going to deal with this mess herself. There was only one thing for it she had to go and see Rita and listen to what she had to say.

CHAPTER NINE

WORM AND JOHNNY were driving way to Moston Lane. Worm was quieter than usual and he didn't have a lot to say, he was distant. Johnny broke the silence. "I need you with me on this one mate. Monty wants to meet me today to talk about some work he's got lined up for me. Are you up for it or what?"

Worm stuttered. "Do you really want to get involved in all this shit? I bet your mam is just partying somewhere, you know what she's like."

Johnny saw his arse and banged his clenched fist on the steering wheel. "Oh, thanks a fucking bunch. I thought you had my back like I have yours. Brothers in arms, my arse. You chat shit."

Worm knew he'd upset him and tried to make amends. "Listen, I have got your back but let's stick to the stuff we know about. We make enough money doing what we do don't we? What's the point in working with Monty when he's into everything, stuff that will get us banged up for years. Do you really think he's looking out for you, give your head a shake, he'll have us on all the shit jobs, you know the ones carrying the biggest risk," he gasped and dipped his head low. "I'm not going back to jail for anyone. Fuck me, I've only just got over the last stretch I did and here's you trying to get me back in the big-house."

Johnny opened his car window and spat a mouthful of phlegm out of his mouth. He banged his rounded fist onto his chest and coughed to clear his throat. "So I'm on my own then am I?"

Worm turned his head away from Johnny, he'd let him

down and the guilt was kicking in. "No, I'm not saying that. I'm just saying if you need me I'm there but don't expect me to lick Monty's arse. And any risky jobs that come along I'm not doing it. I'm not putting my neck on the line for anyone, especially that cunt Monty."

Johnny smirked. He knew Worm wouldn't let him down when it came to the crunch. They were mates, they always there looking out for each other. The car drove past "Moonlights". Johnny spoke to Worm as they went past. "I went in that gaff the other week. A girl called Martina works there and she was telling me a bit about how things worked."

Worm sniggered and covered his mouth with his hand. "Since when have you been into seeing brass? I thought Sandy was giving you plenty now, why you even going there?"

"I just had to see the place for myself. She told me about a farm where all the new girls go. It's full of foreigners he has working for him, young girls who he grooms and lies to."

Worm was on edge. His eyes were wide open and he was unsettled. He sat back and listened with eager ears as Johnny told him all about his visit with Martina. "Fuck me Johnny and you want us to get involved with all this. I'm not a nonce and I can't have people thinking I'm a sex trafficker." Johnny let out a laboured breath and he too realised what was at stake here. Worm was right, this was some fucked up shit. The subject was changed quickly. "So, come on, tell me about Sandy, you've never been away from her since you've met her, is it love or what?"

There was a hint of jealousy in his eye and he was watching Johnny closely. "She's a nice girl, well-educated if you know what I mean."

Worm nearly choked. "Fuck telling me about her

education I want to know what she's like in the sack. Is she a dirty bitch, is she kinky, come on spill, tell me."

Johnny smirked, this was just the normal thing for them to discuss. Worm had always spoken about the women he'd slept with and he always went into full details, he was hoping Johnny did the same. "Nar, I've not even shagged her yet. I've told her to sort it out though. I feel like a monk. We do bits of stuff but she's just not had the big meat yet."

Worm's face creased. "What, and your still bothering with her, what's up with you? Back in the day you would have slung her to the kerb and moved on."

Johnny sat thinking about what he'd just said. "What do you mean by that, I was always with Natalie and sex was on tap. I've never had to go without pussy for years."

Worm loved a good debate and he was putting the world to rights. "So sling her then and come out with me tonight. I'm off to a party in Harpurhey, some kid I know has invited me. There will be pure snatch there who will definitely be up for some filthy antics. What are you saying bro, you having it or what?"

Johnny was thinking about this. Worm was right in a way, sex should have been on tap but he had to keep Sandy sweet. If she got a whiff of him playing around it would be game over. He had to tread carefully, cause no friction between them.

It was time to go and meet Monty in the boozer. Worm and Johnny were all set for it and they discussed that they wouldn't be doing any donkey work for him no matter what it entailed. Worm and Johnny were grafters; robberies, snatches, giving someone a crack, or breaking someone's legs was their field of work but if Monty thought they were doing anything other than that he could suck a fart right out of their arses, they were nobody's fool. The Thatched

House pub was situated near the top of Moston Lane. It was a well run boozer; modern and scally-free. Brian the landlord was on the ball, he could smell a rat a mile away and he was the eyes and ears for Monty and his men. The police had been watching Monty for years but not once had they made an arrest. Don't get me wrong, he'd had a few close shaves but he always came out smelling of roses. Brian was well paid for his vigilance, he could smell an undercover copper a mile off. All it took was one look from him to the boys and they left the pub. Just to make sure he wasn't rumbled, Monty had a few police officers under his wing too but with all the local press regarding the area at the moment they had recently told him they couldn't turn a blind eye to his antics anymore. The two officers who were working for him had moved from Moston months ago. It was for the best too, they knew too much. Monty knew it was just a matter of time before he got his collar felt again. There was always some nosey cunt waiting to turn him in the moment his back was turned.

Monty sat in the corner of the pub with three other men. They looked to be in some kind of meeting when Johnny and Worm walked into the pub together. By the looks of things, something serious was going down. Monty didn't look happy and he was snarling at the two men he was sat with. Johnny walked to the bar and ordered his drinks. Worm nipped to the toilet. He was always like this when he was nervous, he would shit like a new born baby. Johnny took notice of his surroundings, where people were sat, who looked like they could be connected with Monty. He was always one for planning ahead and even at this early stage he was plotting an escape route. That was the thing with some criminals, they didn't think before they jumped into anything. He'd been sloppy in the past and he swore to himself he would never fuck things up again. Prison had taught him well. Each inmate had a story of their downfall and how just one minor detail had landed them in the clink. All the stories were more or less the same; coulda, shoulda, woulda were the last words of a fool...

Johnny stood with his back to Monty. It wasn't time yet to make an appearance. He could hear his loud voice from where he stood and just the sound of him made the hairs on the back of his neck stand on end. Worm was back now and he reached over the bar to get his bottle. He was on tenterhooks and small beads of sweat were starting to form on his forehead. He leaned near Johnny and whispered, "My arse is twitching. I don't know about yours but this just doesn't feel right."

Johnny felt it too but there was no way in this world he was going to admit it. He had to keep his cool, play his cards right and gain the trust of this firm. Johnny swallowed a mouthful of beer and nodded. "Right, come on, let's do it." The two of them walked over to where Monty was sat and stood at the corner of the table. Monty didn't see Johnny at first and he was still talking to the man at the side of him. However, the other man clocked them both straight away. He growled and he was ready to strike. "What's up boys, you looking for someone?"

Worm looked like he was going to faint. Johnny saved his bacon just in time and spoke in a confident manner. "Yep, I've come to see Monty so sit yourself back down."

The man was just going to swing for him when Monty chuckled loudly. "Whoa, Eddie, calm it down will you. He's come to see me. He's our Sandy's boyfriend."

Eddie was still angry and it took a few seconds before he let them both past him to sit down. Monty smiled over at Johnny. "That cocky mouth of yours will get you in trouble one day, lad. You have to learn a bit of respect for your elders."

Eddie was at it again and he went nose to nose with Worm. "You're lucky he knows you otherwise I'd have put you on your fucking arse. Tell them Monty, I've knocked men out for less." Eddie sat back and chuckled to himself.

Perhaps in his day he was top dog but now he was old school and there was no way Worm was taking this from him. "Yeah, respect comes both ways pal. And, I've put men on their arses for less too."

This was all getting out of control and Monty had to step in. "Eddie these two young pups are just like we were when we come on the scene, so cut them a bit of slack ay?" Monty sat up straight and looked Worm up and down. He was sure he'd met him before, but where, he couldn't remember. He shot a look at Johnny. "Who's this then?"

Johnny was taking a swig from his bottle of lager and didn't rush to answer him. Once he'd wiped his mouth with a quick swift flick of the wrist he chuckled. "This is my sidekick Worm. We work together and I was hoping that any job you had could be split between us."

Monty liked this kid already, yes, he was like him when he was younger, cocky, and full of himself. Worm was in the zone now and his nerves seem to have subsided. "Yep, me and this lad go back a long way."

Monty sat back and folded his arms in front of him. These two were just what he was looking for; fearless and ready to tackle anything flung at them. But first there was the question of confidentiality. He had to remember who Johnny was and the contact he had with his daughter. Monty had to tell him straight, there was no beating around the bush. "Sandy doesn't get to know anything about what we discuss or what goes on around this table. I don't usually work this way but you need a break and my daughter deserves the best of everything."

Johnny was in agreement. "I know how things work

and you have my word, she won't find out anything from me."

Worm jumped into the conversation too and now he'd found his feet he was making sure he was involved too. "That goes for me too."

Eddie still wasn't happy at the way he'd been spoken to and he still had a beef with Worm. "So, hold on Monty. Let me get this right in my own head. You don't even know these two ball bags and you're letting them in. Are you right in the head or what?"

It was time for Monty to show his true colours now and if the truth was known Eddie was doing his head in lately, always questioning things, never letting him finish talking. He punched his fist hard into the table. "I said they're both in. Since when did I have to run things past you?" Eddie realised he'd dropped a bollock and held his hands up, he'd stepped out of line. Money was tight and there was no way he could afford to rattle his boss's cage. Eddie dipped his eyes and listened to the conversation. Suddenly his mobile started ringing and he turned his body away from the table to take the call. "No worries. Let me have a look at her tonight. She better not be like the last one you brought, a fuckin animal she was who could have done with sheep dipping."

Johnny was listening in on Eddie's conversation and was taking mental notes of everything that was being discussed. The phone call ended and Eddie was involved with the conversation now. The lads all sat talking together and their guards dropped. Eddie even seemed to be lightening up now but he kept giving Worm the evils when nobody was looking. Monty wasn't as bad as Johnny first thought and even though he was there for his own reasons he was warming to his power. Monty shot his eyes over to the bar and let out a moan under his breath. "Eddie, don't look now but Sarah is at the bar. If she starts to make her way over to me please fuck her off. I can't be doing with any drama tonight I've had enough to last me a lifetime." Eddie was alert and had his ears pinned back as he kept his eyes on the woman. She was attractive, had a big set of knockers and lovely, shiny dark hair. She was in her early thirties and even in this boozer she was getting a lot of male attention. Monty carried on talking and Eddie left the group. Johnny watched him from the corner of his eye. Monty's wingman took hold of the woman's waist and escorted her to a different part of the pub. Whatever he was saying to her she wasn't happy about. Johnny was getting impatient and time wasn't on his side. He was meeting Sandy soon and he didn't want her standing around waiting for him on her own.

Johnny checked his phone and there were numerous missed calls from June. It was probably something and nothing anyway, she always phoned him for daft things. He was sure it was to just have someone to talk to. He shoved his phone back into his pocket and got straight to the point. Worm was eager to hear this too, they were all ears. "So, can we talk about work Monty? Sandy will go ape if I'm late to meet her and you don't want me upsetting her do you?"

Monty raised a smile, he was liking Johnny more and more each second he knew him. He sat forward and licked his lips slowly, his tongue gently brushing along his top lip. "I need some money picking up, the guy's being a bit of a prick about it so I need to put a bit of pressure on him. Nothing too harsh for now, just a few broken ribs if he's not willing to cooperate that's all." Worm nodded, this was the kind of job he loved, especially if Johnny was by his side. Johnny was as hard as nails and if anyone could make someone part with cash he was the man for the job. Johnny nodded and puffed his chest out. "Consider it done, just give me the details and I'll sort it. What's the till on this, it's got to be worth my while?"

Worm agreed and added his two pennies worth. "Yep, we don't work for peanuts. We've all got to make a living haven't we?"

Monty checked nobody was listening and kept his voice low. "Do the job and I'll look after you both. And, if this job gets good results I could be putting a lot of work your way in the future."

This was music to Worm's ears. The graft in the area was slow at the moment and to have something regular was a right result. He did have a side job though, not something he was telling anybody about. But the money was crap and not worth the hassle, he wanted out of it as soon as possible. Johnny shook Monty's hand, it was a done deal. He was in the circle of trust.

June sat in her front room waiting for Rita to turn up. Over an hour ago she should have been here yet still she was waiting for her. June sat munching on a packet of cheese and onion crisps. Her mouth was full and she was struggling to fit a large fistful into her mouth. There was a banging on the window and she nearly choked as she rocked about in her seat trying to stand up. Rita's face was squashed up against the window and she was eager to get inside. Rita held a cocky look in her eye when she confronted June. This was a whole different ball game now and June had to eat a big slice of humble pie. Oh yes, she had to lick arse. "Come in love, I've been waiting ages for you."

Rita smirked and stepped inside the house. "Sorry I'm

late, I was watching Coronation Street and then EastEnders came on."

June snarled as she walked past her. Here she was worrying and this cheeky bint was sat watching the soaps. June had to hold her temper, there was no way she wanted to upset her again. "Sit down love, do you want a drink or anything?"

Rita declined, she knew why she was here and she wasn't going to beat about the bush. "So, what's changed your mind then? I thought you said I was lying about Annie?"

June sat on the edge of the coffee table and dropped her head. "I just thought you were trying to get her in trouble. She's not been home in days and her phone is just going to voicemail. I got a text from her the other day saying she's staying at her friends for the weekend and she'll be home soon. You know me Rita, usually I don't bother where she stays but after what you'd told me I just have a gut feeling that something is wrong."

Here it was, the moment Rita would save face and be the hero of the hour. She was enjoying this and she wanted to see June's expression when she told her again that she was right all along. Revenge was sweet and Annie was going to pay for her betrayal this time. Rita was a Judas, a snitch. "His name is Colin. I met him when I was in a club in town. He's a right sweet talking fucker June, he had me fooled anyway. I believed everything he told me." This was killing June, the truth about her niece made her want to spew her ring up. She was green and rubbing her chest as if to ease the vomit that was rising. Rita stood up and placed her hands on her hips, this was her time to shine and she was making the most out of it. "I can take you to the club where he goes if you want. He always there."

June had to think about this, should she just hand this

over to the police or should she take it on herself? She needed to know more about the man she was dealing with. This was dangerous, very dangerous ground she was treading on. "Tell me more about this Colin, would he hurt her or anything like that?"

Rita shook her head and sadness filled her eyes. She rubbed slowly at her arms as if a dead body had just walked over her. "Colin is a gentleman, he would never hurt Annie. I think he just likes younger girls that's all. He's not ugly, so I don't know why he doesn't get women his own age. Money is no object too, he's always flashing the cash about. June," she stressed, "he bought me so much in such a short space of time. Honest he got me this "Michael Kors" watch," she rolled her sleeve up and flashed her prize possession, "and, a new iphone just weeks after I met him. We went to all the top places to eat and each time we went out he always bought me a new outfit." Rita was pissed off now and the thought of her friend betraying her trust for gifts and money was something she couldn't get her head round.

June sat staring into space, she was thinking out loud. "Perhaps she's just lonely, you know missing a father figure in her life. Why else would she be seeing an older man? Yes," she blew a hard breath, "she's trying to replace her own dad if you ask me. I mean, all girls like an older man don't they? I remember when I was growing up and I had a crush on my friend's dad. He was an ugly fucker when I think about it but honest to God he used to make my heart flutter." June was waffling on now and Rita was listening to her with a blank expression. "I used to fantasize about him too. I'm blushing even thinking about him. I used to imagine that he would just come up to me and kiss me when nobody was looking. I suppose I would have slept with him given the chance too. Perhaps I was looking to replace my own dad as well."

Rita looked at her watch and June clocked that she was boring her. "Do you want me to take you to the club or what? If you do, I'll have to nip home to get changed first." June was so mixed up, was she overreacting? This wasn't out of character for Annie and she was just like Elsie for going on the missing list. She would stay out for days and come back home when it suited her. Elsie used to call her a tom cat. June thought for a minute and declined the offer of going to the club. At the end of the day if she went speaking to him about Annie he would probably just deny it all anyway. What man would hold his hands up to say he'd been sleeping with a sixteen year old girl? She was just pissing in the wind and if she didn't hear from Annie soon she was going to tell Johnny and let him deal with it. She didn't need the extra stress in her life at the moment. Life was hard enough without adding somebody else's drama's to it too.

Annie sat shivering behind a locked door, knees held tightly up to her chest. The room was pitch black and the only vision she had was the yellow light creeping in from under the door on the corridor. She'd been locked inside this room for hours now and her head was bleeding at the side, red drops of blood dribbling down the side of her cheeks, deep purple bruises all over her body. Annie had been had over.

How on earth hadn't she seen this coming? It was all too good to be true. Colin had groomed her, lied to her and let her believe he really cared for her. What a conniving bastard he was! All the way to the farmhouse he was telling her just how much he loved her and how much this weekend was going to mean to him. Annie actually thought he was going to propose to her; get down on a bended knee and pop the question. From the moment they got to the farmhouse he changed and she should have seen it coming. As they walked down towards the farmhouse he held a tight grip on her hand, making sure she was never far from his side. Annie was so oblivious to it all though, love does that, it makes you blind and unable to see the real facts about somebody. Annie walked into the farm oblivious to what was waiting for her. There was a group of men sat there who seemed to be expecting them. They all stood up when she came into the room, circling her like vultures. She thought they were just Colin's friends, the good friends who said they could spend the weekend there together. Colin walked from her side and poured himself a large glass of brandy. He then turned to face her and an evil smirk filled his face. "Take the watch off her boys I'm sick of forking out cash for these money grabbing bitches." Annie was shell-shocked and before she knew it she was being wrestled on the floor by two men, she didn't stand a chance. Eddie was there and he rolled out a wad of cash and passed it to Colin as they watched Annie being attacked. Johnny's sister pleaded with Colin to help her but he just stood watching as the men ravished her body. They ripped her clothes off and bit hard into her soft pink skin. She tried to fight back of course but it was no use.

A blow to the side of her head knocked any fight out of her and she just lay staring into space. She could still see the silhouettes of her abusers and hear their voices but she was unable to move. Colin walked over and gripped her cheeks tightly together and spoke. "You were a good shag too. I was going to keep you but business is business isn't it."

The man who he called Fred pulled him back up and

chuckled loudly. "You're always the same with these young 'uns Colin. You always think you love them until you remember the cash."

Colin rubbed his hands together and licked the side of his lip. "It's all about the money pal. I've got a few more girls lined up so you need to keep the cash rolling," he stopped dead in his track and held a serious look. "This one's from near Moston Lane, so don't be sending her back there, keep her here until she's ready to be moved somewhere else." Colin picked the watch from the table and rammed it back inside his pocket. "Right, I'm off. You need to watch this one too she's a handful, well, she was in the sack anyway, a proper dirty fucker."

Fred shot his eyes to the body on the floor and smiled. She was a pretty thing and as soon as he got the chance he was going to slip one up her too. He was like that, he was a proper pervert who lusted after young girls. Colin made his way to the door and before he left he turned his head slowly back to the men. "I'll be back when I can. Tell the man what I said." Colin was gone.

Now Annie sat sobbing behind the door. Punching her clenched fist against the door she pleaded with her attackers. "Please, let me go back home. They'll be looking for me soon and once they know I'm missing God help you because none of you will be left standing. I swear, just open the door." Annie dropped her head onto her lap, her words fell on death ears and nobody was going to save her. What lay behind the door was something she could only imagine in her worst nightmares. It was just a matter of time before she found out exactly what an evil world she'd entered. Annie could hear sobbing from the next room. She crawled over to the wall and pressed her ear closely to the cold surface. "Is anyone there, please if you can hear me, answer me?" Nobody replied.

That night, Johnny and Worm sat watching a house not far from Moston Lane. Johnny was quiet and he was ready to take someone out. There was silver claw hammer in his hand and he was stroking his finger slowly against the cold steel. From what they'd been told, Morris Kenyon owed four grand to Monty and he was pissing about paying his debt. Monty had given him a chance to repay the money but as of yet he'd not kept his word. Worm was rubbing at his nose constantly, he always did this when he was nervous. "What's the plan for this Johnny, are we waiting until he comes out of his house or are we going in through the front door?"

Johnny watched the terraced house in view and never flinched. "Nar, we don't go in his house, we wait for the cunt to come outside. I'm not into terrorising families. It's Morris we want, nobody else."

Worm popped a cigarette into the side of his mouth, he opened the car window as he lit up letting the cold air inside. "How did it go with Sandy, did you bang her or what?"

Johnny shook his head and he was in a mood. "Nar, nothing down again but I can't push her can I? I need to keep in with her until all this is over. If Monty hears I've upset her he'll be down my neck. She's a nice girl but fuck me she's frigid. At first, I thought I could cope with all this no sex game but it's doing my head in."

Worm watched him closely and felt confident enough to ask him about his old flame Natalie. Blowing a mouthful of smoke through the car window he spoke in a low tone. "Do you ever think about Natalie anymore or are you over her now?"

Johnny inhaled deeply and turned to face him. "You

need to remember what that girl meant to me. Sometimes if I'm being honest all I want to do is kick her fucking head in and yet at other times I want to sit down with her and see what happened. I swear, she hurt me bad. Okay, I get that she moved on with some geezer but don't fucking get pregnant to him, that's just a piss take. Who's the dad anyway, do you know him or what?"

Worm flicked his cigarette butt from the window and shook his head slowly. "No, I just know when you got slammed she announced she was pregnant. There was no mention of any man in her life or fuck all. But think about it Johnny, she must have been seeing this guy when she was still with you because like I said you just don't meet a man and get yourself pregnant do you? I bet it was just a one night stand. Anyway, you know Natalie better than me and she never came across as a player did she?"

Johnny gripped the claw hammer tighter in his grip, he sat up straight in his seat and jerked his head back slowly. "So, you're saying it's someone I know, or someone who she knew."

Worm swallowed hard and his jaw dropped. "Nar, I'm not saying fuck all mate. It's you who's saying that, so don't be putting words into my mouth. If I knew who the dad was I would tell you."

Johnny was angry now and he couldn't hide it. "Yeah, like you told me in the first place! I'll tell you what, just shut the fuck up and stop reminding me of it all. Fuck me, as if I need to hear all this now, why the fuck did you even bring it up anyway. You've put me on a right downer now. Cheers for that, fucking super." Worm dropped it. They seemed to be waiting for ages. Worm zipped his coat up and snuggled down into it. It was freezing in the car and he was shivering. Suddenly, Johnny reached over and tapped at his knee rapidly. "Here we go. Look, that's him isn't it?"

Worm scanned the man walking down the garden path in the distance. "Yep, that's the fucker." Johnny flicked the ignition and they were ready for action. Monty had told them every move this guy made and tonight he was going to a club. Johnny crept from the roadside and followed the black BMW down the road. There wasn't a lot of traffic tonight and he had to make sure he wasn't spotted. Johnny was a confident driver and he kept a safe distance. Morris was speeding down the road and he seemed in a hurry to get to his destination. He pulled up in a car park not far from the club. Johnny quickly turned the engine off. Worm was eager to get this over with and they both had their hands on the door handle ready to strike. Morris got out of his car and locked it up. Here it was, the moment that was ideal to take him down. Johnny sprinted across the car park and he was at his victim's side in seconds. It all happened so fast and Morris didn't stand a chance. Morris was dragged by his feet to the car and flung in the boot. He was still alive but at this moment he was dazed. Johnny jumped back into the driver's seat and spun off from the car park. Nobody was about and there were no witnesses. "He was a big cunt, Johnny. I thought we were going to struggle."

Johnny kissed the end of his hammer and rammed it back under the seat. "Right, now we've got him we need to make him pay up."

Worm was sweating and talking the talk. "It's going to be like taking candy from a baby. Take him to the Boggart Hole Clough just near the lane and we'll make sure he coughs up. It's quiet there and nobody will disturb us." The car pulled up just inside the park gates with its lights off. There was an eerie silence and it was pitch black, owls hooting in the dark of the night. Johnny opened the boot of the car and Morris covered his face with his hands.

"What the fuck is going on, who are you, what do you want?"

Worm stepped forward, this was the part he loved, the fear, the weakness of his victims. "You owe fucking money and we want it. Monty has given you chance after chance and you've just taken the piss. It's pay up or be fucked up, your choice." Morris was trying to sit up but Johnny secured him with a tight grip around his windpipe. "So, are you sorting this out or are we burying you here?" Worm chuckled and started to walk away from the car. "Get the spades," he shouted over his shoulder, "it will only take a few minutes to dig a hole for this cunt."

Morris was terrified, he was trying to speak but no words were coming out. Johnny gripped his arm to remove him from the boot of the car and he started screaming. "No, I'll pay. I've got the money in my house. I swear, I'll give it to you. Fuck me, there's no need for this."

Johnny froze, was this muppet trying to have them over or what? He looked him deep in his eyes. No, there was fear there and Morris was going to pay. The guy had pissed his pants, big wet patches appeared all over his jeans at the front. Worm marched back to the car. He shot a look at Johnny and nodded his head. "What's happening is he going under or what?"

Morris repeated himself and he was pleading with his attackers. "I swear on my children's life, I'll pay the money I owe. Tell Monty this won't happen again, you have my word on it."

Johnny closed the boot and smiled over at Worm. "Let's take him home. We'll go in the house with him and make sure he's got the money. If he's lying we need to finish him off, we're not taking any shit." Johnny was aware that Morris could hear him in the boot of the car and they could hear him screaming that he wouldn't lie to them.

Morris paid up just like he said he would and once Worm left his side Johnny could see him falling to his knees at the front door. Morris was nearly having a heart attack. He couldn't believe he was finally a free man. The debt was settled. Johnny and Worm sat in the car and they were laughing about how scared Morris was. This was the thing with guys like him, they talked the talk but when push came to shove they shit themselves. Johnny made the call to Monty and he was laughing down the phone. The lads had done him proud and they were now a step further to finding Elsie.

CHAPTER TEN

ANNIE COWERED IN the corner of the room as she heard keys jangling outside. She was alert and ready to protect herself. The door opened slowly and Fred was stood there sneering at her. "I hope you've settled down now. You try anything and you'll stay in here for days, do you hear me?" Annie's heart was pounding inside her chest and she knew she had to obey every word this man said or he would attack her again. Fred walked into the room slowly and stood over her. "Stand up, get on your feet."

"Where are you taking me," she asked as her body trembled.

"Don't ask questions, do what I fucking tell you too and you get to live."

Annie was petrified, her lips were trembling and she was unsure of what was happening. Fred walked her out of the room and led her to another room at the side of the corridor. She could hear voices outside and she knew whatever was behind this door she wasn't going to like it. Fred snarled at her and came to the side of her face. His warm stale breath circling her nasal passage. "You need to learn to be nice. The girls who are nice always get the work." Annie swallowed hard as the door was unlocked. There were five girls lay about and they all stood up gawping at Annie as she was pushed inside. Fred stood guard near the door and clicked his fingers over his head. "Linda, sort this new one out for tonight. She's a nasty bitch so you'll have your work cut out with her." The door was slammed shut and Annie was stood there shivering.

Linda looked her over and raised her eyes to the ceiling. "Get over here and let me see if I can sort you out. Melanie, get her something to calm her down, a vodka, with a little sprinkle of something in it." Linda was around thirty years of age and she looked like she'd had a hard life, her eyes were dark and deep-set wrinkles all over her face and tattoos up her arms. Melanie was rushing about the room and getting the drink ready. She's been through the induction herself and knew if she stepped out of line Linda would have knocked ten tons of shit out of her. The vodka was poured into the glass and Melanie reached over to the small table nearby and grabbed a small bag of powder. She emptied the full contents into the glass and used her index finger to stir it around. Linda looked the girl up and down and gave her a long jumper. "Here, get this on you look perished." At last, a friendly face, someone who cared about her, Annie thought. Her teeth were chattering together as she slipped the garment over her head.

Melanie was here now and she passed Annie the spiked drink. "Why am I here, what's going to happen to me?"

Melanie was about to answer her when Linda reached over and slapped her hand over her mouth. "Button it you. I'll do the talking." Melanie shut up. She was so thin and even though she had make-up on you could see she was only young, fourteen maybe. Linda urged Annie to take her drink. She hated that she was involved in the sex trade but how on earth was she ever going to find a job that paid like this one? She was brought here herself when she was younger and it just made sense that she stayed here. She had no home, no family, no one who cared about her. At least here she felt important. Linda sat admiring her newly painted red nails. "Darling, there are things you need to do while you're here to make sure you stay safe. If you don't listen, they'll just kill you, trust me, I know and I've seen it happen so many times before." Annie took a large mouthful of her drink and she was hanging on Linda's every word. "You just have to look good and entertain the men who come and visit us. Some want you to dance for them and some want to talk to you."

Linda wasn't telling the full truth and Melanie couldn't help herself. She just blurted it out. "You have to sleep with the dirty old bastards too. They make me feel sick, go on Linda tell her the truth. Don't try and cover up what really happens here."

Linda launched a hair brush at her and it connected with the side of her head. "Keep it shut," Linda screamed.

Annie was starting to feel a bit light headed and her heart was pumping inside her ribcage. Linda gave Melanie the eye and she came to her side. "We need to start getting you cleaned up Annie. I'll help you with your make-up."

Annie was led to the corner of the room and she was aware that her hair was being brushed. Her eyes were clouding over and she was trying to push Melanie away but her body wasn't functioning right. Linda was here now and she was holding her down and tying something around her arm. A hypodermic needle was pushed into her vein and slowly brown liquid was injected inside her. Melanie turned her head and tears rolled down her cheeks. She looked at her own arms and she too had track marks all over her pale white skin. The heroin hit Annie's body and her head dropped to her chin, her mouth was wide open and saliva hung from the corner of her mouth. Melanie dropped to her knees and rocked her body to and fro, the other girls in the room didn't bat an eyelid. They'd seen this so many times before and this was just another girl who was taken from home and brought to this dirty, horrible place. Each girl there had been misled in some way or the other. Their life was set in stone and without a miracle happening they would always be trapped here. There was no way out, no escape.

Elsie sat with her legs up on the bed. She was reading a magazine and appeared to look glowing as she casually flicked through the pages. Her cheeks had colour in them for a change, pregnancy clearly agreed with her. Her eyes lifted as the door was unlocked from the outside and she was about to sit up. Monty walked straight over to her. "I hope you've been behaving. Fred said you've been handful since you've been here."

Elsie snarled and pushed him away. "Fuck off and leave me alone. I've told you before. I'll have this kid and then when it's over I want to leave. You can't hold me a prisoner here forever you know."

Monty sat down on the chair at the side of her and studied her longer than he should have. "Why did you ever think you could get away with my money? Didn't you think I would find you?"

Elsie swallowed hard and closed her eyes slowly. Her life was in such a mess and she knew she was in deeper than she could handle. "I didn't mean to take the money. I was bringing it back to you. I just had a manic moment with myself and got on my toes without thinking, you know what I'm like. I don't think sometimes. I would have come back. I would never steal from you."

Monty sucked hard on his gums. He knew she was lying, he could never trust her, not now, not ever. "You were going to abort my child, your words not mine. Do you think I would have let you do that?" his expression changed. "I loved you Elsie and you said you loved me. You knew this baby would be the icing on the cake for us both."

She opened her eyes wide and gritted her teeth closely together. "If you loved me then you would have told her about us and the baby. How many times did you say you were leaving her and you never did? I'm not some fucking idiot who will sit about waiting for you to find the balls to tell his wife."

Monty cracked his knuckles. He'd given Elsie a slap in the past and he wasn't arsed if he had to do it again. This woman got right under his skin when she started with, she never let him have the last word. He darted his eyes over at her. "I would have told her, it was you, rushing things, pressurising me all the fucking time. Jackie's got problems as you know. I can't just desert her can I?"

Elsie was never one for holding back and she told him straight. "Her problem is the drink love. You don't know the half about her, she's not as daft as you think. So what if she can't have kids anymore, that's not my problem. She has to deal with it not me."

Monty was livid, this woman was evil, she had no compassion whatsoever. Elsie definitely had something else to say but stopped at the last minute, her jaw was moving about but she was holding something back. Monty was onto her and urged her to continue. "Go on then, you tell me about Jackie. You seem to know a lot about her."

Elsie had said too much already and she changed the subject quickly. "Oh, just fuck off and leave me alone. When this baby is born I never want to see you again. You promised me Monty, so you better stick to your word. You can have the baby I'm not arsed anymore."

Monty was besotted with this woman and she made his heart flutter every time she looked at him. He had never meant to fall in love with her but it had just happened and he had no control over it now. She was his guilty pleasure, an addiction that he could never give up. Monty had met Elsie years ago when she was working in the clubs. She as a cocktail girl and from the moment he set eyes on her, she was his heart's desire. Elsie was always stunning and she could have had her pick of any man she wanted. Her bright red hair complimented her green eyes and her long slender figure always had men drooling over her. Jackie knew Monty fancied Elsie from the minute she first saw them together. He'd never looked at her like that and she knew this woman would destroy her marriage in the end. After a long time flirting, the actual affair started four years ago and at first Monty looked like he would lose everything for this woman. She got right under his skin and inside his head. He thought about her twenty-four-seven. Elsie loved the high life, she loved being on Monty's arm and there was no way she was going to share him for long. Monty didn't know the half of it. The fights she'd had with Jackie, the telephone calls, the money his wife had given Elsie to leave her husband alone. Elsie was lethal and she would do anything it took to get what she wanted in life.

Monty lay down next to the woman he loved and stroked his hand over her stomach with a soft touch. "I do love you Elsie. You're just a fucking liability. You're a ticking time-bomb and I don't know what you're going to do next. I'm not arsed that you stole my money if I'm being honest."

Elsie jumped into the conversation and stopped him dead in his tracks. "I've told you a fucking hundred times before that I wasn't nicking your money. Yeah, at first I thought fuck it, I'll take it, but you know I was just doing it for attention. You know me I don't think sometimes."

Monty chuckled and looked her in the eyes. "Yeah, dead right. I wasn't born yesterday. If you wasn't planning taking my money then why were you found at the train station on your way to fuck knows where?"

Elsie licked her lips and stroked a single finger over his ripe red lips. "Like I said, I wanted to scare you. I never got on the train did I, stop going on."

"No you never did but if I hadn't caught you just in time then I think you would have been on your toes with my money and my baby."

Elsie spoke softly, she always did this when she wanted something. "Monty, just let me go home. I've not seen my kids for ages, they'll be worried. Just let me ring them to tell them I'm safe."

Monty smiled softly at her, she was a right cunning cow and he knew she was up to something. "Give me June's number and I promise I'll send her a text telling her you're safe. It's the best I can do for now."

Elsie snarled and her nostrils flared. He could see right through her. "Just let me go home. I swear, if you don't I'll get out of here and you'll never see me again."

Monty stroked her red silky hair and lifted it up to his nose. He loved the smell of her locks and it always sent a warm sensation through his body. He leaned in to kiss her, staring deeply into her eyes. Elsie was still in a strop but she knew she had to keep this man happy. Her lips touched his and they shared a long lasting kiss. Elsie jotted down her sister's phone number. She passed it to Monty and sniggered. "Tell her this bastard is keeping me hostage and I'll be home as soon as I can."

Monty smirked and shook his head. "You're a bad apple you are Elsie. I don't know why I even bother with you." He folded the piece of paper and shoved it into his jacket pocket. He stood up and edged closer to the door. "I'll be back later to see you soon. Is there anything you want me to bring you?"

Elsie's heart sank, she was sick of sitting in this room

on her own. She hated him with a vengeance but she was glad of company, even his. But she could never show him she cared, to show her weakness, no that was never going to happen. She picked the magazine back up and carried on reading it. "Piss off, since when have I needed anything from you?"

Monty opened the door and left. He was used to her moods and just took her comment on the chin. While she was where he wanted her, he had nothing to worry about. Elsie punched her clenched fist into the pillow the moment the door was locked behind him. She stood to her feet and tried to look out of the boarded up window. There were small crack in the boards – squeezing her eyes closer she could just manage to get a glimpse of the world outside. She could see hills, trees, moorland, she didn't have a clue where she was. Where the hell had he brought her, would she ever break free from his evil grip?

Monty walked from the stables next to the main farm house. The wind was howling and he fastened his coat up as soon as the wind hit his body. Trudging over to the building he walked straight inside through the main entrance. Fred was there waiting to greet him and he was stressed. "Did you tell her to stop launching things at me, she nearly caught me earlier with a fucking brass ornament, she's a crank."

Monty smiled, he knew what Elsie was capable of and tried to calm him down. "I'll have a word with her later. You know what women are like."

Fred forgot who he was talking to and let out his true feelings on the matter. "I can't see why she can't stay over here with the rest of the girls. I'm sick of trudging over there every bastard hour to see if her ladyship is alright."

Monty wasn't happy, the vein in the side of his neck was pumping with rage. "Oh, so you think my woman should mix with all the brasses and see what goes on over here. She knows nothing about this place, so if I was you, I'd keep it shut before I shut it for you."

Fred had overstepped the mark and he knew it, his cheeks were beetroot. "I'm sorry, I meant to say, wouldn't it be easier to take her somewhere else? Like you said yourself you don't want her finding out what's happening here do you?"

Monty stomped about the room and ragged his fingers through his hair. There were only a handful of people who knew about what was going on here and he knew Fred was right. If Elsie had got one sniff that he was involved in this she would have been off like a shot. Yes, she knew about the brothel on the lane, but this was on another level, it was sick and something he would much rather not talk about. Monty sat down and folded his fingers in front of him. "Who's the new girl, Colin said he was brought one last night?" Fred was glad Monty was calming down and came to join him.

"Yes, he did. The girl is going to need to calm down a bit first, she's a bit of a live wire. I've told Linda to give her a bit of the hard stuff to calm her down."

Monty went white and a look of disgust filled his expression. "I thought you'd stopped all that shit after last time. I don't want another death on my hands. Fuck me, just give the girl some vodka or something light, don't be using smack anymore on them."

Fred chewed on his fingernails. He wasn't happy and hated that the boss thought he could just walk in here and start telling them how to run things. He was here well before Monty took over and he hated having to answer to him. This was the way it had always been done and if this prick thought he could start changing things, he had another thing coming.

CHAPTER ELEVEN

JUNE HAD JUST told Johnny about what Rita had said about Annie. He sat there pumping with rage. "What, and you decide to tell me this now after how fucking long. She could be dead somewhere. What the fucking hell goes on in your head, June?"

His auntie was at breaking point and now he'd actually put it like this she realised she'd dropped a bollock. "Annie always stays at her friend's houses. You wouldn't know that because you've not been here and it's been me who's been left to pick up all the bastard pieces all the time. Your mother just fucked off without a kiss my arse or anything so don't you dare start having a go at me when I've been doing my best."

Johnny had gone over the top but what did she expect, this was his sister and he feared for her life. "I need to speak to Rita about this."

June slammed her hand on the corner of the sofa and she was shrieking at the top of her voice. "For fucks sake, I've already told you what she said. She said it's some guy called Colin who's she'd been seeing. Rita is a smacked arse though and I would take anything she tells you with a pinch of salt."

Johnny reached for his trainers and started to put them on. June got a text alert on her phone and she was anxious to read it. "It's from your mam!" she gasped as she stood up from her chair. June paced the room and swiped the drops of sweat that had formed on her brow. "She said she's alright and not to worry about her."

Johnny sat looking at her waiting for some more news.

He shrugged his shoulders and raised his eyebrows high. "Is that it, didn't she say anything else?"

June shook her head. "No, just what I've read out."

They were puzzled and June went into it deeper. "That doesn't even sound like her. Why has she texted me and not rang. No, something is going on here."

Johnny hurried to her side and snatched the small mobile phone from her hand. He scanned the message and looked at the number it was sent from. Without any hesitation he pressed the number to ring it. June sat on the edge of her seat, she could hear the ringing tone and she prayed her sister would answer the call. Johnny flung the phone on the sofa and grabbed his coat from the side of the table. "I'm going to do a few calls, something isn't right. If Sandy comes while I'm out just tell her to wait for me, I shouldn't be long."

June sat with her head in her hands. Now Johnny was involved everything was going to go up in the air. He had little patience to start with and she knew he would do whatever it took to find out where his sister was. Johnny started to sprint down the street. Worm was out of town and he had no transport to get him anywhere. He was on his way to the club June had told him about. Rita was always there and he was hoping tonight would be no different. He needed to know who this Colin guy was, he needed his sister back at home where she belonged.

Johnny stood in the queue with all the clubbers. South Nightclub was the place to be if you liked to party hard. House music and drugs were the only reasons a lot of the youth went there to get off their head. Magic, pills and ketamine were all the go at a venue like this. Johnny walked past the bouncers on the door and he was pulled to one side to be searched. The security was right on him and he seemed to think he had a parcel of drugs stashed somewhere on him. Johnny held his hands out to the side while he was frisked. He held a cocky smirk on his face as this bouncer rubbed over his legs. Johnny had been to jail and if he wanted to he knew he could have plugged the drugs up his arse to get away with any detection in this gaff. When he was in jail plugging contraband was the normal thing to do. The only real way they could tell if you had anything illegal on your body was sitting you on a doctor's chair in the nick. This chair was like an x-ray machine and it could detect anything you had concealed in your body. This club didn't have anything like this, how on earth did they think they could stop drugs coming into the club? Clowns they were. People were streetwise who came here and even the girls here knew by stashing things up their vagina it wouldn't get detected by these guys. The search was over and Johnny winked at the beefy bouncer. They knew without saying a word to each other that even if Johnny had drugs stashed on him he would never have found it. The noise was deafening as he walked inside. Everyone was talking and shouting at each other. Johnny hadn't been to a club like this in years and he was taken back by how much the club scene had changed since he was last out. Even the way the girls dressed was different, they were barely covered and every time they bent over you could see their arses.

Johnny jogged down the stairs and looked round the club and located the bar. The baseline was thumping in his head and he was struggling to concentrate. He looked around and the people he saw looked like they were prisoners to the beat, eyes rolling, sweat pouring from them, they were off their rockers. Johnny paid for a beer and mingled around the club trying to spot Rita. Stood at a table close to the dance floor he felt a hand tap his shoulder from behind. "I hope you're not going to start with me again?" Diane Sheldon stood grinning at him. She held her drink in her hand and sipped at it slowly. Johnny let her join him.

"Nar, I just went over the top. I apologise, I shouldn't have taken it out on you. I was just a bit stressed that's all."

Diane was relieved and stood closer to him. She liked this lad and she had plans of making him her man in time. Diane tickled the side of his cheek with her finger. "So, you're still single then I take it?"

Johnny pulled her closer and flirted with her for a while. This was just harmless fun to him and he had no intention of slipping her one. He just wanted to see if he could if he wanted to. "Why are you asking anyway? I thought you were Natalie's mate and all that?"

Diane made sure nobody could hear her and made her intentions known. "I am her friend, but you're not with her, so it's all right isn't it?"

Johnny hated girls like this, they had no loyalty, no standards, would do anything to get a bit of attention. He was ready to put her in her place and wipe the smile from her face. "Anyway, I'm not single, I'm all loved up with some girl I've met."

Diane's jaw dropped low. "Fuck me, you didn't waste any time did you?"

"And, why should I? I'm a free agent now. I don't answer to nobody anymore so I'm entitled to see who I want."

Diane looked deep into her glass and spoke with her head dipped. "She still loves you, you know. She just couldn't handle all the shit anymore."

Johnny was gobsmacked, he didn't want to hear this

now. It was too late and he didn't want Diane getting into his head about Natalie. He held a flat palm out in front of him. "Diane, listen to me. Natalie is my past. I'm not really interested how she feels anymore. I've got a girl who really likes me and that's enough for me as it stands."

Johnny opened his eyes wide and he spotted Rita on the other side of the room. He placed his thumb and his index finger into his mouth and wolf whistled over to her to get her attention. Rita spotted him straight away and started to make her way towards him. "Diane, nice speaking to you. I'll catch up with you some other time yeah?" Johnny moved forward to meet Rita and Diane was left alone. Rita was holding her drink above her head and struggling to get through the crowd. This place was packed out.

"What are you doing in here Johnny? I didn't think this was your scene anymore." Rita had grown up so much since he'd last seen her. She had tits now, a shapely arse, she was a woman. He couldn't stop looking at her and he was amazed at how much she'd changed.

"Yeah, I've just popped in to see you about our Annie. June said it's some guy in here she's been seeing?"

Rita was more than ready to spill the beans and she wanted Colin knocked on his arse as soon as could be. Who did he think he was taking the piss out of her like this? She'd told him he would get his comeuppance and she was more than eager to tell Johnny everything he wanted to know about this guy. Colin was always in here making moves on the young girls and it was time someone knocked him down a peg or two and put him in his place. Rita jerked her head back and pulled Johnny by his arm. The music was deafening and she was struggling to hear a single word he was saying. Once they moved to a quieter spot, Rita was ready to tell him just what she knew about his sister and her new man. "He's not in here yet, but as soon as he comes in I'll point him out to you. He's a total prick Johnny, he had me right over. I'm just glad I got out of it before I ended up in trouble. The guy's a weirdo you know and he's into some pretty kinky shit too. He likes spanking." Rita dipped her low and the reality of what she'd done with this man was hitting home.

Johnny cringed, the more he heard about this geezer the more he wanted to knock him on his arse. Rita told him all she knew and she was genuinely concerned about Annie, she moved closer to him and placed her hand on his shoulder. "When you see her, tell her I'm sorry for the things I said but I was just upset at the time and I had every right to be because she nicked my man. You know me Johnny, I'm not the kind of girl to go about spreading shit when it's not true. I just tell the truth."

Johnny could see she was getting upset and comforted her with a hug. He thanked her for her help and watched her leave across the dance floor. Johnny was alone with his thoughts now. What Diane had said was lying heavily on his mind. He ran it over again and again inside his head. 'She still loves you' she'd said. This was some heavy shit and something he couldn't get his head around. He needed to forget what he'd just heard and put Natalie in his past where she belonged. He had a new girl now, he had Sandy. Pulling his mobile from his pocket he texted her telling her that he would be with her as soon as he could. There was no rush though, it wasn't like he was getting any sex from her, she was still playing hard to get. He had all the time in the world.

★

June sat clock watching. Sandy was here now and every second that passed seemed like an eternity. Sandy wasn't that much of a talker and June was already bored, she needed to liven things up. This girl was so boring, she could talk a glass eye to sleep. June smiled over at her in hope to lighten the mood. "Should I crack open a bottle of wine. We may as well, God knows how long Johnny will be?"

Sandy was a bit taken back, it was only a Tuesday and she only really had a drink at the weekend. She was like that, she liked to have a daily ritual. "What kind of wine is it? I only really like Jacobs Creek."

June was already in the kitchen and never replied to her, she was mumbling under her breath. "Jacob's Creek my arse, you'll get whatever I've got, Miss Fancypants." June opened the wine and filled two large glasses and headed back into the front room swigging at her glass. Sandy's head nearly fell off when she saw the size of the drinks June had poured. There was more than her weekly units inside this one glass. Lifting the drink up to her mouth she sniffed up hard trying to take in the aroma of the flavours, there was little fruity fragrance, just the smell of vinegar. This was cheap, trashy shit. June sniggered as she necked a large mouthful of the wine. She quickly wiped her mouth with the corner of her sleeve. "That will put bleeding hairs on your chest, Sandy. It's some strong shit let me tell you. I drank a full bottle of it the other night while I was just sat here on my own," she bent forward and chuckled as she picked her knickers out from the crack of her arse. "I was dead to the world after it. I woke up the following morning still sat here," she covered her mouth and sniggered. This woman had no shame. "I'd pissed myself too, it blew my fucking brains out it did."

Sandy pulled a face as she tasted her first mouthful.

This wasn't wine, it tasted more like paint thinners. She sat nursing her drink for the next fifteen minutes, it was putrid. By this time June was on her third glass. This woman was a lush and loved a good piss up. June stood up and walked over to the stereo. She picked up a CD and read the playlist on it. "Oh, shall will listen to a bit of Adele, I love her voice." June coughed and spluttered and cleared her vocal chords. "Maybe I'll find, someone like you," she sang as she started to play the song. Sandy was lightening up now. She had to make the most out of a bad situation. June saw her glass was empty and she raced towards her to top it up. The music was low and June plonked back down in her seat. She was well on her way to being pissed and her left eye was twitching the way it always did when she'd had a few too many. "So, come on then Sandy, tell me about you and your family. I mean, you're stuck with us all now so we may as well start getting to know each other. Where do you live, have you got parents who are still alive?"

What a nosey cow she was! Just blurting out private questions, she had no manners whatsoever. These questions were personal and not something Sandy really wanted to discuss. Monty had drummed it into her from an early age that she shouldn't discuss their private affairs and usually she kept her mouth firmly shut. Sandy let out a laboured breath. "My mam and dad are still together, well, for now they are anyway. I'm sick to death of hearing them arguing all the time if I'm being honest with you. Day in, day out – it's draining me."

Sandy was opening up, June was surprised and loved every minute of the gossip. She loved hearing about other people's lives and urged her to continue. "We all argue love, that's what happens when it all goes sour, trust me, I know. Who's the one who doesn't want who anymore? It's usually one of them, or is it both your parents?"

Sandy necked her drink and she opened the flood gates. This was the first time ever she really had someone to open up to, somebody who wasn't going to judge her. "My mam's drinking all the time. It's since she lost the baby, she blames him for it. I mean, my dad. She said all the stress caused the miscarriage and I think she's right. Perhaps, it was."

June was sat wide-eyed and eager to hear more. "What stress does your mother have? I mean, from what Johnny has told me she doesn't want for nothing. She has a nice big house, more money than sense, so what's so bad about that?"

Sandy reached over for the bottle of wine and filled her glass, she was getting a taste for it now. "Money isn't everything June, she craves his love, the attention he no longer gives her. He's got another woman too, he thinks she doesn't know, but she does. How can he do that to her? Why doesn't he just leave her for good and have done with it all instead of putting her through all this misery every single day?"

June was a good listener and she'd often thought about becoming a counsellor, she loved listening and she often had some good advice to give. She could always see the solutions to other people's problems. It was just her own life she struggled with. June moved to where Sandy was sat and placed a comforting arm around her shoulders. "Shit happens love. People stay together sometimes for all the wrong reasons. Why hasn't your mam just upped and left him?"

Sandy was ready to tell all, she had been bottling this up for too long… "She has tried to leave him, loads of times. She's been at the front door with her suitcases but he won't let her go. You see, my dad is not someone who would take anything lying down. He told her if she ever leaves him, he will find her and kill her."

June burst out laughing. What the hell was she thinking? Sandy was upset and here she was disrespecting her. June realised that she shouldn't be laughing. "I'm sorry love but my ex- boyfriend always said the same thing to me. It's a control thing with them. As if they would really kill another human being. I told my ex straight, I said, you come within an inch of me or my house and I'll cut your dick off and ram it up your arse. He never threatened me again after that. Mind you, that was after he'd been warned off by the dibble. He always told me if I met anyone else he would cut them up too. Well, what a load of bullshit that was. I've not seen him for ages and I wouldn't care if the bastard was lying in a ditch somewhere dead. I've had enough of men to last me a lifetime. Why do you think I sit in the house every night on my own? No, me and relationships are over."

Sandy was listening carefully and she could identify with June's story. She never really knew if her dad would stick to his word but she was scared that if her mother disobeyed him again how far it would really go. Her dad was a crank and a couple of butties short of a picnic. He was capable of murder, she'd seen his eyes when he snapped. Yes, he was more than capable of taking someone's life. June stood up and was sick of hearing all the depressing stories. She had enough misery of her own and wanted to change the subject. "I've got two mics if you fancy a bit of karaoke. I've got the Grease singalong CD if you think you can hit the high notes?" Sandy was blushing, she was never a confident girl and to sing on karaoke was just something that had never crossed her mind, she thought it was just for geeks. June pulled her up from the sofa and she wasn't giving up. "Come on misery arse, let's get this party swinging." Sandy was giggling, what did she have to lose? She had no one to impress here, she could be who she wanted to be without being judged. She kicked her shoes off and yanked the big clips out of her hair. Shaking it free with her fingers she was ready to rock and roll. June placed the CD in the system and before she knew it Sandy was singing her head off. Karaoke was so much fun, it wasn't just for geeks. It was for anyone who wanted to have some fun.

Zipping his jacket up slightly Johnny necked the last bit of his beer and headed towards the exit. The club was rocking and if he was here under any other circumstances he would have made a night of it. His life was so hard to change. Every time he thought he had everything sussed out, something would crop up and bring him back to the world of crime he'd always lived in before. He never really stood a chance. From the moment he'd been out of jail he was forced to return to it. Johnny had dreams of one day owning his own business, having a family, doing things by the book, but that day seemed further away than ever now. His family needed him and he had to do everything in his power to help them. He was the man of the house, the protector. Johnny left the club with a low heart. Natalie was playing on his mind. Why the hell was he thinking about her again? He had a girl now. He liked Sandy but they were from different worlds, she wasn't the same as him and he knew deep down that he would never match her expectations. He didn't want to go out and eat nice food in fancy restaurants, and he wasn't changing for anyone. Johnny walked along the main road and he stopped and studied the area around him. He should have carried on walking along the road but his legs took him in a different direction.

Johnny found himself on Natalie's street, just a few doors down from her house. There was a light on and he wondered if she was asleep. What would she say if he knocked on the door? How would she react? Natalie was like a stranger to him now, years had passed and things had changed. Popping a cigarette in the side of his mouth he flicked the lighter. What the hell was he doing, he was walking down the garden path. This lad had some balls. Johnny blew a cloud of grey smoke from his mouth and closed his eyes slowly. He had to know, he had to speak to her and find out what really happened. Diane had already said she still loved him so things couldn't be that bad could they? He rapped on the letterbox. There it was, there was no going back now. The deed was done. Johnny stood back from the front door and his heart leapt into his mouth. He'd made a mistake, he should never have come here, what was he hoping to achieve? He turned and he was just about to walk away when the front door opened.

He twisted his head back and there she was, his heart's desire. The woman he couldn't get out of his head. "Johnny, what's wrong, what are you doing here at this time of the night?"

His lips trembled and he couldn't speak. He stared at her, gasping his breath. "I'm sorry, I shouldn't have come. You know me, I just do things on the spur of the moment sometimes."

Natalie smiled at him softly as she tried to straighten her hair. "Do you want to come in for a bit? I can't sleep anyway so you would be doing me a favour. I'd be glad of the company."

Johnny was taken back, he thought she would have gone sick at him. He twisted his head about, where was her new man? He'd never really thought about him being here. He stepped forward and his chest expanded. "Nar, what about your fella. Would he be alright with me being here while he's in kip?"

Natalie placed her hands on her lips and raised her eyebrows. "What fella? I'm her on my own."

This was music to his ears, no man in her life, he could be in with a chance. Natalie walked inside and Johnny followed her cautiously. The light flicked on and Natalie sat down in the living room. "It's bleeding freezing in here, it never gets warm no matter what I do." Johnny sat down and now he was here, he'd clammed up. All the things he wanted to say to her had vanished, his mind had gone blank. Natalie sat smirking at him as she yanked her t-shirt over her bare legs. "You look good Johnny. A bit older but you still look like you."

Johnny smiled, she always had the knack of making him feel good about himself. "You look good too, a bit fatter than I remember but you still look good for it."

Natalie was aware of her body being slightly larger than it used to be and blamed her weight gain on motherhood. Johnny looked like he was going to spew his ring up. Just the mention of her having a kid to someone else made his blood boil. It was time to put his cards on the table here, she owed him an explanation. How could she do that to him when she knew how he felt about her? Sitting forward he took a deep breath and the question that had tormented him since he found out, finally came out. "Why Nat, why have a kid with some random bloke when you know how much I cared for you?"

Natalie was edgy, she sat fidgeting. Johnny urged her for an answer, there was no way he was leaving without knowing the truth. Natalie licked her lips, she just stared at him and the tears started to fall slowly down her cheeks. "It wasn't just some random lad. I loved him. Don't judge me when you know nothing about my life. You've always been the same, you have always presumed you know the truth when in fact you couldn't be more wrong. Johnny," she paused and cringed as if a hot poker had been stabbed deep in her heart. There was pain in her eyes, deep heart felt pain. "I wanted us to have a good life. You told me you would change and you never did. What kind of a life would we have had if you carried on doing what you were doing? I gave you a choice and you chose crime. So, don't you come here shouting the odds at me!"

These two had always been like this. The arguments they had were always heated and none of them would back down, stubborn they were, the pair of them. Johnny went into his protection zone now and any plans he'd come here with went out of the window. He bolted up out of his seat and waved his hands in the air. "Why the fuck did I even come here? The facts are there right in front of me. You've moved on and you've got baggage now. Damaged goods aren't ya?"

Natalie was shrieking at the top of her voice. "Go on, you think you know it all when you know fuck all. Fuck off anyway, why did I even think we could talk again? You're still the same arsehole I left behind years ago."

Johnny was raging and he clenched his fist together and ran to her side. He kept his hands still though and went nose to nose with her. "You ruined it, don't give me the sad story about me giving up crime because when I was earning you enjoyed the money just like I did. If you wanted another man you should have just said you wanted to go and bang somebody else. But no, you waited for me to get slammed and hooked up with someone else. Who is he anyway, go on, tell me his name."

Natalie backed away from him, and sat back down in her seat. "I don't have to tell you anything about my life anymore, you're not my jailer. It's time you left, you're right, me and you would never work. You're just the same old prick you've always been."

Johnny was struggling to breathe, his windpipe was tightening and his heart was racing. He'd not had a panic attack for weeks and he thought he was over them. Sweat poured from his body and he was suffocating, he needed to leave, get some fresh air. Running to the door he yanked it open. Johnny didn't say a word, he was gone. Natalie sat alone in the front room and her head was in bits. Why did it always turn out like this, they just couldn't get on. Once she heard the front door bang shut she gripped her head into her hands and squeezed at her head. "You're a prick, you never listen, you never listen," she screamed at the top of her voice as she launched the pillow at the wall.

Johnny ran into the night. He raced down the side streets, ducking and diving frantically. Finally, he found a bench and collapsed on to it. Sucking in large mouthfuls of air he tried to control his breathing. His coat was off now and he was breathing rapidly as his body folded in two. Johnny was starting to calm down, this was the worst panic attack he'd ever had. It was like a heart attack, he thought his time had come. He needed to get home, get his head together and sort his life out. He couldn't do this anymore.

CHAPTER TWELVE

ANNIE STOOD BEFORE the mirror. Linda stood behind her straightening her red dress. "You look lovely, the punters will love you." Annie was spaced out and whatever they'd given her had taken effect. She was slurring her words and her eyelids looked heavy, as if she was going to fall asleep at any time. She was muttering, trying to steady herself. "I want to go home, when can I go home?" Linda reached her hand up and stroked her fingers slowly across her cheeks. She hated doing this job but sometimes she just had to bite the bullet and do what was required of her. Her job was to make sure these girls kept the clients happy. There was nothing worse than an uncooperative girl. Linda kept the girls inline and if they needed sorting out she wasn't scared of punching the living daylights out of them to show them who was boss. She'd done it in the past and she would do it again, she was a hard nut. Linda had a large scar down her right arm, an old wound that still looked sore. The scar would always remind her that nobody here could be trusted, she always had to watch her back. One of the girls had done this to her, someone she thought was her friend before she turned on her and sank a blade deep into her skin. She was putting her make-up on when it happened and it came completely out of the blue. But what did she expect? She made the girls have sex with men. It had to happen sooner or later.

Annie gawped at Linda. "Where am I going? Please just take me home."

Linda was immune now. At first she had struggled with the job but when she first came here nobody listened to her pleas to go home, so why should she be any different now she was in charge? Linda sprayed Annie with perfume, it was a soft, fruity fragrance. She stood back and looked her up and down. She was ready. Linda took a deep breath and for a moment she was actually feeling this girl's pain, she knew what lay ahead. Taking her by her hand she led her out of the room and down a dimly lit corridor. Linda opened the wooden door to the left of her and walked inside. There was somebody in the room but they were out of sight for now. Linda raised her voice so they could hear her. "She's here for you when you're ready. I'll pick her back up in an hour. She's a new girl so be gentle with her, she's a bit temperamental at the moment." Linda walked back to Annie and gave her a few last minute adjustments and flicked her hair back over her shoulder and led her into the room, shutting the door behind her.

Annie was alone now and trembling with fear. Her feet were glued to the floor, her eyes shifting one way then another, she could hear him but she could not see him. The shadow of a man was now approaching, she still couldn't see his face. Her heart was racing and she knew she wasn't safe. Her mouth was dry, her body trembling. He stepped from the darkness. His tone was chilling and creepy as he spoke. "Come and sit down here with me sweetheart, I won't bite. Come and sit with daddy." His cold hands reached over and pulled her closer, and before they glided slowly over her young skin. His warm breath blew slowly over her breasts. She could see him now, see the whites of his eyes, feel his heartbeat beating next to hers. The man ran his fingers through her hair slowly. "You smell good," he whispered as he inhaled her fragrance. She needed to do something, how could she ever get out of this.

Her voice was low and she looked him straight in the eye. "I need you to help me. I'm not here by choice, they are forcing me to do this. They've kidnapped me and brought me here, please help me to get home."

Her words fell on death ears. This man didn't give a toss about how she got here he just wanted to ravish her. His hand gripped her neck and restricted her breathing, he pinned her down and she could see his true identity for the first time. This wasn't an old man, he was a good looking guy who you would think would never have any trouble getting women of his own. His white teeth sank hard into her skin as he pinned her down and rolled her on her stomach. She could hear the buckle as he undid his belt. The man hooked the black leather belt inside her mouth and yanked it with force, he was in control now. Annie was his prisoner, his sex slave. Her knickers were torn off and her dress was yanked up high. He was still biting at her body and trying to enter her. This wasn't vaginal sex either, the punter was ramming his cock up her arse. Annie's screaming went unheard. He pushed her head deep into the pillow and all she could do was lie there and accept what he was doing to her. He was rough and his nails sank deep into her flesh, scratching and pulling at her. He was groaning, whispering, cursing. Annie felt the grip being released on the belt in her mouth, she was coughing and gagging. Twisting over on her front she could see her attacker lay there trying to catch his breath. Annie kicked her legs away from him and scarpered to the other side of the bed. There was a warm gush between her legs and her eyes were wide open as blood tricked from her back passage.

The man jerked his head forward and smirked. "Plug it up, it will be fine."

Annie gritted her teeth and with every bit of strength left in her body she sank her fingernails deep into his eye sockets. "Bastard, bastard," she screamed at the top of her voice. The punter picked the young girl up from the bed and launched her at the wall. His eyes rolled with madness and he wanted to finish her off. Sprinting to her side he pummelled his fist into her. The noise was sickening and now he was looking to finish her off. Just at that moment Linda ran into the room and stopped Annie's attacker. "Just leave her to me Monty. She's young. I'll sort her out I promise you. Just back off."

Monty stood over her and wiped his finger slowly under his eye. Once he saw the blood he snarled and drew his foot back to boot his victim in the stomach. Monty snapped and he was gunning for Linda. "Get the slag out of here. I thought you'd sorted her out, do your fucking job in future otherwise you'll be out on your arse."

Linda was doing her best to calm him down. He spat at Annie and then walked over to the bed. His eyes were swollen and getting redder by the second. Blood started to ooze down his cheeks. Linda dragged Annie out of the room. Once she was in the corridor she shouted out for help. This girl was in a bad way, she was barely breathing. "Fred, Fred, get your arse down here quick," she shrieked at the top of her voice. There was a dark shadow approaching from the other end of the corridor, Fred was on his way. Linda was in tears and she held two fingers on the girl's neck trying to find a pulse. "She needs to go somewhere, she can't stay here with the other girls. If they see what's happened here they'll be up in arms. Fred, you need to get rid of her. Please, do something."

Fred started to panic. This was bad, what was he supposed to do with her, finish the kid off, bury her alive, his head was in bits. Fred paced the floor ragging his fingers through his hair. "Leave her with me, go on, you sort the other girls out. I'll deal with her."

Linda ran back down the corridor, she kept looking

over her shoulder. Fred picked Annie up and held her in his arms. This kid was probably the same age as his own daughter and for a split second he held so much guilt about his job. "Fuck, fuck, fuck," he yapped as he ran with her from the farmhouse. Fred's eyes were all over the place. It was pouring down with rain and he didn't know what to do for the best. His eyes shot to the hills in the distance. There was a cliff nearby, he'd been there before when things hadn't gone to plan in the past. Annie was coughing up blood as she reached her hand up slowly in a bid to find some compassion. "Help me!" she yelped. The blood was choking her, her lungs filling with fluid. Fred gritted his teeth and he looked up to the heavens as if the answer was looming there. The rain pummelled his head as he knew he had to make a decision and fast, this kid needed urgent medical help. Surely, it would have been easier to end her pain. What was the point in making her suffer any more, she was a goner. Fred secured her tightly in his arms and his mind was made up. The thick black mud sucked around his feet and he was sinking as he made his way across the farmyard. Every step was a struggle and his face creased with every step he took.

Fred opened the door slowly to the barn house. Elsie was locked away in the next room and he knew if she heard a noise outside her room she would be banging on the door demanding to be set free. He rushed over to the single bed and dropped Annie's lifeless body onto it. He stood hovering over her and ragged his fingers through his hair. He had to leave now and hope this young female didn't make it through the night. Fred took one last look at her and left the room. The keys held in his hand were shaking rapidly as he tried to lock the door.

Elsie was hammering at her door as if her life depended on it, she'd had enough. "Let me out of this shit-hole.

Monty, please! I'll do anything, just let me go home. I'm going mad in here, it's seriously doing my head in."

Fred stood with his back against the cold brick wall. Slowly, he edged out into the night. This was a mess, a bit fat fuck up. The clouds hung low in the night sky and he could see lightning bolts in the distance, bright white lights spread across the moorland. He was stressed and knew sooner or later he would have to deal with the girl once and for all. If Monty found her still here he would slit his throat. Fred needed to get his head together and think straight. He stomped back over to the farm in a panic. He was back inside, dripping wet, hair stuck to the side of his cheeks like rat's tails. Linda was in the room and fear was in her eyes. "Did you deal with her?" she asked as she passed him a dry towel. Fred was in some sort of trance, he wasn't with it, his eyes were hollow. Linda poked her crooked finger deep into his shoulder. She needed an answer. "Fred, can you hear me? I said did you sort her out?"

In a daze he nodded, "Yep, nothing to worry about anymore she won't be giving us anymore trouble."

Linda sighed and plonked down on the seat next to him. "Do you want a stiff drink Fred, you look like you need one?"

"Yep, give me the fucking bottle. I definitely need it."

It was early morning and Johnny couldn't get back to sleep. He was lay staring into space, his mind working overtime. Sandy was at his side, she was still fast asleep. By the time he'd got into bed she was well away and he never tried waking her once, not even for a quick leg over. He knew he didn't love her now and even though she was a nice enough girl, he was just using her to discover his mother's whereabouts.

Johnny was alert, someone was outside the room. His eyes were wide open as he watched the end of the bed. The door creaked open slowly and he was ready for war. June's head appeared at the bedroom door. Her hair was all over the place and she was holding one hand on the side of her head. "Oh, my head is banging. I've got a right hangover." Johnny was relieved, he pulled the covers back from the bed and slipped out of it slowly hoping not to wake Sandy. He tiptoed onto the landing and followed her back into her bedroom. June plonked onto the bed and spread her body out like a star fish. "I feel like I've been raped and pillaged. I swear, my legs are so sore from dancing last night. Every inch of me is paralysed," she started to smile before whispering, "I'll tell you something for nothing too," she checked the door to make sure nobody was listening, "that one's dark horse in there, she can't half drink when she puts her mind to it. Five bottles we done in, fucking five bottles."

Johnny sat on the edge of the bed, just like he'd always done in the past when he had a problem. Drawing his knees up to his chest he rested his head on the top of them. His heart was low and he was genuinely upset. "My mam... she's alright isn't she? I mean she texted now so that means she's alright doesn't it?"

June could see the sadness in his eyes and rolled over and placed her hand on his leg. She tapped her fingers softly on his bare white flesh. "Yeah, I think I just blew it all up into something that it's not and as for Annie, I'm sure she's okay too. They're alike them two, no matter if they fell in a pile of shit they always come up smelling of roses."

Johnny looked at his auntie. This was serious and he was trying to get his words out. "I need to get away from here but I can't go until they're both back safe. Rita texted me last night and said this Colin guy came into the club right after I'd left. He's said Annie told him she was going to her mate's caravan in Wales to clear her head, so I think she's fine too."

June looked at him in more detail. He was on the verge of breaking down and not the big man he made out to be. "You just do what you have to do. It's not fair that you have to deal with all this shit all the time. I'm guilty of piling crap on your head as well. So, all I can say is I'm sorry."

A single tear rolled from the corner of his eye and landed on his bottom lip. "It's her, I just can't get her out of my head. I've tried, fuck knows I've tried but it's killing me inside."

June sat and hugged him. Sometimes everybody needs a hug no matter who they are and Johnny was no different. June used a single finger to wipe away his tears with a swift movement. "If that's what you have to do, then pack your stuff and go, fuck everything else. We'll be fine."

Johnny pulled away from her, he hated anyone seeing him crying, he had to man up, stand tall. What the hell was he doing crying like a big mard arse. He inhaled deeply and gritted his teeth tightly together. "I'm going nowhere until the girls are back home. I'm going to find my mam and bring her home and the same thing goes with Annie. You know I won't rest until then don't you. I'm a worrier, I always have been."

June smiled and kissed the side of his cheek. "What about Sandy, don't you care for her. I thought you two were a good match?"

Johnny stared at the space in front of him as if the answer to her question was lurking there. "I thought she was too but my hearts not with her and it will never me. I still love Nat."

The pair froze as a noise from outside disturbed them.

June held her finger to her mouth and jumped up from the bed. She opened the door quickly but nobody was there. Dropping her eyes to the floor she spotted her ginger cat, Dave. Bending down slowly she scooped him up and snuggled her face into his thick fur. "So, you decided to come home then have you Dave? Three days you've been missing. What is it with this fucking family, nobody ever wants to come home."

June walked back into the bedroom and Johnny was stood ready to leave. "I'm going on the lane today and I'll do my best to find out all I can about Monty and his boys. Someone must be willing to talk because I don't think for one minute it's all that it's made out to be. I've got a gut feeling about this."

June dropped her hands low so her cat could break free. "Try the 'Old Loom' pub. Everybody knows everybody in there. Ask for Bacardi Brenda. She's a wise head and nothing ever gets by her, she's knows the lot. Tell her you're my nephew and she'll talk to you."

June chuckled and rubbed at her arms as a cold chill passed over her body. Johnny smiled and watched as she jumped back into bed. She dragged the duvet over her body and popped her head over the top of it. "I'm going to stay in bed for a bit. I can't be arsed moving today. Pass me the remote, Jezzar's on and I want to find out who the dad is. Three men he's got in the firing line for it. It's fucking amazing that people go on the show and air their dirty laundry in public for the world to see. I'd be ashamed to death if I didn't know who my baby's father was, honest, it's shocking."

Johnny chuckled, what was the world coming to when a chat show host was more important than getting out of bed each morning? He sucked in a mouthful of air and left the bedroom with a spring in his step. Getting things off his chest had done him a world of good. He felt stronger now and ready to face his demons. Sandy was stirring as Johnny walked back into the bedroom. She yawned and stretched her arms above her head looking around the room. "What time is it? My head is wrecked. Last night was something else, your auntie is a mad head."

Johnny shot her a look and started to get ready. He knew what he wanted now and his plan was to leave Manchester for good; make a fresh start, get a job and maybe one day a wife and a couple of kids. He had to let go of the past. It was the only way he could move on. Reaching for his mobile he stood and dialled Worm's number. "Yo, can you pick me up mate. I've got a bit of running about to do?" Johnny listened carefully to the voice at the other end of the phone and his jaw dropped, he was gutted. "Fucking hell, right, ring me later when you've sorted it out." The call ended and he didn't look one bit happy. "The engines fucked in Worm's car. I could have done without that today I can tell you."

Sandy looked at him seductively. Enough time had passed and she thought it was time to have sex with him. Sandy sat up and straightened her hair, pushing her perky breasts out in front of her. "Johnny, why don't you get back in bed? We can have some quality time together today if you want. I've got nothing planned if you want to make a day of it?"

Johnny hated hurting anyone's feeling, but this show was over and he wanted to move on. Sandy was just the innocent party in all this and he didn't want to lead her on anymore. He looked over at her and hesitated. Could he tell her the truth? Break her heart? Sit for hours with her explaining the reasons why he didn't want a relationship with her? He stood for a few seconds and edged closer, this wasn't going to be easy. "Sandy, I'm…"

He didn't get chance to finish his sentence, she grabbed his hand and dragged him back into bed. "I thought you wanted this, just be quiet and let's make this moment special." Her warm wet lips connected with his and she was the one making all the moves, she was gagging for it. Johnny just didn't have it in him to turn her down plus he'd not had a leg-over in ages. Sandy planted kisses on the side of his neck, he was aroused and any plans of telling her it was over went out of the window. These two were at it like animals now, his hands ravished every inch of her body and he was desperate to enter her. Sandy was sweating, strands of hair stuck to the side of her cheek, her eyes were dancing with excitement. This was the right time to tell him, she was sure of it. Johnny climbed on top of her and slid his erect member inside her. Before he moved she sank her fingernails deep into his shoulders. "I love you, I really do." Johnny had one thing on his mind and that was to shoot his load, her words fell on deaf ears and he continued, not even acknowledging what she'd just said. The sex was kind of a let-down if he was being honest with himself. He should have just walked away, stuck to his guns and told her it was over. Sandy gripped him in her arms and her legs were wrapped around his waist as his pace quickened. There were no kisses exchanged, no long sensuous moments of two bodies coming together never wanting to part. This was just sex, a sack emptier, nothing more. Johnny's back arched as he ejaculated, his toes curled, and his facial expression changed slightly, eyes closed tightly. Dipping his head into the nape of her neck he bit into her skin softly and enjoyed the ripples of pleasure soaring through his body. It was over now, done with.

Sandy lay as he rolled away from her. He was still catching his breath when he felt her head land on his chest and small kisses all over his skin. This girl wasn't happy with what she'd just had, she wanted more, he could tell. Johnny gasped, usually he would have had a few minutes breather and continued but he was in no fit state to give it her again, any chance of seconds were out of the window. Johnny lifted her head slowly and kissed the top of it. "I'm sorry but I need to go. I've got some important stuff to sort out today."

Sandy pulled a face. This prick had just used her for sex and she knew it. How could she have been so thick? She sat up straight and watched him scarper. She threw a few questions at him just to make sure she was right. "I thought we could have made a day of it?"

Johnny nearly choked. He'd had what he wanted and wasn't arsed about spending all day in the feather with some girl when his mother was still missing but he couldn't be nasty with her, she'd see right through him. Turning his head slowly he replied. "I would love to Sandy but honest I've got a busy day, some other time maybe."

Johnny loved dossing days. He'd done lots of them with his old flame Natalie. DVDs, toffees, crisps and takeaway was all you needed. It was great to cuddle up in bed with the one you loved doing absolutely nothing all day. Sandy knew she was pissing in the wind, there was no way she was begging. She could see he wasn't interested, she wasn't daft. "Right, I'll get out of your way then. I need to go home anyway. It's your loss. We could have had a good day." Johnny slipped his jeans on. He was never one for looking neat and tidy. He enjoyed the rough look, stubble on his chin, clothes creased. Sandy was in a rush to get ready too and she was fully dressed in seconds. She walked to Johnny's side and pecked him on his cheek. "I'll get going, phone me later if you want. Well, if you can be arsed."

This was easier than he first thought, he'd half expected her to be here all day, lingering. "Yeah, as soon as I'm free

I'll bell ya." Sandy didn't even wait for his reply, she was out of the room and heading down the stairs before he'd finished speaking. Punching his clenched fist into a pillow he growled. "Fucking women, argh…"

Johnny was on foot today so he had to get a move on. As he marched up Rochdale Road, grey clouds scudded across the sky and he knew the heavens could open at any minute. Heading through the estate he was scanning the area, looking for anyone he knew that might help him find his mother. This was the Shiredale Estate, he'd spent a lot of hours here growing up and the park where he used to chill looked like a ghost town, it was empty. In the past every kid used to be there; smoking weed, driving nicked cars, up to no good, being chased by the dibble, it all went on here. The park was where he first met Natalie. They were always together and without her he would have probably landed in jail a lot sooner than he had done. Natalie was sensible like that, she always wanted to change him and even from an early age she was always begging him to mend his ways. Johnny loved a good fight and Natalie was always telling him to walk away from trouble, he rarely listened. He was a know it all. Johnny Barker was an angry child. He held so much frustration at the cards life had dealt him. He secretly craved a father figure when he was growing up, somebody to play football with, someone to toy fight with but it wasn't to be. The only men that had been in his life had been arseholes. Men who held no respect for his mother, men who were just there for a shag. From the age of thirteen Johnny took no shit from anyone. The last man his mother had brought home, an ex-copper called Simon, took it out on Johnny. It started with clipping him around the ear at first but gradually the guy was knocking ten tons of shit out of him. Elsie didn't believe Johnny when he told her about the abuse and he was alone in facing this monster every night after school. A person can only take so much and Johnny plotted his revenge. Every move was planned to ensure he got his own back against his abuser – to bring him to his knees and ensure he never laid a finger on him again. Plans were something Johnny loved, he always had a Plan B at hand in case anything ever went wrong.

One night Simon was sat in the chair watching TV when Johnny came home from school. As soon as he walked through the door he was on him like a rash, picking on him, finding faults, terrorising him. Johnny shot his eyes to where he'd stashed his tool and casually sat down. He knew the moment this prick raised his hand to him he was getting it. He didn't have to wait long either. "Get me a can from the fridge," Simon snarled at him. Johnny ignored him at first and in his own mind he was testing him, knowing he would kick off any time soon. A shoe was launched at his head and he could see Simon from the corner of his eye getting ready to strike. Johnny was quick this time, he scarpered to get his iron bar from its hideout and once it was in his hands he was like a mad man. He was out to do some damage. Johnny struck the first blow and stunned his opponent, he put him on his arse and with all his might he swung the bar back and pummelled it into Simon's body. He was like a man (or should that be boy) possessed, eyes bulging from their sockets. He twatted the guy with the weapon and very quickly he was calling the shots. He was no longer the underdog. With the bar in his hand he pressed it firmly against Simon's neck.

What he did next was chilling. Far from being flustered, Johnny was calm as you like. Cold. "There will be no more of that, you prick. That's the last time you ever lay a finger on me…" there was a pause for effect. One of Simon's eyes was closing and already turning black, "now get your stuff together and fuck off before I finish you off. I swear, if you don't I'll finish the job." Johnny had let him have it alright and by the time he'd finished with him Simon was a quivering mess. That day changed Johnny. He had learned the hard way and knew from then on he would never let anyone treat him like that again. He would always stand up for himself. Of course when Elsie came home from work she said it was all his fault. Simon had concocted some bullshit story saying he was attacked by her son. He left that day and Elsie pleaded with Simon not to go but it fell on deaf ears. To this day his mother never really believed his story and she held a grudge against her son saying he ruined the best relationship she'd ever had. What a joke she was!

The memory of that first clash with a grown man came back to Johnny as he started to pick up speed. He was now at the bottom of Moston Lane. There were so many people out today, the place was buzzing. The Old Loom pub was just in sight. Johnny dug his hand inside his pocket and checked he had enough money for a drink. Monty had paid them well for the job they'd done for him but the money hadn't lasted long. A few new rig-outs, some new trainers and a few other bits and bobs and it was more or less gone. Johnny walked into the boozer and smiled as he spotted a few geezers he recognised. Tony Hamilton had always been a piss-head and as far back as he could remember he was always one of the first people in the pub as soon as the doors opened each day. Johnny ordered a drink and made his way over to Tony. This guy had aged so much since he'd last seen him. His nose was bright red and his skin looked like sandpaper, it was rough and full of spots. Johnny shouted over to him and raised his hand above his head. "How's it going Tony? Long time no see."

Tony squeezed his eyes together tightly and tried to focus. His expression changed when he realised who it was.

He was up from his seat in seconds shouting at the top of his voice. "Where the fuck have you been hiding, it's been years. When did you get out of the nick?" The men hugged and Tony invited him to sit down and join the group of men. Johnny was so happy to sit with some of the old boys from the estate – some were missing and the pain in his heart was overwhelming as Tony spoke about the good old days. Mark Abbott had been was one of Johnny's best friends back in the day but at the age of fifteen he had lost his life. Sad really, a case of misadventure the coroner said. He was just a young lad trying ecstasy pills for the first time. The poor bleeder just passed out on the dance floor and died. Johnny was by his side too, he witnessed every single second of it. It had traumatised him for years and even talking about it today caused a lump in the back of his throat. Johnny changed the subject quickly, he hated doom and gloom and he'd had enough of it to last him a life time. The things he'd seen in his past would make your toes curl; gruesome things, people dying and being abused. No, he wanted to put it all this behind him. The beers were flowing and it was like the lads had never been apart; they were laughing, joking, telling stories about their youth.

Johnny picked his moment wisely and pulled Tony to the side away from prying ears. "What do you know about Monty?"

Tony swallowed hard, he rubbed vigorously at his nose and sniffed. His voice was low as he replied. "Mate, he's bad news, ask anyone."

Johnny punched him in the arm playfully. "Tony, fuck off with the bullshit. Just tell me straight what you know, he's not untouchable is he?"

Tony was singing like a budgie. This guy knew the crack and he was telling him all he knew. Everything he told him led him back to the brothel on the lane. No matter how he looked at it, this place was the heart of Monty's empire. Tony pointed out Barcardi Brenda on the other side of the bar. He remembered what June had told him about her. He slurped his lager slowly and stood up but paused, unsure of his next move. Did he really need to speak to this woman? He wasn't sure. Johnny smiled over at her and gave her a wink – no, his mind was made up, he had to leave no stone unturned.

Brenda thought she'd copped, she straightened her hair and made sure her cleavage was on show. She liked a younger man and given the chance she would have had this lad in her bed before the night was over. Johnny placed his pint on the bar and turned to face her. "Hiya love, I'm June's nephew. She said to mention her name when I saw you."

Brenda smiled and ran her finger slowly around the top of her glass. "I know June, she's a lovely woman." She looked Johnny up and down and licked her lips slowly. She was attracted to him. "You're a good looking lad if you don't mind me saying."

Johnny was uneasy, he knew what she had on her mind, it was written all over her face. Desperate she was, gagging for it but it was probably best if he led her up he garden path for a bit..."Can I have a quick word with you Brenda? June said you know a lot about the lane and I'm hoping you might be able to help me."

She studied him, what on earth did he want to know, was it safe to talk to him? She didn't want anything coming back to bite her on the arse. Brenda necked her drink in one and banged the glass on the bar, she raised her eyes. Nothing in life was for free and she was making sure she got something in return before she opened her mouth. Johnny knew what she wanted and shouted over to the barmaid. "Can I have a treble Barcardi for this lovely lady?"

The barmaid chuckled and went to get a clean glass. She was used to Brenda and it was very rare she paid for her drinks, she always had an admirer willing to stand her a drink. Brenda beckoned Johnny into a quiet corner of the pub. She sat down and crossed her legs in a seductive manner. This woman was mutton dressed as lamb; short skirt, high heels and a tight top. Brenda had had a hard life, there was no denying the fact. She'd done some bad things to keep her head above water too, some things she was not proud of.

Johnny sat down and dug in his pocket for his cigarettes. He passed one to Brenda. Slowly, she popped it into her mouth and sucked hard onto it. "So, what can I do for you?" Johnny wasted no time, he had to be straight with her, tell her the script so she could help him. Johnny asked the same question about Monty and his men and sat back with his arms folded tightly in front of him. Brenda's expression changed, she knew she would have to delve back into her past to give this lad the answers he needed. "I'm not going to lie to you love, Monty is someone you should steer clear of but it's up to you if you chose to challenge him." Brenda took a deep breath and sat thinking for a few seconds. She double-checked nobody was listening. "There's a farm where they take the young girls. I've been there once when I used to work for him." Johnny was listening now and knew he'd hit the jackpot. "I only worked in Moonlight for a short time, just to clear a few bills. You know how it is when you're on your arse?" Johnny nodded, there was no way he was judging her. She took another blast from her cig and her expression changed, sadness clouding her eyes. "I worked on reception mostly and sometimes the clients asked me to come in the room with them just to watch, probably to spice things up. Usually it was just to get my tits out, nothing special. Even I have standards." Johnny chuckled, this woman just said it like it was… "Anyway, there were always calls from two guys, one called Fred and the other one called Colin, for Monty. I think they're the ones who get the girls for him. Sick bastards they are too. They used to come to see him on the lane and I told Monty straight that I couldn't stand either of them. I had a gut feeling, honest, they made my stomach churn." Johnny was alert, and eager to hear more, he rested his elbow onto the table with his head placed on top of his hand. "The farm is near Ramsbottom. I can't remember exactly what the road is called but it's quite easy to find it as it's the first exit when you come off the motorway," she closed her eyes and mumbled under her breath.

"The name of the farm would be handy, Brenda" Johnny urged, he was so close now. He just needed the exact location.

Brenda was trying to visualise the place she'd been. Bingo, she remembered. Eyes open wide. "Homestead Farm, it's called. Fancy remembering that after all this time! " Brenda was very pleased with herself, "Yes, that's what it's called. If your mother is missing then that's where she'll be. They take all the naughty girls there. Honest, if any woman gives them shit they go there and most of them never come back. It's tight really the way it all works, these foreign girls haven't got a clue what they're letting themselves in for when they agree to work for these guys. It's a shame, a fucking crying shame."

Johnny rubbed his hands together. At last he had a place to look for his mother. She had to be there, there was no other place left to look. Johnny's mobile phone starting ringing and his face dropped as he recognised Monty's phone number. He walked outside with the phone held tightly to his ear. "Hiya, what's up?" Johnny was listening carefully and tickled the end of his chin. This must have been another job, an earner. "Right, leave it with me. As soon as I get some transport I'll nip over to see what I can do." This was strange, it wasn't the normal kind of job he was usually asked to do. Arson wasn't really his game, but to blow a car up was easy money. He took the job, no questions asked. Everything was coming together now and his life was starting to look a lot clearer. Johnny smiled and walked back into the boozer. He got the round in for Tony and the lads and carried on talking about all the changes that had happened in the area since he'd been in prison.

CHAPTER THIRTEEN

ELSIE LOOKED ABOUT the tiny room. Lifting her jumper up slowly, she looked down at the small mound inside her stomach. How on earth had she ended up like this? She didn't want any more kids in her life and this bastard was making her have this one. She'd already had two abortions to this guy. He never knew about those though, he would probably have killed her if he'd found out. Elsie lay thinking about the days gone by. She had never sat still long enough to think about her life properly until now. She was starting to see how many mistakes she'd made in her life and how much she'd let her kids down. She had regrets, so many regrets. Monty had fucked her head up so much. He'd made her forget just what was important in life. There was no way she could stay locked up in this room for the rest of her pregnancy, no way in this world. Standing to her feet she scratched her head and started to look for a way out of this shit-hole. Elsie looked at the boards covering the windows. She gently gripped her fingers behind them and tugged seeing if they could be moved, they weren't budging. She needed a tool, something she could stick behind them and prise the boards from the window. Elsie was in the zone, she was on a mission to break free. Searching high and low she needed to find something to help her. Elsie froze, she could hear crying and sobbing noises. Her head twisted around like a barn owl and she walked slowly to the wall at the other side of the room. There it was again, somebody was in the next room. "Hello, who's in there," Elsie shouted. She pressed her ear firmly against the wall, still no reply.

Elsie hammered her clenched fist into the wall hoping to get a response. "Is somebody there," she stressed. This was so frustrating, no one was answering her.

Elsie started emptying the draws, looking under the bed and in every nook and cranny of this tiny room. At last, having removed every drawer from the dresser, she found a small pen-knife hidden away on the floor beneath it. Quickly she pulled it out and studied it. There were silver screws in the boards and she unfolded the rusty blade out and tried to unscrew the boards. Elsie pressed the knife deep into the screw and tried to twist it. Her tongue was out and she was really concentrating. This was a nightmare. The knife kept on slipping and it only turned the screw slightly. This was going to take a lifetime! Elsie pulled a nearby chair over and stood on it. She'd only been at it a short time and already her hand was hurting, her fingers bleeding at the end. She needed a break to figure out how she could complete this task. Lying back down on the bed she started to cry, she was so frustrated. This was so unusual for her and it must have been her hormones playing up because under normal circumstances this woman was as hard as nails and she would never cry over anything, she was a heartless bitch. Elsie was exhausted, she was sweating, her heart was racing and she realised that her body was no longer as fit as it used to be.

Monty would be here soon and she knew if he spotted anything different in the room he would have moved her from it. This baby was all that Monty ever wanted and he would do anything to protect it, anything. His wife Jackie could never give him an heir to his empire, she was his last hope of fathering a son. When Elsie first fell pregnant, Monty had promised her the world. It was the happiest he'd been in a long time. He even told her he was going to leave his wife and finally they could be together, no more lies, no more hiding. So what had changed? It was the money, her greed, her need to break free to try and change her life. Elsie closed her eyes and started to go over her life and how she'd ended up in this horrible mess. She was a fool, she hadn't thought about the consequences. It was just a normal night at "Moonlight" and she was helping out until Monty got there, just making sure all the girls weren't taking the piss and actually working. That's when she got call the phone call. The call that changed her plans. Jackie was always harassing Elsie and there was no surprise in her knowing about Monty having an affair with her. The two women had been at loggerheads several times in the past and Jackie had nearly scratched her eyeballs out the last time they'd met. Elsie should have just stayed put, never left the building. But Jackie told her money was involved and she couldn't not go and miss this opportunity to be quids in. The women met on a street not far from Moston Lane. It was dark and Elsie was a bit scared for her safety as she trudged down the side streets to meet her. The lane was well known for attacks and every other week there was a story in the local paper mentioning another woman who'd been raped and robbed. Elsie was so hard faced and cocky and refused to show fear to anyone.

The moment she saw Jackie sat in her car she walked straight up to it and jumped inside it as if she was the one in the right. She had no shame. Jackie was a classy women, even the smell of her perfume told you she had money. Her hair was neatly styled, her fingernails immaculate and she wore top class clothes. She was everything Elsie wanted to be… Jackie pulled her seat back and made sure she had enough room to move if she needed to punch her husband's mistress. Jackie stared at her at first, taking in every inch of Elsie, cringing inside knowing her husband had fallen in love with this tramp. She wasn't anything special, she wasn't a patch on her. Maybe in her day she had it all but today she looked washed up. Why was Monty going out for mincemeat when he had steak at home?

Elsie could feel her stare and sat fidgeting. She sat twiddling a piece of her hair near her cheek. She hated the silence, she had to speak. "So, what is so important that you needed to see me tonight? If it's another fight you want then you're wasting your time. I'm pregnant and that's the end of it. There you go, I've said it. I'm having Monty's child."

Jackie creased up and her hands gripped the steering wheel with force, so much rage was pumping inside her. She already knew about the child, people had talked and her worse fears were confirmed. Her heart was shattered into a million pieces and for hours she'd been sat there staring into the bottom of an empty glass trying to make this problem go away. Jackie had been drinking. You could smell the alcohol on her breath. She leaned forward and spoke directly to her. "I want to offer you a lifeline. I've got some money here, more than enough for you to fuck off and start again somewhere else, away from my husband." Jackie looked her up and down. "I drew the money out of the bank earlier, it's Monty's money but I'm sure you won't mind where it's come from as long as you can spend it." Elsie sniggered, was this woman for real or what? Did she really think any amount of money would cause her to leave the man she loved? Jackie opened the bag and there was more money there than Elsie had ever seen in her life, enough to start again just like she said. "Get rid of the kid and leave Manchester and it's yours." Elsie was thinking about it now. The only real reason she was ever thinking about having the baby anyway was to have a meal ticket from Monty. Okay, she'd loved him once but he was so possessive and controlling and her life would never be happy as long as he was in it. The honeymoon period had finished ages ago and now all she had were false promises. Jackie waved a wad of notes under Elsie's nose, taunting her, "twenty grand is a lot of money, imagine what you could do with that – you could get new tits – well I mean you could do with a boob job, they're like fucking spaniel's ears."

Elsie wasn't taking any shit from this woman because after all she was the one holding all the cards here. She inhaled deeply and give it her right back. She was evil with her mouth when she wanted to be. "I don't need a boob job love. Your husband loves them just the way they are. Whose bed is he in most nights, go on ask yourself that?"

Jackie had heard enough, she gripped Elsie's hair wrapping her fingers deep into her thick locks. Jackie was aggressive and she could have easily ended this woman's life the mood she was in, the red mist had come down and she was at the point of no return. "Listen to me you cocky slut. You take the money and go otherwise I'll make sure you never spend another night with my fucking husband. I mean, how much would it cost to have you done in?" She sniggered and threw Elsie's head crashing into the dashboard. She sat staring at her and gritted her teeth tightly together. "Monty has taught me a lot over the years and to deal with a slag like you is child's play. You're not special you know! Do you think you're the only one he's sleeping with?" She had her now, Elsie was listening, she was alert and hanging on her every word. "He's had endless women, he likes the young girls too, has he told you about that?"

Elsie licked her lips slowly and the thought of her lover cheating with somebody else made her stomach turn. She had to fight back, it wasn't in her nature to be the underdog. "Stop talking out of your arse Jackie, Monty loves me. He's told you enough times, so stop shit stirring and just let us get on with it. Your marriage was a sham well before I came along, so don't go blaming me for your husband's infidelity."

It was time to show Elsie her ace card, to knock the smile right from her face. Jackie flicked some invisible dust from the top of her shoulder. "Do you know when we first got married Monty couldn't get enough of me. It's me who told him I didn't love him anymore and it was me who wanted to end it all. I bet he never told you that did he?"

Elsie stared down at her fanned out fingernails. "Yeah, blah de fucking blah, whatever you want to believe. You know the truth and so do I."

Jackie kept her voice low and got ready to deliver the killer blow. "We were both out on a night out and I was carrying my second child. We always had a young girl called Stacy who babysat for us and she was only fourteen years old at the time." Elsie pulled a strangled look and she wondered where she was going with this story. Jackie wound her window down slightly and sucked in mouthfuls of the night air. "He's a sick twisted bastard, sick, tapped in the head. Clever he is though, cunning and sly." Elsie was getting bored and she started to open the car door to leave. Jackie reached over and gripped her jacket and pulled her back inside. "Fucking listen to me. I haven't finished yet." This was getting out of control and Elsie was scared, she'd never seen Jackie like this before, usually she was too drunk to string a sentence together. The car door was closed again now and Elsie sat up straight in her seat with her hands folded tightly in front of her. Jackie raised her eyes to the moonlight outside and the whites of her eyes seemed so bright, her eyes clouded over. "He must have thought I was thick. But, I had a gut feeling the moment he asked

Stacy to stay at the house," she chuckled sarcastically and let out a laboured breath. "He said he was too drunk to drive. What a load of crap that was, he'd only had one glass of wine." Jackie was kicking the arse out of this story and Elsie couldn't see where she was heading with it. She opened her handbag and passed a cigarette over to Elsie and smiled. "Come on, get one, you're going to need it." Elsie always smoked when she was pregnant anyway, she ignored all the health warnings and never really cared what anyone thought about smoking during pregnancy, she was so selfish. Jackie held her cigarette between her fingers and sucked hard on it. She blew her smoke towards Elsie as she continued speaking. "It was late. I'd been asleep for hours and I must have woken up for a wee. I noticed he wasn't in bed with me. I just thought I was dreaming at first. But no, he wasn't in bed next to me. I walked along the landing trying to find him and I could hear noises." Elsie was intrigued now, she was sat on the edge of her seat and the colour was draining from her cheeks. Jackie was staring into space and her eyes never flinched. "I opened the bedroom door slowly and there he was fucking her."

Elsie gagged and held her hand over her mouth. "What, he was shagging a fourteen year old girl?"

Jackie nodded. "Of course he was, are you thick or something? He's always had a fixation for young girls, the man is a kiddy fiddler. Anyway, after that night I told him I was leaving him. I hated him. I couldn't look at him, he made my skin crawl. Monty would never let me leave though and he gripped me at the top of the stairs begging me not to go, begging for my forgiveness. I lost my footing and slipped, head over heels I went down the stairs and I was lucky I wasn't seriously hurt." Elsie flicked the butt of her cigarette out of the window. Jackie tried to hold back the tears but they were flowing now. "I lost the baby that night and he pleaded with me never to speak a word about what he'd done to me, to our relationship. Stacy went home but before she left she told me all about his affair with her and what he'd promised her for having sex with him. He groomed her, a fucking nonce he is, not the hard man he makes out to be."

Elsie let out a laboured breath. "Are you lying to me or what? If you are, then that's sick. You can't say stuff like that when it's not true?"

Jackie nodded. "It's the truth, why do you think he's never left me or let me leave him? He knows his secret will be out and then everyone will know what a spineless prick he really is."

Elsie felt sick in the pit of her stomach. It all made sense now. The way he looked at the young girls in the brothel, the way he always liked her pubic hair shaved off. Yes, she believed every word Jackie had told her. This was a different ball game now. Jackie was right, she could make a new life for herself. This money was all she needed to break free. Jackie reached over and stroked her hand softly. It was such a shame for this woman. "I know you think I'm mad but me and Monty will always be together. It's just the way it is. It's pathetic really but he's my life and I have to stand by him. For better or worse."

Elsie snarled and punched her hand deep into the side of Jackie's seat. What a complete dickhead she'd been, why hadn't she seen what was right in front of her eyes? Elsie knew there was something not right with this guy but she had got carried away with the money and she had just overlooked it. This was some sick shit and she was finding it hard to deal with. Her heart was racing and her throat was dry. Taking a few seconds to think she agreed to take the money. She could never stay with him now, she could never trust him. Jackie handed the money over and didn't say a word. She dropped her head onto the steering wheel and looked like she was sleeping. Elsie was gone. Jackie was alone.

Elsie stood holding the wad of money in her hand. She had choices to make and time wasn't on her side. She rang Monty and asked him to meet her, she didn't tell him why, just that she needed to speak to him as soon as possible. That night she was so mixed up, she didn't know which way to turn. What should she believe? She had to go with her gut instinct. Stood underneath the arches waiting for him her mind was racing. Should she wait and tell him what she knew or should she get on her toes? Elsie saw Monty approaching and her mind was made up. She could never tell him what she knew, she would never tell anyone about the man she loved. Jackie had bought her silence and she would never breathe a word for as long as she lived. Elsie ran into the night and her plan was to leave Manchester. All she had to do was grab a few things from her house, just the bare essentials to get her over for a few days. This was the worst mistake she ever made, she should have known he wouldn't be far behind her. Elsie swung her bag over her shoulder and headed back into the night all ready to leave Manchester. She was a nervous wreck. Elsie peeped out from the doorway near the train station just to make sure the coast was clear. Hid away in the shadows of the night Monty was there waiting to capture her in his evil grip again. The minute she stepped from the doorway he grabbed her. Elsie screamed out and told him she was leaving him. Monty just picked her up in his arms and carried her punching and screaming to his car. She was going nowhere. It turned out that Jackie had double-crossed her in any case and she'd rung her husband and told him she'd given his lover the option of them staying together or taking the money and that Elsie had chosen the money. What a cunning cow Jackie was!

Monty had taken her straight to this room and she'd been here for months, it was hard to know exactly how long. Elsie knew she had to be smart where Monty was concerned. She couldn't tell him she hated every inch of him even though she now knew the truth and was already planning a future without him. The child inside her was the only thing keeping her safe. If she hadn't been carrying his child he would have kicked ten tons of shit out of her, and probably dumped her in the canal. She knew how much he wanted this baby and he would do anything to make sure she carried it full term. Elsie trembled inside. There was a noise outside the bedroom and she sat up on the bed watching the door handle for any movement. She could hear somebody in the next room, chairs scraping along the floor, whispering and furniture being moved. She jumped from her bed and ran towards the door. She'd had enough, she was ready to blow. "Fred, is that you? I need you to get me some more stuff. Monty said I can have anything that I want while I'm here so you need to sort me out! Don't ignore me! I know you can hear me! Fred!" Elsie paced around the room and a plan was hatching inside her head. There was a heavy brass candlestick on the side of the table nearby and she knew if she was quick enough she could take Fred down with one fatal blow. Keys jangled outside her door. Elsie ran over to the bed and lay with her hands looped over her head. Her chest was rising and she was doing her best to remain calm.

Fred stood at the door and he was stranger than normal. Usually he was on the ball and wouldn't take any shit from her but today he was stressed out, he clearly had other things on his mind. "Can you let some bleeding fresh air in here? I can't breathe. I'm sweating all the time, it's a wonder I'm still alive." Fred scanned around the bedroom and started to walk to a small air vent on the other side of the room. Elsie stood up and edged towards the candlestick. She had it in her grip, she had to be quick, no time for mistakes. She needed to be precise. Fred was reaching up to open the vent and she knew as soon as his foot touched the ground she would strike a blow. Fred was taking ages, he was shaking the small lever with force. It was stuck and he couldn't budge it. He stepped back down and was just about to turn around. Elsie held the candlestick high behind her head and with all her might she belted him right over the head with it. Fred was in shock, his eyes were wide open and he was unsteady on his feet. She sprinted to the unlocked door and for the first time in ages she was free. Looking left, then right she was unsure of which way to go. She hesitated. She could hear crying from the open door not far from where she was stood, she rammed a sweeping brush under the door handle, that should keep Fred at bay for a while, she thought.

Spinning on the spot Elsie heard the crying again. This time she popped her head inside the door and scanned the room. There was a bed and she could see somebody's head sticking out from the top of it. Elsie didn't have time on her side, she needed to leave but the body in the bed needed her too, she couldn't just walk away. She moved into the room and she was now stood at the side of the bed. She couldn't see the female's face due to the black hair dangling in front of it. "Help me," the body whispered. Elsie should have left right at that moment but she hesitated and needed to see who this was. She stood shaking and gently wiped the hair back from the girls face. Elsie's jaw dropped low and her eyes were wide open. Her lips trembled and she was struggling to breathe. Annie opened her swollen eyes and she gripped her mother's hand. "Please, help me." Elsie felt sick and light headed – the room was spinning round. A hand from behind gripped her throat and her windpipe was being tightened with every breath she took. Fred swung her about the room. "You dirty slut, did you think you could get away from me?" Blood trickling down the side of his cheeks and he looked like he was going to finish her off. Elsie was flung on the floor and her knees were held up to her chest as she scarpered to the other side of the room. She cowered as Fred stood over her and swung his foot back in the air. He toe-pecked her right in the stomach. Not just once, he repeatedly booted the living day lights out of her. The sounds of her screams echoed the room, deep, piercing cries of desperation. Fred was struggling to breathe. The gash on his head was pumping blood and he needed to sort it out. He left the room in a hurry and the door was closed quickly behind him. Elsie could barely move, she dragged her body closer to the bed and touched the hand she could see dangling from the side of bed. This was bad, so bad. Elsie's face creased with pain as she gripped her stomach. Dipping her hand between her legs she brought it back up to her eyes, she was bleeding. She was losing the baby. Annie lay staring into space and she was not in any fit state to move. "Mam, mam," she sobbed as her eyes closed slowly.

CHAPTER FOURTEEN

WORM WAS MOBILE again after spending an arm and leg getting his precious motor fixed. He and Johnny made short work of Monty's next job and as the pair walked away from the BMW now in flames it had been a piece of piss. They were straight in and out, it was ten minutes work, tops. Johnny was hyped up and ready to face his fears. He sat cracking his knuckles, chewing heavily on his lip. He'd already told Worm about the farm and tonight he planned to go there to see for himself just exactly what went on there. His mother had to be there, he had a gut feeling. No matter which way he looked at it everything led him back to this farmhouse. Worm was quieter than usual and he was unsure of what Johnny had planned. Yeah, he was his mate, but this guy was asking him to put his neck on the line against a man who could kill him. Make him suffer. Things had changed so much since Johnny had got out of jail and even his friendship with Worm was something he wasn't sure about anymore. Worm wasn't the same friend he left behind, something had changed. He just couldn't put his finger on it, he was always going missing, unable to contact him.

Johnny reached under his seat and pulled out a small bag. His hand dug deep inside it and he pulled out a silver pistol. He squeezed the trigger slowly. "I've got to do what I have to do. If my mother's there then I need to step up. Monty has her, I'm sure of it. I spoke with Martina again and she told me a lot more stuff about this farm. Worm, I'm not going to lie to you, I need you on this one. I need to know you have my back. I know my mam is a fucking idiot sometimes but if she's in some sort of trouble I need to sort it out. You know I would do the same for you don't you?" Worm nodded, there was no doubt about it. If he needed Johnny he'd be by his side all the way - one hundred per cent. Johnny squeezed the top of Worm's shoulder and smiled. "It means a lot to know you have my back. We go back a long way me and you and once this is over I will never ask for your help again."

Worm was confused, he held a puzzled look. "There's no need to thank me. I will always be there for you no matter what. Did you get me a gun as well?"

Johnny reached under the driver's seat and there it was, another firearm. These men were ready now to do whatever it took. They were brothers in arms and ready to tackle Monty and his boys. Johnny's phone was ringing and Sandy's number was displayed on the screen. He raised his eyes over at Worm. "I've got to take the call, I've been ignoring her all day." Sandy was crying her eyes out and he couldn't understand a word she was saying as he answered the call. "Just slow down, take it easy and tell me what's wrong. Sandy, just take a breath." Johnny listened carefully and he was doing his best to get her to calm down. The call ended and he let out a laboured breath. "Her mam's gone missing. She said she's just got in and there are empty bottles of gin all over the place but no signs of her mother."

Worm shrugged his shoulders, "And what does she expect you to do about it?"

"I don't know but I have to sound concerned, don't I?" Worm was ready for it now, his head was in the game and he was ready to kick some arse. Turning the ignition over Johnny revved the engine. The lads looked at one another and nodded. It was time to go and find Elsie.

June was on her own when she heard someone knocking at the front door. She fastened her cardigan tightly around her body and made her way to the door. "June, I know I'm the last person you want to see but can I come in and talk to you for a few minutes. I promise I won't keep you long?"

June snarled, she was in no mood for this today. She couldn't hide how she felt and she told her straight. "You've got some bleeding cheek coming around here after all the trouble you've caused. Say what you have to say and piss off. Johnny will be home soon and I don't want you here playing with his head again. You've got five minutes, tops, start bleeding talking." June held the door opened and Natalie walked inside. She stood fidgeting as June came into the room after her. "Park your arse then," she growled.

Natalie was so nervous and her eyes were red raw through crying. "June, do you know what time he's home? I'd prefer it if I spoke to him directly."

June sat down and leaned forward, she cupped her hands together and tapped her feet rapidly. If the truth was known she wanted to rag this scrawny cow all over the front room if only to make her feel the pain her nephew had felt when he was locked up, unable to do anything about the situation he was in. There was no way she was letting her call the shots, this was her house and her rules. "You don't need to wait for Johnny. I'll tell him anything he needs to know. He's happy now and he doesn't need you fucking his head up again. He's in love. Yes, he's found someone who deserves him."

Natalie creased up as June's words shot straight through her heart. This was such a mess and things had just got out of hand. Natalie had to say something. She had to lay her cards on the table, confess all. "June, Johnny called to see me the other night," she paused and dipped her eyes.

June was chomping on the bit and she wanted to hurt

this girl even more now, rip her hair out, bite her face. "Yeah, he will do, you're an easy leg-over that's why, what did you expect?"

Natalie sniffed hard and licked the tear that had landed on her lip. "Why are you being nasty to me, June. You know how I felt about Johnny. It was his choice to get put away, not mine. I wanted a better life for us, to not have to be scared every time someone was knocking at the front door."

June raised her eyebrows and spoke in a sarcastic tone. "And did you get that life with your new fella? Like fuck you did. You can't polish a turd, love. Face it, you carted Johnny so you could move on with this new guy of yours. You had a baby with him. Johnny had not even made his bed up in jail and you were tubbed."

Natalie was fighting her corner now, she sat up straight and looked June straight in the eye. "Is that what you think? Go on June, say it like it is. I don't owe you an explanation about how I choose to lead my life. Like I said, Johnny was the one who ruined us. I asked him to pick between me and the life he was leading and you know what June? He picked jail. I can't see me shouting from the roof tops about that can you?"

June saw red, she didn't know anything about this but there was no way on this earth this cocky bitch was shooting her down. "Fuck off home, come on, do one from here. Nothing has changed. You go and live your life and let Johnny lead his. What is it, has the baby's dad fucked off? Aww, poor you." Natalie was pissing in the wind if she thought she was getting any sympathy here. She should have known better than thinking she could talk to June. She always thought the sun shone out of her nephew's arse and she'd never have a bad word said about him.

Natalie stood up and placed one hand on the side of

her hip. "Just tell him to come and see me June. This needs closure. Once I've spoken to him he won't see sight or sound of me again."

June clapped her hands together slowly. "Well, thank fuck for that. I can't say you'll be missed. Come on, I'll walk you to the door. I don't want you here longer than you need to be."

Natalie gasped her breath and started to make her way to the hallway. Just before she turned the catch she turned around and looked at June. "I did always love him and I probably always will."

June pushed her out of the door and she was ready to punch her lights out if she said another word to her. She'd got right under her skin and she was fuming. "Save you breath love, go and tell someone who gives a fuck because I don't."

Natalie hurried down the garden path and she wary watching her back. June couldn't be trusted and she half expected a half brick landing on the back of her head. June slammed the door shut and marched back into the front room. She ran to the window and pulled back the net curtain making sure Natalie had left. "The bleeding cheek of her," she muttered under her breath.

It was nearly midnight and Johnny and Worm had hatched a plan to follow Monty all night long to see if he led them to the secret hideout. They were parked up on the lane and they knew any time now he was about to leave to go on his travels. Worm was slouched down in his seat and Johnny was sat with his hood pulled up covering his identity. Music was playing softly inside the car. The lane was quiet tonight and just a few people were about. The shady residents and those up to no good. There was singing to be heard outside the car and as Johnny turned his head slightly he could see a group of girls falling out of the Ben Brierley pub blind drunk. This boozer was always full at weekends and most of the youths went there to finish off their night out. It was a free and easy pub and Karaoke and cheap beer always kept the punters happy. The three girls were staggering down the lane, one step forward and two steps back, they were steaming drunk. Worm nudged Johnny in the waist with his finger and smirked. "Check these lot, twisted the lot of them. I bet their game as fuck for a knee trembler."

Worm squeezed at his crotch and he was aroused. The girls were wearing the biggest heels known to woman, how on earth they walked in them is beyond me. Their skirts were like belts too, just covering their arses, leaving nothing to the imagination. Worm wound his window down slowly and he just couldn't help himself. He loved women and never missed a chance to flirt with them, especially with the younger girls. "Yo, sexy ladies, what's going on?"

The ringleader of the girls wobbled over to the car and bent her head down slowly. Her tits were nearly popping out of her bra and they both got an eyeful of her great knockers. Her eyes were all over the show and she took a while to focus. She gripped the car to steady herself and began to speak. "Orr, I don't suppose you've got a cigarette I can nick from you? The shop's closed now and we're gasping. We could do with one each if you're being generous."

Worm dug into his packet and pulled out a full deck of "Mayfair" cigarettes. He pulled the wrapper from them slowly and pulled out three cigarettes. "There you go lovely, don't say I don't give you anything." This girl was on fire, full of confidence and out to impress. She stuck her head further in the car and clocked Johnny. She smiled at him and slid her index finger down her cleavage in a seductive manner. "What are you saying sexy, do you fancy coming to a party at my house or what?" She twisted her head a little over her shoulder and spoke to her friends. "We'll look after him girls won't we?" The other girls were all pushing their heads through the small gap to try and get a better look at the eye candy. Johnny wasn't interested and didn't reply. He had his mind elsewhere and a gang of drunken females was something he could do without at the moment. Worm, however, was fanny mad and he was interested in anyone who would give him the time of the day. He usually pulled a lot of girls, but usually they were mingers, those who were desperate to have a man in their life. Worm licked his lips and he was buzzing. He'd bagged himself an easy fuck buddy. "Give us your number then. I've just got a bit of running about to do and I'll call around to your gaff later."

The girl pulled a face and turned to her friends. She was loud and laughing her head off. "Nar, sack that. I was talking to your mate not you. No disrespect mate but I'm fed up not hard up."

Worm was fuming and he tried grabbing the cigarette back from her hand but she was too fast for him. She'd rattled his cage now and she was getting told. He was fuming. "Oi, you've got a face like a bulldog chewing a wasp, so do one." Why didn't he just keep his big gob shut? These girls were ruthless and there was no way they were being spoken to like that. The car was shaking and they were trying their hardest to turn the car on its side. They were booting at the door and smashing their hands against the windows.

Johnny was up in arms. How on earth could they keep a low profile when this lot were bringing it on top for them?

Johnny flicked the ignition on and wheel spun from the side street. As he looked into his rear view mirror he could see the three girls doing a moonie. Yep, their knickers were pulled down and they were showing the cracks of their arses and slapping their bum cheeks. Johnny was trying to keep a straight face but he just couldn't do it. These girls were raw and at any other time he would have been glad of their company. He loved girls like this. They were his kind of people. Worm had a face like a smacked arse, his confidence had been rocked. He stuck his head near the wing mirror and started to examine his appearance. "Cheeky bitches. I mean Johnny, there's fuck all wrong with me is there?" Johnny was still chuckling and he looked like he had a feather stuck up his arse. This was so funny to watch, Worm was devastated.

About an hour later Monty came out of "Moonlight". It was late now and both Johnny and Worm were nodding off. It was freezing and the car temperature was below zero. Worm stretched his neck, he spotted Monty. He slapped Johnny's arm rapidly. "Here we go, lad. Wake up, he's here." Johnny rubbed his knuckles deep into his eyes and focused. Monty was dressed in black and in his hands he held a bunch of flowers. He was carrying some shopping too. Johnny was eager to follow him, he just hoped and prayed that tonight he was going to the farmhouse. Monty stood speaking to a woman at the door. He was there for ages talking and it looked like he was never going to leave. At last, the conversation was over. Monty unlocked the car door and jumped inside it. Worm and Johnny were on tenterhooks, their eyes were twitching one way then another. This guy was taking ages. Monty pulled away from his parking spot and they could see him talking on his mobile phone. "Come on you slimy cunt, take us where we need to go," Johnny mumbled under his breath as his fingers gripped the steering wheel. Monty was heading towards the motorway and he was putting his foot down too.

Worm rubbed his hands together and slapped the end of his knee. "Result, let's go and get your mother. If Elsie's there, then she'll be coming home with us. There's no doubt about it. Let's sort this shit out once and for all." Johnny's nostrils were flaring and he didn't say another word. His head had to clear, he had to be focused, make no mistakes. Worm watched Johnny from the corner of his eye and he seemed agitated.

Monty slowed down as he hit the country roads. It was pitch black and hard to see anything. The boys were not far behind him and kept well out of sight. Monty's indicator started flashing and Johnny pulled over at the side of the road. In the distance he could see the lights inside a farmhouse set in the middle of the moorlands. He sucked in large mouthful of air and nodded his head slowly. "So, this is it, the famous farmhouse where it all happens. Martina said there must be at least ten girls working here. It's a cushy little set up when you think about it really. I mean, look where it is in the middle of fucking nowhere, no pressure, no dibble lurking. This guy's got his head screwed on."

Worm was chain-smoking, he'd already smoked four cigarettes whilst they were on the motorway. Johnny got out of the car and walked over to a wooden fence on the opposite side of the road. He leant on it and held his head in his hands, thinking. Elsie needed to be here because if she wasn't, what the hell was he going to do? Monty had trusted them both. As soon as he spotted them there he would know they were trying to double-cross him. This job had to be quick and clean, they had to be in and out like ninja warriors. Johnny walked back to the car and popped his head inside. "Get what we need. The car can stay here. We'll have to jib across the field. They'll see us if we go down the path." Worm tucked the gun down the front of his trackie bottoms and patted it with the palm of his hand. He pulled his hat down just covering his eyebrows. They were ready, it was time to make every second count.

Monty was on the phone to his daughter. All night long she'd been ringing him telling him about Jackie being missing but he wasn't arsed. She was always going off on her own when she was like this and he couldn't be bothered with it anymore. Different day, same drama. Elsie was all he cared about now. Elsie and his baby. Locking his car up he made his way to the farmhouse. The gravel crunched under his feet with every step he took. Monty sniffed the flowers and smiled. His woman loved flowers and hopefully once she'd seen all the nice food he'd brought her she'd change her tune and start doing as she was told for a change. Elsie was a live-wire there was no doubt about it.

Fred sat near the open fireplace watching the logs burn away slowly. The open fireplace was so calming to watch and many a night Monty had looked into the flames trying to find the answers to his problems. Fred turned his head slowly as the door opened. He wasn't his normal lively self. The job was getting to him, there was stress, so much stress. He looked like he had the worries of the world on his shoulders. Back arched, head dipped low. "Cheer up mate, it might never happen," Monty sniggered as he sat down near him. Fred had something to say and his mouth kept opening and closing but nothing came out, not a single word. Monty was that full of his own dramas that he never noticed how quiet he was. "So, have you got any girls who you think are ready to go and work on the lane yet? What about that Alenka, she's been here for months, she should be ready by now."

Fred nodded. "Yes, she's good to go. But, what about old Albert who comes here to see her, he always wants her, he'll be gutted if she's gone. We're fucked now for getting new girls here because Colin has gone away for a few months to clear his head."

"Tell that dirty old cunt that we've got some new girls for him," Monty snapped, "just say they've got tighter pussies that should sort him out."

Fred agreed, and sat playing with his fingers. His voice was low and he never looked at his boss as he spoke. "Monty, when you've got a minute can I have a word with you?"

"Fucking hell pal, just let me have a shower and that first. Elsie will be having kittens if I don't take this lot over to her, she'll skin me alive if I'm not there soon." Monty left his shopping on the floor and his car keys on the table. He left Fred alone with his thoughts.

Fred had decisions to make now, should he stay and face the music or get on his toes? He slid his finger near the car keys and touched the end of it softly. He was hovering, unable to make his mind up. Holding his ear to the door he could hear the working girls arguing. They were always like this and before now there had been some bad injuries between them all.

Alenka was top dog here, she took no messing about from anyone. When she first landed here she had been a handful and it had taken a few beatings from Fred before she finally agreed to work her debt off. Alenka had just turned seventeen, blonde hair, blue eyes and a great slim waistline. She'd had dreams when she made the choice to leave her country and one day she was hoping to make her family proud. That day would never come now. She hated her life and the person she'd become. Dirty bastards touching her body every night, making her do things that made her sick to the pit of her stomach. She had no choice though. It was either do as they say or be beaten and thrown into a room on her own for weeks with little food and no one to speak to. Fred told her that in few months she would have worked her debt off. Of course he was a lying fucker and he had no intention of ever letting this girl go. She was a good earner and the punters loved her. Fred stood and walked to the door. He walked back and paced the room slowly as he ragged his fingers through his hair. He'd hurt Monty's woman, this wasn't good. He knew how he felt about her and he couldn't take the chance of waiting about. His mind was made up, he grabbed his black leather coat and quickly snatched the car keys off the table," he paused and let out a laboured breath. It was no good, he would find him. He had to stay and face the music.

Monty stood tall in the mirror as he got out of the shower. This place was so cold and even after having a red hot shower, he was still freezing his balls off. Quickly, rubbing his body dry with a thick white cotton towel, he started to get dressed. There was no doubt about it, this guy was handsome, he had a thick neck and that bad boy look in his eye. His chest was toned and the hours he'd spent at the gym were paying off. Opening the old oak bathroom cabinet he scanned inside it. He'd left some toiletries here previously and he was hoping Fred hadn't used his stuff to spruce himself up. His head dug deep in the cabinet, his hands moving everything about. Monty smiled as he found his favourite "Hugo Boss" aftershave. He loved this stuff. He always felt clean and special when he wore it. It was Elsie's favourite fragrance too and when they first met she'd commented on how good it smelt. Women liked a man who smelt good, it was a sign that they cared about their appearance and personal hygiene. There is nothing worse than sitting next to someone who stinks like a monkey's arse. Monty ruffled his hair with his hands. He didn't like it when it was neat and tidy, he liked the rough look. He was all set to go now. One last look in the mirror and he was ready to see the love of his life. His future wife maybe. Monty had spoken about marrying Elsie in the past. Well, in the early days when he worshipped the ground she walked on. Okay, he'd gone off her in the time they'd been together but now she was carrying his child, he was trying his best to do the right thing by her. Monty would always be a womaniser. It was just something in his blood. His father was the same and even when he was growing up he remembered the endless arguments between his parents about his father's extra marital affairs. It was very rare these days to find a man who believed in the true vows of marriage.

For better for worse, for richer and poorer, in sickness and in health.

What a load of crap that was, this was fairy tale stuff and in the real world it was complete bullshit. Happy endings very rarely existed. The women were just as bad as the men. Oh yes, they were just as bad as the men. They wanted equal rights and they sure as hell got them, they were players too. Monty slid the small black iron lock from the middle of the oak door. It was stiff and he had to use some force to get the door open. He was singing as he left, serenading anybody who would listen to him. He had a good voice; a crooner, with a soft melody that melted the heart. Monty's father was a big music fan in his day and growing up in the family home every Sunday night the family would sit around the radio and listen to Frank Sinatra and the rest of the Rat Pack. Monty was clicking his fingers as the song hit its peak, he even did a few dance moves too, spinning and shuffling. Walking back into the front room he spun on the spot. He had the moves, he had rhythm there was no doubt about it. Monty finished singing and shot a look around the room, he coughed a few times to clear his throat. "Fred," he shouted through the open door. Monty stood waiting for a reply but there was nothing, silence, no response. Rolling his eyes he picked the flowers up from the table and swung his jacket casually over his shoulder. It was time to go and see his Elsie.

Johnny and Worm were hidden away in a tall hedge not far from the farm. Worm was moaning and it was hard to keep him quiet. "Will you shut the fuck up, someone will hear us," Johnny growled.

"I've stood in cow shit, look all over my new trainers, it fucking stinks. Don't tell me you can't smell it?" Worm was gagging. Johnny snarled at him and shook his head but he was still going on. "One hundred and ten quid these trainers cost me. You owe me a new pair, it's your fault. There's no way I'm wearing them now they're covered in cow dung. Fucking ruined they are."

Johnny held a single finger up to his mouth and poked his head slowly out from the hedge. He could hear someone whistling. His neck stretched and he was trying to get a better look at who it was. His eyes were wide open and his chest was rising frantically. "It's him, watch the fucker and see where he goes." Worm was twitching. This man put the fear of God in him. You could see the fear in his eyes. He zipped his coat up tightly over his mouth and blew warm breath about his face. There was another building not far from the main farmhouse. It looked like an old barn conversion. The lighting was faint and very hard to see. Monty walked along holding a bunch of flowers down by his side. The shopping bag he was carrying looked heavy and every now and then he changed his grip to get a better hold of it. Monty disappeared from view.

Johnny stepped out from the shadows and crouched over slightly. He gave the eye to Worm and jerked his head forward. "Pssss, come on, let's check it out."

Worm swallowed hard, he was shaking inside and all of a sudden his arse had gone. He'd not thought this through and regretted ever saying he would be Johnny's wingman. He spoke in a trembling voice. "I'll check the main building out. You follow Monty and see what he's up too."

Johnny was in no mood for arguing, he tiptoed over the gravel and made his way to the barn house. Worm kept a low profile and proceeded to the farmhouse. Johnny was there now, his heart beating like a speeding train. There was no time to think. No time to change his mind. He had to see with his own eyes if this was the place his mother was being held hostage. There was a small window near where he was hidden away. He cupped his hands around his eyes and tried to get a better look inside. He could see nothing, it was pitch black. With caution he crept around to the door where Monty had entered. Somebody was in there, he could hear noises. Chilling sounds that made the hairs on the back of neck stand on end. His back was pressed up against the cold brick wall and he dug deep in his coat to get the gun. Johnny had used a shooter before in his past, a shot gun, a firearm that could blow a man's head from his shoulders. He'd never killed anyone though, it was just to frighten his victims. His last charge was for armed robbery and even during that time in the local supermarket he knew he could never end another human being's life. But things were different now, his mother's life could be at stake. He needed to do what he had to.

Holding his ear to the door he stepped back and prepared himself to blow the cunt's head off. There was no time for thinking, the minute he opened the door he had to be quick. Take him down, make sure he never got back up. Johnny gripped the brass door handle and his face creased as he slowly pushed the handle down. He was ready, it was do or die time. Johnny swung the door open and pointed the gun one way then another. What the hell was he doing, shoot, shoot, shoot! He could see his target sat on the floor holding a woman in his arms. Monty was sobbing. At first he didn't seem to notice the gun in Johnny's hand. "Look at what they've done to her, my Elsie, my baby."

Johnny was white, his jaw dropped low. Elsie lifted her head up slowly and her eyes were just about open. "Johnny," she whispered as she spotted him.

Monty picked Elsie up in his arms and ran from the room with her. "She needs to go to the hospital, she needs a doctor." Johnny stood frozen as if he was in some kind of deep trance. Had this really just happened? His mother, what was wrong with her, why was she was in a bad way?

Johnny was just about to leave the room when his eyes flicked over to the bed at the other side of the room. There was a body underneath the covers and he ready to shoot whoever it was under the covers. Johnny walked a few paces forward and used the end of his foot to yank the covers back from the bed. What had he seen? He sank to his knees, his breathing nearly non-existent. He leaned back and ragged his hands through his hair. "Annie," he shrieked at the top of his voice. Johnny dropped the gun on the floor and plonked down on the side of the bed. He had no fight left in him, he was in bits. With caution he pulled her body onto his lap and sat slowly stroking the top of her head. A single bulky tear rolled from his eye. "Please no, please don't be dead."

Monty ran with Elsie over to the farmhouse. He was screaming at the top of his voice. "Help me, somebody fucking help me."

Alenka rushed into the room wearing only a red silk housecoat hanging from her shoulder. She could see this woman was in trouble and ran straight to her side. It only took one look and she was aware that Elsie was on her last legs. "Phone a doctor, she needs medical help," she stressed.

Monty knew he could never get an ambulance to come here. This was a safe house that he wanted to remain unknown. If anyone came here they would put two and two together and he'd be slammed in the nick for years. Monty placed Elsie's body on the floor and started to run around like a headless chicken. "Where are my car keys, fuck, fuck, somebody help me find my bastard car keys."

Alenka was in too much of a shock to do anything. She sat by Elsie's side and sobbed. This was terrible, her worst nightmare. Placing her delicate hand on her head she stroked it softly. "Come on lady, don't give up. Just hang on."

Monty ran back to where she was and dragged her from the floor by her hair. His eyes were bulging from their sockets. "Don't you dare touch her, take your dirty hands away from her."

Alenka backed away and stood with her back to the wall. Monty was desperate and he was finding it hard to cope. Alenka shot a look to the open door. Her eyes were wide open and she was licking at her lips constantly, breathing increased. She flipped her eyes one way then another. There was no sign of Fred and this chance may never have come again. Monty looked into Elsie's eyes as she tried to speak. "Johnny, get my Johnny," she mumbled as she held the bottom of her stomach. Monty was so engrossed in Elsie he never saw Alenka leave.

Johnny sat sobbing. His sister was dead. She was cold and not one bit of breath was left inside her. Kissing the top of her head he held a look in his eye that was scary, menacing. His nostrils flared and his ears pinned back as he placed his sister's lifeless body back onto the bed. He gripped the gun and let out a scream like an injured animal. Worm come to the door and shot his eyes towards Annie. He dipped his head as the arm of another man pushed him from the door's entrance. Johnny didn't stand a chance. Fred was all over him and he wasn't letting go. He was punching him, kicking him, there were head butts and several blows to his skull. The silver blade Fred held in his hand plunged deep into Johnny's legs and bright red claret pumped from the wound almost immediately. There was no way he was moving now, he was a goner.

"Worm, fucking help," he screamed at the top of his voice. Worm just walked casually into the room and sat on the bed watching Johnny take a beating. He sat forward and hummed a tune, tapping his feet to the beat of it. What the hell was going on here? Why wasn't he kicking ten tons of shit out of this guy? They were brothers in arms, he was his wingman. Fred had wasted him. Johnny was barely conscious and every now and then he tried to fight back. He had nothing left though, not one bit of strength left in him. Fred sat down exhausted on the side of the bed. He was gagging for breath and sweat pumped from him, there were sweat marks all over his grey t-shirt. He snarled at Annie's lifeless body and casually threw the blanket over her head. He had no remorse for his actions.

Fred held the end of his chin and his nostrils flared wide open as he tried to gasp mouthfuls of air. "Finish him off, Worm. Put a bullet in his fucking head. Do it, fucking finish him!"

Worm walked over to Johnny and bent down to his eye level. He lifted Johnny's head up in his hands and looked deep into his eyes. "Johnny, I just couldn't do it. I've been working with these lads long before you come back on the scene. You were banged up pal and I had to make money somehow. I only line the young girls up. Nothing more, nothing less and they pay me well."

Fred sniffed hard behind him and licked the blood from his knuckles. "You do a bit more than that you dirty bastard, you fuck them too," he chuckled as he held his head back. Worm closed his eyes slowly, Johnny didn't need to hear this and he cringed as his secret was out in the open.

Johnny could barely see as his eyes swelled. His voice was low and it was hard to make out what he was saying. "You Judas, you fucking dirty no good bastard. Karma mate, fucking karma."

Worm was unsettled. What was all this mumbo jumbo shite about karma? This was just a business deal with the lads, nothing more, nothing less.

Fred walked up to Worm and placed his hand on his shoulder. "Come on, we'll leave this rat to Monty."

Worm wasn't ready to leave just yet. He was trying to buy some time but Fred was having none of it. "I said move it. To tell you the truth, I don't know if I can trust you myself now. Fancy bringing the fucking idiot here, are you right in the head or what?"

Worm swallowed hard, there was no way he was upsetting the boys. "He followed Monty here. I had fuck all to do with it. I shit you not, he found this place on his own."

Fred studied him a bit longer than he needed to. Worm was a double-crossing bastard and he didn't trust him as far as he could throw him. Fred stood at the door and held his hand on the door frame. "Monty will want to deal with it himself. God help this cunt, he will torture him for what he's tried to do to him."

Worm choked. He never told Fred what was going on. He never thought it would get this far and now he'd had time to think he realised he'd dropped a bollock. No one would believe his story anymore, it was on top.

Monty drove like a maniac, he had to get Elsie to the hospital as soon as possible. She was lying on the back seat just staring into space, she looked like she was in a coma. "Hang on in there baby girl. Just hang on. Don't you dare leave me." Elsie was coughing and spluttering. It didn't look good for her. Monty put his foot down and he was driving like a mad man. His mobile was ringing and whoever it was on the other end of the phone wasn't giving up. It was just ringing and ringing.

CHAPTER FIFTEEN

JACKIE LAY ON the bed staring at the ceiling. Her eyes were red raw and she looked like she'd been crying for hours. There was an empty bottle of gin at her side and she'd clearly had one too many. Suddenly, Jackie sat up as if boiled water had been poured over her; she was alert, agitated. She wiped her mouth with a swift movement and staggered from the bed. Wobbling over to the wardrobe she opened it and ran her fingers over her husband's expensive clothing. "Bastard, dirty no good, lying bastard," she sneered. Oh, this woman was on one, she was like a woman possessed, eyes dancing with madness. Flinging every bit of clothing he owned onto the bed she ran to the bathroom to get a pair of scissors. Jackie had lost the plot, strength seemed to have returned to her body as she sat with a cunning smirk slicing at his expensive trousers, shirts and anything else she could get her hands on. He would be fuck all without his clothing, absolutely nothing. No woman would ever look at him again. She was going to make sure he paid for every tear she cried. She was going ballistic. Jackie cut and sliced at the clothes, jabbing the scissors into the crotch of his pants. Finally, the job was done, every last item from his wardrobe was destroyed.

Jackie moved onto his boxer shorts next. Holding them up in the air she chuckled to herself, she was off her head. She cut out a pretty snowflake pattern from the crotch of every pair of boxers he owed. She was always creative and took her time with each pair, making sure the job was done. Slowly, she started to put everything back into the wardrobe, exactly the way she found it. This woman wasn't of sane mind. Eyes dipped she looked at the safe fixed to the wall concealed in the back of the wardrobe. Jackie smiled and reached inside the secret compartment for the key to open it. As the black steel door opened her jaw dropped low. There was so much money in here, more than enough to buy anything she ever wanted, to keep her well looked after until her dying breath. Her hand trembled as she pulled out wads of cash from it. Lifting the money up to her nose she inhaled the aroma. This was dirty money, cash he'd earned from people's misery; drugs, prostitution and hooky deals. Money that he'd used to show his sluts a good time. At the back of the safe she could see a small pistol. This was just what was needed to put him in his place. He would shit a brick when she pointed this at him, maybe she'd ram it down his throat. Yes, that would make him see what he was doing to her. That would make him stop. Monty always had firearms hidden away at home. Every nook and cranny had some form of protection in it. He was paranoid like that, he knew sooner or later his front door would be boomed in and a gang would be there to take his title, his money. Monty wouldn't think twice about using a gun, he'd blasted lots of men away in the past, pricks who thought they could take him down. Men who thought they could take liberties. The man Monty had previously killed felt the barrel of the gun rammed down his throat before they had their brains blown out. He had no remorse, he never flinched. He just watched his victim shake as they took their last breath. The police took weeks to identify one particular victim too, he was such a mess. Jackie held the gun as if it was a baby in her arms, she stroked it and kissed the end of the silver barrel. It was time to take control because if she couldn't have her husband, nobody could.

Jackie walked over to the bed and secured the pistol under her pillow. She froze as she heard someone downstairs. Jackie was in a state of panic and her face was bright. She had to look busy, she couldn't let anybody know what she was up too. Reaching over for the photo album she placed it on her knee and smiled as she looked at her family in happier times. They were happy once. Yes, these two adults were love's young dream. Monty would have done anything for her back then but things changed. The money and the power had over taken what really mattered in life. Jackie was just tossed aside like an old pair of trainers. She chuckled as she slowly ran her finger over a photograph. She was actually talking to herself, tapped in the head she was. "Orr, look at you there Jackie girl. You look hot, bloody gorgeous." The smile didn't last long and now the depression kicked in again. She was like that, one minute she was on top of the world and the next thing she was down in the dumps. The doctor had prescribed her some anti-depressants but the tablets didn't touch the pain she felt in her heart. Heartbreak is something nobody can cure. The sleepless nights, the loss of appetite, the pain in her heart every time she thought of the she loved. Monty's death would have been easier to cope with really. If Monty would have been six foot under she could have at least learned how to live again. Jackie had not had a full night's sleep in years if the truth was known. That's why she started drinking in the first place, to drown her sorrows, to blank out the life Monty was leading her. She'd thought about having him done in. She'd been to see people who could have done that for her too, she meant business. Jackie knew the script when it came to the world of crime and she wasn't behind the door with her knowledge of getting things done. Monty always held meetings at his house and she sometimes listened in to anything that was going on;

deals, heists, shootings. Jackie knew enough to have them all slammed for years. Murders, robberies, drug deals, it all went on in her house but, what about her daughter? Could she really do that to her, to ruin her life knowing her father would never be there for her again when she needed him? Who would walk her down the aisle when her wedding came around? Who would protect her whenever she needed help? No, she could never do that to Sandy.

Jackie looked at the door as she glimpsed a shadow from the corner of her eye. "Bleeding hell, you scared the life out of me then! What the hell are doing creeping around the house at this time of the night?"

Sandy edged into the bedroom and it was obvious that something was bothering her. "Mam, I'm worried about you. I can't sleep just in case you go out on your own again. You could kill someone driving the car when you're drunk. Give me the keys. I need to know you're safe."

Jackie patted the side of the bed with her flat palm. "Come and sit over here with me. It's been ages since we had a good old chat. Come on, come and sit with your washed out mother." Jackie rummaged about at the side of the bed and hooked the car keys around her finger. "There you go, I'm going nowhere. You can relax now."

Sandy let out a laboured breath. Lying down on the bed Sandy dragged the duvet over her and rolled on her side. She was freezing cold, goose pimples all over her arms. Jackie turned to face her and gently moved her fringe from her forehead. "You've got your dad's eyes, did you know that? Every time I look into them all I can see is him."

Sandy raised a smile and snuggled into the bed covers. "Mam, is this ever going to end? Life would go on if you two split up. I know you've stayed with him for my sake but honest, I'd much rather have to happy parents living apart than two living together arguing every day."

Jackie choked up, she swallowed hard. "It's not me, it's him. You know how much I loved him and he treats me like a dollop of shit on the bottom of his shoe." Jackie had something to say now, she took a deep breath and lay down beside her daughter. Her words stuck on her tongue and her eyes clouded over. "He loves Elsie. I should have just let him be happy, but I couldn't do it. I can't share my husband. I'm not like that. He wants me to turn a blind eye to it all but do you know how that makes me feel inside? I hate myself. It's so degrading." Sandy was listening and she could see the pain in her eyes as she continued. "Do you know how it feels when he climbs into my bed each night after being with his fancy piece? I choke on her perfume and he just turns over and goes to sleep without a care in the world. He's heartless, he cares about nothing but himself."

Sandy reached over and rubbed the side of her mother's cheek. "Mam, if you carry on like this you'll end up making yourself ill. You're drinking every minute of the day. It has to stop."

Jackie switched, rage pumping from her body, the red mist descended again. "He has to stop, not me. Do you know he has a brass business and," she paused and thought about her next sentence before she delivered it, "he's involved in taking young girls from the streets to have sex with dirty perverts. Yep, the sex trade," her eyes were wide open. Sandy sat up and tried to digest what she'd just said. She'd heard whispers about this in the past but she never really knew if they were true but here it was, right from her own mother's mouth. It had to be true. Sandy felt sick inside and the colour drained from her. This was her father they were talking about, her old man, her dad.

Sandy dragged the covers from the bed. Something was niggling at her and she was restless. She stood up and placed a single hand on her hip, she was getting told. "And you stayed with him knowing he's a paedo. You're just as bad as him in my eyes!"

Jackie was sorry she'd ever opened her mouth. She forgot how sensitive her daughter could be. She tried to change the subject. "Where's Johnny these days? I've not heard you speaking about him for a while now?"

Sandy was beetroot, she hated talking about her private life and she was embarrassed that the man she loved no longer loved her back. Something must have happened that she missed. She racked her brain for days but nothing was adding up. How can a guy be all over you one minute, then blow you out the next? Jackie picked up the photographs and carried on looking at them, she was in the zone now and wanted to be alone. Nothing else seemed to matter except her own self- pity. "It's all Elsie Barker's fault, she's a dirty slut. A life wrecking bitch."

Sandy twisted her head slowly, she heard that name before, but where? The surname was so familiar too her. "Mam, what did you just say, who is it, what is she called?"

Jackie slurred the name slowly. "Elsie Barker love. The biggest slag that has ever walked this earth."

Sandy was back over to the bed now, she had a gut feeling she was right. "Mam, where does this Elsie live, does she have any kids?"

Jackie raised her head slowly and sucked on her bottom lip. "She's lived all over but when I first saw her she was living in Collyhurst with her loud mouthed sister June. A pair of low lifes they are, both of them as rough as the other."

Whoa! No, it couldn't be, could it? Sandy clenched her fist together tightly and bit hard into her knuckles. It all made sense now. What an idiot she'd been! This was the only reason Johnny was dating her, to find out about her life, to help his mother score points against her family. To take her father away. Sandy stroked the top of her mother's head. She needed her to go to sleep now so she could relax. "Come on mam, put those photos down and try and get some sleep. I'll lie with you for a bit if you want."

Jackie nodded. It was so nice to have some company for a change, someone who would listen to her misery. Jackie slipped her shoes from her feet and lay fully clothed on the bed. She very rarely got into bed. Usually she was that pissed that she slept where she fell. Sandy cuddled up to her and tried to make herself comfortable. Sliding her hand under the pillow she felt something cold next to her hand. With caution she pulled it and tried to get a better look. Her eyes were wide open, she stared into thin air as he mind was doing overtime. Tucking the pistol down the side her pyjama bottoms she smirked to herself. "I'll show them. I'll show them all."

It was the early hours before Monty came home. Sandy could hear him rummaging around downstairs. She'd been restless all night long and now her father was home it was time for her to confront him. He owed her some answers, she needed to know the truth once and for all. Jackie was dead to the world for a change. Slipping out of the bed Sandy sneaked from the bedroom.

Monty was sat at the dining table and his head was in his hands. There was no lights on in the room and he was at in the darkness. Sandy flicked the light switch on and stood at the door just staring at him. Was he really as bad as her mother made out? Was he the beast everyone hated? "Dad," she whispered in a soft voice. "What are you doing sat down here on your own, it's nearly time to get up?"

Monty lifted his head up and once he saw his daughter stood there he started blubbering. "It's all fucked up, nothing matters to me anymore. Anything I touch, I ruin. She's my everything. She's my world."

Sandy couldn't just stand there and do nothing, he was bawling his eyes out she had to comfort him. She hurried to his side. "Dad, whatever it is that's gone on, I'm sure in time it will be alright. I need to speak to you. I need to know the truth about who you really are. I want to know everything."

Monty tipped his head back and sighed. He was having a meltdown. Even the strongest of men had their limits. He shook his head slowly and pulled his cigarettes from his shirt pocket. This was bad, he only smoked when he was stressed. Popping one into his mouth he sucked hard on it as if his life depended on it. "Sit down princess, you're right, we need to talk."

Sandy was wary of him, he was acting strangely and she didn't know how to take him. She couldn't hold her tongue though. She needed her questions answered, her mind was racing. "Dad, is Elsie Barker Johnny's mother?"

Monty looked puzzled as he blew a grey cloud of grey smoke out from his mouth. "What, who's Johnny?"

"Johnny, my boyfriend."

He closed his eyes tightly, thinking. His eyes wide open. The penny was dropping now. This lad was at the farmhouse, he remembered seeing him there. Elsie had said his name. How did she know him? What the hell was going on here? Was it a big conspiracy? Monty's heart was in his mouth. He needed to ask more questions. "I don't know, what makes you say that?" He was on edge now and looked her straight in the eye.

"It's Elsie Barker isn't it?" Sandy reiterated.

He nodded, his mouth open in shock. Everything

was coming together now. Sandy nodded slowly, she was speechless as well. "My mam told me her name before and it all clicked together. It just all fell into place. Johnny's surname is Barker too."

Monty stood up and kicked the chair away from his feet sending it crashing into the wall. "And, what does that mean then?"

Sandy was tearful and sniffled as her fears were confirmed. "It means Johnny was only with me to find out about our family. It all makes sense now, the endless questions, his fixation on you."

Monty punched a fist into a nearby cupboard. He'd had the wool pulled right over his eyes. His arse smacked by this guy. He walked around the dining table ragging his fingers through his hair. "Do you mean he planned all this to get at me?"

Sandy looked at him and hunched her shoulders. "It looks that way, there is no other reason for it is there?"

Monty paced the floor, twisting, turning, unsure of his next move. Then it dawned on him. The full story was coming together now. "He's at the farm. Arrgghh... He's a dead man. Fuck, fuck, I need to get back there."

Sandy was petrified. This was all some fucked up shit. It was like something you only saw in the movies. The time she's spent with Johnny had all been a lie. She knew that now. No wonder he kicked her to the kerb the moment he found out all he needed to know. Monty grabbed his car keys, he turned slowly towards Sandy. "Lock all the doors and don't let any cunt come in here. If anyone turns up ring the police. Do you hear me, ring the fucking police."

Sandy ran after him as he left the room. "Dad, I'll come with you, you can't drive in that state. You'll end up dead. Let me drive you."

"No! Just do as I said and lock all the doors and

windows. Tell your mam what's gone on, she'll know what to do."

Monty rushed out of the house. Sandy peeped through the window and watched him struggle to get into his car. He was fuming and ready to kill somebody. The engine roared as he drove away. Time wasn't on his side and he knew if he didn't get back there in time, his empire would be destroyed. Sandy stayed at the window until the car left the street. She pressed her fingers against the cold glass pane and dragged them to the bottom of the glass. Her mother's car stared back at her and she had an evil look in her eye. Running back up the stairs she headed straight into her bedroom to get dressed.

June sat next to the hospital bed and she was struggling to keep it together. As far as she knew Elsie had been dropped off outside the hospital in the early hours of this morning, just dumped there, left to die. Just before she lost consciousness she'd managed to give the emergency team her name and address. June looked at every deep purple bruise on her sister's body and she was distraught. Someone had given her a right going over. She was in a bad way. Elsie's eyes were closed and every now and then she gasped for breath. June made sure the doctors couldn't see her and leant over the bed. "Elsie, it's me June, can you hear me?" Elsie didn't' reply, she just lay frozen, lifeless. She reached over and grabbed her hand. Touching every finger she kissed the tip of them. These were old hands, wrinkled with veins popping through the pale transparent skin. "The doctors said you're lucky to be alive, whoever has done this to you wanted you dead. What the hell have you been involved in? Time after time you've landed yourself in the shit. Don't you ever learn?"

Elsie twitched and she was responding now. She took a couple of deep breaths and twisted her head to the side. Her eyes opening slightly. "Annie, they killed Annie. Get the police. Monty, the farm, get the police."

Elsie was talking in riddles. What was she going on about? What did Annie have to do with all this? Nothing was making sense. June sat running her sister's words over in her mind. Something wasn't right and she couldn't settle. Reaching inside her pocket she pulled out her mobile phone and sat staring at it. From the moment the police had informed her about her sister being in hospital she'd been ringing Johnny constantly trying to tell him what had happened. There was no reply, nothing, straight to voice message again. What was he playing at? Surely he'd seen the missed calls on his phone. Why hadn't he rang her back, the tosser? Two police officers came into the side room. They stood next to June and they were hoping for some kind of statement to try and piece this mess together. June clocked them with their notebooks and pushed her shoulders back. There was no way she was going to be a grass. It just wasn't the way it was done in her world. Johnny would sort this out. They had their own law of the land and talking to the rozzers was out of the question. This was to be sorted out internally, no police involved, an eye for an eye.

The two female officers started to ask June some questions about Elsie. Who was she involved with? Who did she have a beef with? Who was her partner? June told them straight what she thought about the justice system. "I know nothing about anything. So you're pissing in the wind if you think I can tell you what's happened. All I know is she has been gone for ages and fuck knows where she's been. She always goes on the missing list so she could have been anywhere."

One of the officers sat down next to her and looked over at Elsie in the hospital bed. "You do know your sister might not make it don't you. So, if you know anything about this you need to let us know. Do you want this to happen to someone else?"

June swallowed hard, she was biting her tongue. She shrugged her shoulders and stuck to her guns. There was fuck all these officers could do anyway, she'd seen it so many times before when residents had given statements about the crimes in the area. It was all about paperwork. No arrests were made. It was just a formality. "Like I said, if I find out what's gone on I'll make sure I let you know but as of this moment, I'm as much in the dark as you are." The officer knew she was lying through her teeth but they had a procedure to follow and asking these questions was part of the process. They knew the code of silence wouldn't be broken here and shot a look at each other shaking their heads.

The officer started to write on a piece of paper. "I will leave you my number in case anything pops up. Remember, there are dangerous people out there and if they've done this to your sister, your life could be in danger too."

June swallowed hard, her arse was twitching now. She'd never really thought about her own safety. Say the attackers knew where she lived, what if they come around to her house and did the same thing to her, she was terrified. June stayed true to herself though and let the officers leave. Holding the piece of paper in her hands she screwed it up and rammed it into her coat pocket. "I'm no fucking grass," she mumbled under her breath. June stood up from her seat and cautiously edged to the door. She peeped outside and made sure the officers had gone. She pulled her mobile phone from her pocket again and dialled Johnny's number again, still no answer. "Fuck, Johnny, where the hell are you when I need you?" she stressed as she left the room.

Monty could see the farm in the distance. Nothing looked any different. His heart was in his mouth as his long chunky fingers gripped the steering wheel tightly. Reaching under his seat he felt around, his head dipped low. Here it was, the lump hammer he always kept here just in case he ran into trouble. Monty screeched up outside the farm house. He jumped out from the car and sprinted to the front door. The hammer was swinging by his side and his eyes were dancing with madness. Somebody was going to get it, he was going to knock someone clean out. Monty boomed the front door open. He was ready for whatever lay beyond the heavy oak door. The hammer was held high over his shoulder and he was ready to swing it into action, club someone to death. "Where the fuck is Johnny? Tell me where he is?"

Fred jumped to his feet and Worm started to back off into a corner. Monty was gunning for him now and he wanted answers. "You fucking little rat, you set me up! You knew what he was up to and you led him right to me." Monty wasn't waiting for any answers. No way, he was getting it. Worm screamed out as the weapon crashed into his skull. He keeled over as every blow connected with his body. This was a massacre, a blood bath. Fred chewed on the end of his knuckles. Was he next? Monty really went to town on his victim, blood surged all over his body as he whacked him half to death. There was no way Worm was surviving this. Even if he did he would be brain dead or paralysed, he'd be a cabbage.

Fred backed off, he was getting ready to run. Monty

caught his eye as he struck the last blow to his victim's head. He stood up and yelled out like a mad man, blood trickling down the end of his nose. "Go on, tell me. Did you know too?" Fred was shitting himself, he was actually shaking. Yes, he could fight but he wasn't ready for this. He had a family, he wanted to live. He would do whatever it took to save his bacon but did Monty know about Elsie, had she told him he was the one who'd beaten her half to death. Had Monty seen the young girl too? The girl he should have dealt with and got rid of. It was do or die time. Monty edged closer to him. His stale breath tickling the end of his nose. Sweat pumping from his lean torso. "Well," he growled.

Fred stuttered and his hands were held up high ready to protect himself. "I knew fuck all about anything. I don't know what's been going on here honest. I'm as much in the dark as you."

Monty stood thinking for a few seconds. His nostrils flared, teeth gritted tightly together. "Where's Johnny, tell me he's still here. I'll break the fucker's neck, snap the cunt in half."

Fred choked and swallowed hard. His throat was dry and his heart was pounding inside his ribcage as he answered him. "He's locked away in the barn house. I kicked fuck out of him the moment Worm confessed all to me. You know me mate. I'm loyal to the end. Worm would have got it as well but I was waiting on you to come back before I smashed the fucker up." Fred was licking arse, trying anything to calm this man down. He trudged closer to him and placed a firm hand on his shoulder. "Monty, you need to trust me. I'm your wingman, me and you have always been straight with each other, no lies. Just trust me."

Monty wasn't thinking straight, so much was going on inside his head that it was going to burst any second now.

He had pains at the front of his head and stabbing pains in his heart. "Take me to him and get me the shooter."

Fred didn't even have to think about the request. He never asked questions. He just left the room and obeyed his every word. Worm was moving slightly. Monty could see him from the corner of his eye. With a menacing look he walked over to where he was and drew his foot back one last time. Worm shuddered, his clenched fist unfolded slowly like a flower in full bloom. He moved no more. He just lay there frozen. Fred passed the gun to Monty. "I've done the cheeky twat in already so I doubt you'll need that. I swear. I left him for dead. A right beating I gave him. It's a wonder he's still breathing. I bet you he's snuffed it already." Monty pushed his chest out in front of him and let out a roar like a caged lion. He marched across the room ripping his shirt from his back. He was running across the yard now like a gladiator. This was going to be easy, nobody crossed him, nobody.

Fred pulled the silver key from his pocket and his eyes were wide open as they approached the door. He was up shit street now – once Monty saw the girl he was bound to start asking questions. He needed to think quickly, sort out his story. Get his facts straight. Before the door opened he held his hand on the brass handle and looked Monty straight in his eyes. "I need to get rid of that dirty little bint's body too. I threw her in here the other day until I found a place to stick her." Monty pushed passed him. The girl meant fuck all to him anymore. He wanted the Judas. The man who thought he could have him over. The door flung open and smashed into the wall behind it. Monty's eyes were all over the place. He clocked the body in the bed and walked further into the room. "Where is he? I thought you said he was here!"

Fred was all over the show now, head dipping under

the bed, looking in all the cupboards, under the bed. But nothing, he was gone. Monty was alert and aware that any minute now Johnny could leap onto him and take him down. Fred scratched at his head, puzzled. "I swear to you, he was here. I left him half dead in here." Monty wasn't sure about this, was this another plan to take him out? He snarled over at Fred and walked slowly to his side. Lifting the shot gun up he rammed it deep into the side of his head. His finger was easing at the trigger. "Nar, none of this makes any sense. Something is not right." Fred was slammed against the wall and his eyes were nearly popping out from their sockets. Monty went nose to nose with him. "Start talking. I swear, I'll cut you up and feed you to the pigs if you try and feed me any bullshit."

Fred pissed his pants. A large puddle appeared near his feet, this guy was going to kill him. All of a sudden an army of police officers raided the room. They were like flies around shit. Monty was twisted up and he was put straight on the floor with his hands secured behind his back. Fred was having a panic attack, he folded in two and tried to seek some comfort from the officers. "He was going to kill me. You saw it all. I'm the innocent party here."

Alenka trudged inside the room with a female officer closely by her side. She lifted her hand up and pointed her finger over at Fred. "He's the one and that bastard on the floor is the main man, Monty."

Fred was hysterical, he was sobbing his heart out and realised he would never walk away from this. He pleaded with the officers, "It's Monty's gaff. I just come here every now and then to bring food and that for the girls. That's not a bad thing is it?"

Alenka broke free and walked over to her abuser. "He's lying, he's just as much involved as he is," she sneered down at Monty. "These two are evil men. They take young vulnerable girls and make them do things." Alenka was upset and the female officer by her side was trying to comfort her. "They ruined my life, my dreams. They said I could go home but that day never came. Lock them both up and throw away the key. I hope they both rot in hell." Monty was dragged to his feet and led out of the room. Six officers had to restrain him. He was like a wild animal, even now he was still fighting with them. The farmhouse was now a crime scene and the police were swarming the area. All the working girls were being led outside and some of them just couldn't take it. They were crying, screaming. At last this ordeal was finally over for them. Monty was going down for years for this, his days were over as Manchester's criminal king. All he would be now was just another prison number.

Johnny crawled along the muddy field. He was barely breathing. He'd found a way out of the barn house through the ceiling. His head was swollen like a balloon and he could hardly see. He'd been out of the barn for over an hour and he was making little progress. There was a vibration in his pocket. Johnny lay on his back and stared at the early morning sky. Dawn was breaking but the clouds mostly black and he could feel splashes of rain on his face. His hand reached inside his pocket and he pulled out his phone. The battery was low and he didn't know if he could take the call. He pressed the button and held the phone to his ear. "Johnny, it's me Sandy. Where are you? I'm near the farm and all I can see is police. Has my dad been nicked what the hell is going on?" Johnny was trying his best to talk, he was coughing and spluttering. With his last bit of breath he managed to tell her where he was. She was his last hope of getting away from here alive.

The police were dealing with a blood bath. Two bodies were pronounced dead by the ambulancemen. This was now a murder scene. The news crew were all over it and vans were pulling up every few minutes trying to get a scoop for the national papers. There were ten girls in total rescued from the farm house. The youngest was thirteen years old. "Moonlight" on Moston Lane was also raided and another seven girls who'd been forced into the sex trade were freed from there as well. This was turning out to be some case. Monty was fucked, they had him bang to rights. His house had been ransacked too but all they found was an empty safe. No guns, no money, nothing. Jackie was crying her eyes out when the police raided her home. She actually thought she was being kidnapped and held for ransom. Jackie was hysterical and all she kept saying was 'where is my daughter? I want my daughter!' Jackie was arrested and taken to the police station. The police knew once they slammed her in a cell for a few hours she'd sing like a canary, women like her always did.

Sandy crept along the country lane in her mother's car. She was barely moving at one point. She couldn't see Johnny anywhere and for the last ten minutes she'd been driving up and down the same road. From the corner of her eye she spotted a hand held up in the bushes on the left of the road. It was there one minute and disappeared the next. Was she seeing things or was Johnny really there? She brought the car to a halt and stretched her neck. There it was again, the hand floating about in the air. Sandy pulled the car keys from the ignition and slowly crept towards the body. Her nerves were on edge and every step she took she was debating her next move. Finally as she got close enough she recognised Johnny. Sandy motored to his side and fell to her knees. She scooped him up into her arms and rested his head onto her lap. "Has he done this to you? Johnny, why, why, did you have to get involved? You knew what he was like."

Tears dropped from her eyes and landed on his cheeks. He wasn't saying anything he was just shaking his head slowly. Sandy had to think fast. The police were all over and time wasn't on her side. With every bit of strength left in her body she dragged him closer to the roadside. Her face was strained and she looked like she was going to give up at one point. At last, she got him to his feet and just about managed to get him in the back of the car. There was blood all over the place. He was bleeding badly and if she didn't get him medical attention quickly it was obvious he wasn't going to make it. But, she couldn't take him to the hospital, they would ring the police. She had to think quickly. Sandy started driving, she could take him to one of her dad's hideouts, a flat where they could lie low and let him recuperate. She'd ring the family doctor and explain the situation. He'd done things like this for her father in the past and she knew his silence could be bought with a couple of grand. Johnny was mumbling in the back of the car. He kept trying to sit up. Bubbles of blood seeped from his nose and every now and then he coughed up thick red clots of blood. This was bad, he wasn't going to make it.

Doctor Walker examined Johnny and his expression said it all. "He's lucky to be alive Sandy. I've sorted him out the best I can. The next twenty-four hours are crucial. He's got some nasty wounds and if they get infected," he paused and started to pack his medical equipment up. "Let's not cross that bridge until we have to. Just make sure he does everything I've told him." Sandy walked the doctor to the door of the flat. Sandy often came here to study and clear her head. This was a nice little setup. A two bedroom studio flat that had everything. Elsie and her father must have stayed here occasionally as well because there were traces of a woman all over the house; perfumes, hair sprays, underwear. Sandy walked back into the bedroom and sat on the edge of the bed. This was all so fucked up and she didn't know where to start. She'd heard on the radio that her mother and father had both been arrested and for now she just needed to keep a low profile until her head was clear. She would deal with the police when the time came. All her life she'd had them at her family home, she knew how to put on a show. She was good like that. Even from an early age she'd learned to cover up the truth and keep her mouth shut.

Sandy looked at Johnny's swollen face. He looked peaceful as he slept. Something was niggling at her, she needed to speak to him. She wanted to hear it from his own mouth that he'd only got with her to find out about her father. Her voice was low. "Johnny, can you hear me. Are you awake?"

Johnny squeezed her fingers tightly and twisted his head to face her. "Thanks Sandy. I would be fucked without your help. This is all a mess."

She took a deep breath and here it was, the moment of truth. "I know about you only getting with me to be near my father." Johnny cringed as he lay in the bed. How the hell did she know about this? He licked his lips slowly and closed his eyes as she continued. "I thought you loved me. Honest, what we had was special and you just ruined it all to get what you wanted. I love you Johnny."

He had to get this off his chest. He was never a good liar to the people he cared about. He just couldn't do it. "It's true Sandy, I'm not going to lie. But, I didn't find out who your father was until after we started seeing each other. I had to do the things I did to find my mother. What other option did I have?"

Sandy looked beyond him and spoke into thin air. "So, it's your mother who ruined my family. All this time it's been her. Do you know what my mother has been through because of her? She cries every night. She's on medication because of it all. And, now she's ruined us too. I don't know your mother Johnny but to me she seems better off dead. She cares only about herself."

Johnny was having a coughing fit, he was trying to sit up. Sandy sprang to her feet and helped him lean forward, she patted the small of his back. Sandy looked at the time and knew she had to leave. She had places to go and people to see. Walking over to the other side of the room she flicked the TV on. The news was on screen and there it was, the story of how her father was involved in the sex trade and how he had lured young girls to work in his brothels. This was more than she could take. How could she ever look people in the eye? Everyone would judge her, call her behind her back. Looking down near her feet she slowly opened the black sports bag she'd brought with her. There was enough money in it to walk away, to start again. But what about her poor mother? Who would look after her when she'd gone? Monty wouldn't get out of jail for years and she'd just be left on her own. Sandy picked something out from the bag and slid it into her pocket. She sat looking at Johnny for a few seconds and let out a laboured breath. "Time to face the music I suppose. Johnny," she whispered as she shook his arm slightly. "I need to go. I'll be back soon. Just you stay here and rest." Johnny was away with the fairies, the painkillers he'd been given had knocked him for six. He was out for the count. Sandy left quickly, it was time to look after herself now, nobody else. It was time to get her ship in order.

Elsie was awake and sat up in the hospital bed. She'd been sick a few times and every time she moved her head she felt dizzy. The last twenty-four hours had been life or death for her but she had responded well to the medication and seemed out of danger for now. She still had a long way to go but at least she was able to talk now. Elsie knew Annie was dead and she'd been told how she ended up at the farm. She would never forgive herself for this. For the first time in years she had looked at her actions and could see the peril of her ways. Everyone was right about her, she was self-centred and cared only about herself. The shame she carried was there for everyone to see. She would never get over this...

June stood at the door, her hands gripping the doorframe, her knuckles turning white. She knew about Annie's death and had agonised about what her niece had suffered before she met her gruesome end. Looking over at her sister she wanted to strangle her, end her life, to make her feel pain like Annie had. Why was she still alive when her own daughter was dead? Life wasn't fair, why didn't she die instead of Annie? June gritted her teeth tightly together and marched to her sister's bedside. There was no more holding back, she was telling her straight. "It's broke my bleeding heart all this has. When is it all going to stop? Don't you realise what you're doing to us all. How many people have to die before you see how fucking simple you are?"

Elsie choked back tears, her eyes were red raw. "I know, don't you think I know already. Johnny's still missing. If he's dead as well then I may as well be dead. How can I ever live with myself if they're both gone?"

June wasn't allowing her to have her say. Self-pity was something Elsie had always been good at and she could kiss her arse if she thought she was getting any sympathy here today. This was serious, people had died. "Fuck off Elsie. I swear, I'm washing my hands of you. All my life it's always been about you and your needs. Not once have you ever give a flying fuck about me and what I needed. It's always been the same with you - take, take take." Elsie tried to reach over and touch the side of her arm but she was having none of it. "Don't touch me, just leave me alone. I'm done with you. As far as I'm concerned I've washed my hands of you. You never deserved them kids, you was never their mother, I was."

The truth hurt and every word she spoke stabbed deep into Elsie's heart. She held her head in her hands, and closed her eyes as the words hit her. "Please, don't say that June. You've all I've got to keep me strong. If you leave me then I'll be alone."

"You should have thought about that before you left me with your kids while you slept with every Tom, Dick and fucking Harry. I could have been happy if it wasn't for you and your problems. I could have got married and had kids of my own, but no, every fucking day I was running around after you making sure you and your kids were alright. You've never been a mother. Your kids thought more of me then they did of you. Go on, what have you ever done for them, when have you ever been there for them when they needed you most?" This was going off big-time and the nurse came in the room to try and take control of the situation. June stood over her sister and pointed her finger deep into her chest. "We're finished. Don't you ever darken my door again. I hope for your sake Johnny is okay otherwise I'll kill you myself and make sure this time I finish the bleeding job."

The nurse was shocked, she didn't know what to do for the best. She was aware families argued but these two were on a different level. Elsie was trying to get out of the bed to go after June but it was too late, she was half way out of the door. She screamed out from the pit of her stomach and punched her clenched fist into the bed. "June, please don't do this to me. I need you. I'm sorry." June was gone and the nurse thought it best to sedate Elsie, she was hyperventilating and struggling to breath. The nurse pressed the red button for the emergency team and within seconds they were wrestling with Elsie trying to restrain her. This was a job and half and not what the medical team needed during this busy shift. The needle slid into Elsie's vein and slowly she started to drift away; her eyes rolled back and her heart rate slowed. The doctor wiped his brow quickly and shot a look to the medical staff. "Hopefully she'll be out for the rest of the night. What is wrong with some people, don't they ever learn?" One by one the staff left the room. Elsie was alone now and her eyes were twitching. The baby inside her was kicking and she never once comforted it with a caring hand.

Sandy parked some distance away from the hospital. It was mad busy in Elsie's ward and nobody saw her jib into her room. She had to see this woman, she had to tell her just how much she'd destroyed her family. The lights were low as she entered the room. She just stood there at first looking at her father's mistress. Then she spotted the baby-bump and knew what she had to do. Her blood was boiling, she hated this woman with a passion, hated her for all the pain she had caused to the people she loved. Sandy crept over to the bedside. She was agitated and kept checking the door behind her. She didn't have long.

"So, you're the famous Elsie Barker then are you?" she whispered menacingly, "the slut who's been keeping my mother awake for years!" Elsie stirred in her sleep, her eyes were half open. Sandy leant over the bed and looked straight into her eyes. "You're not a patch on my mother and you never will be!" Sandy spat into her face and stepped back from the bed. Her teeth gritted tightly together as she picked up a white pillow and squeezed at it with all her might. Slipping her hand inside her pocket she pulled out a small silver pistol. Sandy paused. Was she was really going to do this? Getting a second wind she remembered all the heartache this bitch had caused and snarled as she gripped the ends of the white pillow, her knuckles turning white.

Placing the plump pillow over Elsie's face she pressed hard down onto it. Elsie wasn't moving. Holding the gun deep into the pillow she eased the trigger slowly. She'd seen this on TV and knew there would be little sound. The bullet left the end of the barrel and Elsie's body shuddered as her last breath was taken, no one would have heard it on this busy ward. Sandy made sure she covered her tracks and pulled her hood up as she rammed the pistol back in her pocket. "That's for my mother, she should have done this a long time ago." she whispered as she hurried from the room.

Johnny couldn't stay in bed any longer. He needed to get home, to see his family and let everyone know he was alright. As he stood up he wobbled about and he nearly landed on his arse a few times. He wasn't strong enough, his legs just gave way and he had to crawl on all fours back to the bed. Johnny needed to get in touch with June. She'd be worried out of her mind about him. He owed her that much, he needed to tell her he was still alive. Someone was here, keys rattled outside the door. Johnny held his breath and prayed this wasn't more trouble. He couldn't defend himself, he was too weak. His heart was in his mouth and he prepared himself for the worst. His eyes were on the door, he awaited his fate, his fingers gripping the side of the bed. Sandy rushed inside the room and she was panicking. Her words were rushed and something wasn't right. "Johnny, we need to get away from Manchester. Come with me, we can make it work. You'll grow to love me. I just know you will." She was heartbroken and acting strangely. She rested her head on his chest. Lifting her head up slowly Sandy slid her hand into the bag at the side of her and pulled out a wad of cash. "I've got money and plenty of it. We can leave now and never look back. I've got nothing left here anyway. I've just been to see my mother and she'll stand by my dad, no matter what. I need to find me again. I just want to be normal."

Johnny looked at the money and his eyes were open wide. Sandy wasn't thinking straight, she was on another planet. Something had upset her. "I'm not doing anything yet Sandy. I want you to take me home to see June. I need to know my mam's alright. I can't just leave them all without knowing they're safe."

Sandy was distressed. "If I take you now, can we leave tonight?"

Johnny shook his head. "No, I need to sort things out first. I can't just leave. My sister is dead are you forgetting that?" Johnny was having a panic attack and his breathing was fast and furious. He sat up straight blowing his breath rapidly. She'd seen this type of thing before with her mother and helped him calm down. "Johnny, just take deep breaths, long breaths, come on, blow, blow." It was working, he was calming down. Sandy swung the car keys around her finger and touched the side of his cheek. "I'll take you home but I need to know if you're leaving with me. We can have a good life with this money, no more sadness, just me and you."

Johnny struggled to get out of bed. His main concern was getting home, nothing else seemed to matter. He asked her again. "Just take me home."

June broke down and fell to her knees when Sandy helped Johnny into the house. She couldn't speak as her emotions took over. There were so many questions she needed to ask him, there was so much to sit down and talk about. Sandy led Johnny into the front room and helped him lie on the sofa. "He's going to be fine June. I'm sure he will tell you all you need to know." Sandy bent down and kissed him on his cheek. "I'll be waiting for your call Johnny. Remember, me and you and our new life." June didn't hear a word she said as she was blubbering on the other side of the room. Sandy didn't speak another word she just upped and left.

June lit two cigarettes and popped one in her mouth as she went to sit on the end of the sofa. She passed one over to Johnny and dipped her head. "The Lane has been all over the news. That dirty bastard wants his balls cutting off for what he's done to all those young girls. Johnny," she snivelled, "our poor Annie, what the hell am I going to do without her?"

Johnny's eyes clouded over and for the first time he opened his heart and cried his eyes out too. The pair of them were devastated and no amount of time or medication would ever take the pain away they both felt in their hearts. Death was so final, knowing you will never see your loved ones again. To never hold them in your arms, to smell them, to kiss them. Yes, death was a horrible thing for anyone to deal with. June kept gagging into her hands, she'd not eaten proper for weeks and the weight had dropped off her. Her usually full face was thin and withdrawn, she had dark circles around her eyes, more wrinkles than had been visible before, she'd aged years in a few weeks. Poor June had been through the mill. The two of them huddled together on the sofa and that night they cried themselves to sleep.

It was soon morning time. Lots of kids were shouting outside. Johnny was awake and just lay staring into space. The curtains were closed and it was still dark in the room. The ashtrays overflowed with cigarette butts and empty bottles of wine were scattered about the room. There was knocking at the door, someone was desperate for them to answer. Johnny rolled onto his side and shook June by her arm, he kept his voice low. "June, wake up, someone's at the door. They're knocking like the dibble. Quick, have a look."

June was still half asleep. With one eye still shut she made her way to the window. June had a knack of not being spotted. She'd had loan men all her life and knew the tricks of the trade, she was very careful. "It's the filth. Two of them."

Johnny's eyes were wide open. They must have found out about him being at the farm too. He was fucked, he could hardly move. How could he get on his toes, there was no way in this world. June helped him up the stairs in a panic. "Get in bed and stay there. I'll just say I've not seen you. If they see you like this they'll put two and two together and you'll be nicked. Go on, quick, piss off."

Johnny staggered up the stairs. June straightened her hair as she went shouting into the hallway. "Fucking hell, what you knocking like that for! I'm here, I'm bleeding coming." She swung the front door open and stood there with her hand resting on the doorframe. "Do you know what time it is? People have to sleep you know!"

The officer blushed and knew it was way over the top the way they'd knocked at the front door but they needed to speak to her, what did she expect? "Can we come in for a few minutes?"

"No, I've told you all I know. What's the point in pestering me when I can't help you any more than I have already?"

The police officer took a step forward and spoke in a low voice. "It's your sister, June. We need to speak to you about her. You might need to sit down. It's not good news."

June let out a laboured breath. "Oh, has she reported me for the way I shouted at her. She's lucky I didn't bleeding knock her block off. I'll swing for her one of these days, trust me. I'll put her six foot under."

The female officer led June into the front room. This was never going to be easy, she took a few minutes to compose herself, to make sure she delivered the news with as much compassion as she could do. "Elsie is dead June. Someone murdered her in cold blood in her hospital bed. A single gun-shot to the head."

June looked at them both. Was this a wind-up? Someone was having her over. June smirked and sat back in her chair with her arms folded tightly. "And, you expect me to believe that do you? Listen, if this is some kind of sick twisted joke to get me talking then you're wasting your breath."

The officer repeated herself and June rubbed at her arms, she had goose bumps and the hair on the back of her neck was standing on end. It was true, her sister was dead. June had nothing more to give, her heart couldn't take any more grief. She stood up and snapped. "Get out! Leave me alone, go on, fuck off!" The officer tried to comfort her but June was swinging punches into the air. Their job was done here and there was nothing more they could do. They offered to sit with her, to make her a hot cup of tea but she wasn't having any of it she just wanted them out of her house. She was like a wild woman now dragging them by the arms towards the front door. June collapsed the moment the front door was banged shut. Her knees held up to her chest, she just sat rocking to and fro like a small child. Johnny was sat on the top stair and he'd heard everything that had been said. What was happening? Was June at risk too? His head was fucked and Sandy's offer of leaving Manchester and starting a new life seemed to make more sense now. Johnny had nothing left, his immediate family was gone. How would he ever come back from this? He was a broken man Easing his body down the stairs he sat at the bottom and howled out in pain. The walls shook as his screams smashed against the walls.

CHAPTER SIXTEEN

JACKIE SAT OUTSIDE the prison and checked her make-up in the mirror. She looked different today; at ease, calm. Monty was on remand in Strangeways and his solicitor had already told her it was going to be a life sentence for him, there was no way out. The day she heard Elsie Barker was dead had been the happiest in her life. She couldn't stop smiling. Some would say she was sick in the head but she couldn't help the way she felt inside. Karma was something she believed in and she knew someday that bitch would get what was coming to her. Jackie had stopped drinking now, not completely, she still had a few gins in the evening time but she'd stopped caning it in the day. Jackie knew she had a second shot at life and now Monty was in the slammer she planned to start making the most of it again. Jackie should have let her husband rot in jail on his own but she just couldn't do that to him. In her heart she knew he loved her but prison was the best place for him. Monty was evil and he needed to pay for the heartache he'd brought to others.

Jackie stepped out from the car and looked up at the clear blue sky. Swinging her handbag over her shoulder she made her way to see her husband. She was the one calling the shots now. She was the one who held the power. Maybe in future she could get herself a new man, she liked the younger guys and to have one in her bed would have been fun. Jackie had found herself again and even though Monty's life was set in stone, hers was only just beginning. She'd taken the precaution of withdrawing most of Monty's money over the years and anything of value had been sold. The police were still trying to track down the rest of Monty's cash but it was safe to say Jackie was minted and planned to enjoy every last penny of his ill-gotten gains. At last she had something to smile about.

Monty lay in his cell. He didn't look the same. He was half the size he used to be and the last few weeks had taken their toll on him. He was a shell of the man he used to be and any power he held on the outside had disappeared in here. He was just another number now. Fred had sold him down the river and turned Queen's evidence hoping to get a lighter sentence. What a grassing bastard he was! He was telling them everything, things that they didn't need to know about. It was always the same in the criminal world once the shit hit the fan. Everyone looked out for themselves, there was no loyalty. It was a dog eat dog world. Monty, looked at the small clock on his bedside cabinet. Jackie would be here soon and he needed to get ready. He lay on his bed with his arms looped over his head. There was no way out of what lay ahead for him, no amount of money or force could stop the sentence he was likely to receive. The inmates were eager to knock him down several pegs. He was a nobody, worse than that he was a nonce. The word was out about what he'd done to the young girls at the farm and he was living on borrowed time. The screws had put him on a protection wing with the other perverts, he was isolated. Monty was going to die a lonely old man with nobody by his side. Pulling the grey blanket over his head he hid from the crimes he had created for himself. Night after night he was on suicide watch as he'd already tried to take his life twice. What did he have to live for anymore? He was better off dead.

On the other side of town the sun was shining for the funeral of Elsie and Annie Barker. The news of their deaths had hit the neighbourhood badly and nobody could believe what had happened. Moston Lane was deserted today. The police had closed the road down due to a fire at the brothel. Arson it was, someone had seen a woman leaving the scene of the crime in the midnight hour. All night long the building had been blazing and the fire services had struggled until the early hours of the morning to control the flames. This was the best thing that could have happened to the place. The building was evil and what happened inside its walls would be talked about for years. Monty's story was on everybody's lips. The residents were up in arms. They wanted the bastard hung drawn and quartered for the crimes he'd committed. All the young girls who worked there were safe now and were undergoing counselling. Their stories were all over the national press and it really hit home how bad the world could be sometimes. The residents kept their children closer than ever now and this was a big wake-up call for everyone in the area. This could never be allowed to happen again.

June sat in the hearse with Johnny by her side. The two coffins were in separate cars in front. Everybody was out on the street to pay their respects to the family. There were numerous people attending the funeral. Rita was here today and she openly told everyone she blamed herself for her best friend's death. It was so much stress to put on her shoulders and even to this day she was still crying herself to sleep every night. Johnny sat next to June and he held her hand tightly. He still had injuries and he had a long way to go before he would be fully recovered. The police had never connected him with the massacre at the farm and as far as he was concerned he was in the clear regarding any crimes that took place there. Sandy would be waiting for him today. He was all set to leave Manchester and start a new life with her. Throughout the ordeal Sandy had been his rock, she had helped him cope and kept his mind sane. June was upset when he told her his plans but she couldn't stop him. In a way she was relieved that he would be safe and away from the area. He was right, he needed a fresh start.

When the coffins were lowered into the ground and the priest began his prayers, there wasn't a dry eye among the mourners. Sobbing and snivelling could be heard - this was such a sad time for all involved. Johnny looked down at the brass plaque with his sister's name on it and the date she had died. His emotions took over and his body folded in half. It was final now, he would never see his mother or sister again. Before the funeral he'd spent hours at the Chapel of Rest speaking to them. Somewhere during this time he'd cleansed his soul and got a lot off his chest. They just looked so peaceful, as if they were sleeping. Their faces would always be in his mind and he would never forget the good times they shared. Yes, there had been some good times in his family, it wasn't all bad. It's just sometimes life takes over and destroys any happiness a family can have. Poverty, drugs, affairs, selfishness – they all play a part in destroying a family. Johnny had a chance now to walk away from his old life and never look back. Each day he stayed on the streets of Manchester he knew that temptation would finally get to him. There were just too many opportunities to earn a few quid on the side. Johnny moved away from the graveside and stood tall with his chest puffed out. Everyone's eyes were on him and even at this sad time he hated that people could see his weakness. June was by his side now and the funeral was over. There was nothing left to do or say, it was over. The mourners walked back to the cars and headed to the "Bluebell" pub for the wake.

Johnny knocked back a double brandy. He was shaking inside and he needed to calm down. Sat in the corner of the pub he watched the world go by. He was in a world of his own, eyes dipped low into the bottom of his glass. He just wanted to be alone. "Hello Johnny," a female said in a low voice. He lifted his head up and his heart was in his mouth. "I'm so sorry about Annie and your mother. Honest, I feel like I've lost part of my family too. They were a big part of my life growing up."

Johnny picked his glass up and slurped the last few drops of brandy out of it. "Sad isn't it? But what can I do now. Shit happens and I just have to deal with it don't I?"

Natalie moved slowly and sat next to him, her hand resting on his knee. "Johnny, I need to tell you something. Something, I should have told you a long time ago."

Johnny stood and picked his glass up. "I need another drink. Do you want one?"

Natalie declined and watched him head towards the bar. From nowhere June appeared and she was poking his finger into Natalie's chest with force. "Listen you, he doesn't need any more shit in his life. Today he's buried his mother and sister and this isn't the time or place for you to start about things from the past. Johnny's leaving tonight and I want his head as clear as possible before he goes. Don't upset him, just leave him be."

Natalie casually moved June's finger from her chest and her eyes were wide open. "June, I would never hurt him intentionally. We're just talking that's all. I mean him no harm."

"Good, just keep it like that because if I hear one word from you causing him any grief I'll put you on your arse!" June sneered at her and stood tall and continued talking. "It's something I should have done years ago if I'm being honest with you."

Natalie gasped. This woman was hard work and she always had to have the last word. The two of them just stared at each other for a few seconds and not another word was spoken. June left.

Johnny was back now and he had two drinks in his hand. He slid one over towards Natalie. "You still drink Vodka don't you?" She smiled and smirked, he still remembered their time together, how sweet. Johnny looked into her eyes and for a split second he was back in his past. A time when he loved her so much that he would have done anything for her. He shook his head slightly and he was back in the moment. "I'm leaving Manchester later, so you won't have to see my ugly head on the streets anymore."

"Who are you going with? On your own?" she asked in a frightened voice.

"I'm going with Sandy; she's a good girl, faithful, loyal. Not that you know what that means."

Johnny was still having a pop at her, even after all these years. He couldn't let the past go. Natalie was sick to death of hearing his shit, it was time to come clean, to tell him how it was. "Why are you speaking to me like that? We both know how much we meant to each other. We had plans Johnny, we had a future together."

He growled over at her and his clenched fist banged hard on the table causing his glass to move. "That's bullshit, you never cared about me otherwise you wouldn't have ended it. Come on, let's have it out in the open, how long did it take before you were banging somebody else behind my back. I just landed in jail and some guy was slipping you one. That's not love, that's taking the piss in my eyes." Natalie let him have his say, she just sat back and listened as he rambled on. "Every night I cried about you Natalie for months, in fact, years. I was on my arse, at an all time low and you nearly killed me off." Natalie was getting frustrated and she was eager to tell her side of the story. Johnny told her everything about how she broke his heart and now it was her turn to speak. He shot a look at her after he'd finished speaking and raised his eyebrows. "So, there you go. At least you know now how I felt," he smirked and nursed his drink in his hand. He could see he'd upset her and tried to backtrack. "But ay, I'm so over you now and time's a good healer and all that. Life goes on doesn't it?"

Natalie let out a laboured breath and licked her lips slowly. It was time for her to speak, time for her to put her cards on the table. Natalie checked about and made sure they were alone. She looked deep into his eyes and reached over the table and touched his cold hands. "Johnny, I wanted you to change so much but you weren't listening. It was always, just one more job, just one more drug deal. It was never going to end and I couldn't live my life like that anymore. I've seen my mother do exactly the same with my dad and I hated that I was becoming her." Johnny sat back in his seat and he was listening, for years he'd wanted the answers to his questions and at last he was getting them. Natalie took a sip from her glass and continued. "On the night before you got nicked I begged you not to go out. I told you it was the criminal life or me," she paused as her eyes clouded over. "You chose crime, the graft."

Johnny wasn't taking this lying down. No way on this earth, he had reasons for his choice, real reasons. "We were skint Nat, we had no money, no electric, no gas, no cigs, where did you expect me to get the money from? We didn't have a fucking money tree growing in the back garden you know."

Natalie swallowed hard, she had to get this off her chest. "I had reasons for what I did and if you close your big trap for one second and let me finish I'll tell you why." Johnny pulled his cigarettes from his pocket, he was getting stressed and needed to calm down. He lit a fag and blew the smoke directly into her eyes. He knew she hated that and he was trying to wind her up. Natalie wafted the smoke from her face and tapped her fingernails on the table. "That morning I'd taken a pregnancy test and it was a positive result."

Johnny was puzzled, he tilted his head to the side and chewed on the side of his lip. He was never the sharpest tool in the box and the penny hadn't dropped yet. "What you was having a kid, so, why didn't you tell me?"

"Would it have made any difference? You would have still gone out that night and done whatever you were doing. I gave you the choice and you carted me." Johnny's eyes were wide open, he knew now, it registered that the baby she was carrying must have been his. This wasn't real, surely he would have known. "You got arrested that night and I never got chance to tell you. Even though you left me, I wanted the moment to be right when I told you that you were going to be a father. I had made us a special tea, I borrowed a tenner from my mam and bought candles and everything. Johnny, you never came home." A single tear streamed down Johnny's cheek, was it happiness or sadness he was feeling, he wasn't sure. He was gobsmacked and let her carry on. "I was alone Johnny. I had to do the best for me and our child. I didn't want the police knocking on our door every night, I wanted her to have the family she deserved and if that meant doing it alone then I was ready to do that. I made the choices for the right reasons - a better life for her."

Johnny was blood red. He had a child, Natalie hadn't been sleeping with anyone else whilst he was locked up, she was still his Natalie. The girl he loved with all his heart. Something was happening inside him, a warmth rising from his toes straight to his heart. He stuttered. "So, she's my kid, I'm her dad?"

Natalie smiled and gasped her breath. "Yes, she is. I should have told you the moment I found out but I just kept putting it off. Days turn into weeks and months into years and before I knew it you were due home. It's been so hard for me too. Don't you think I wanted to tell you about her? But, I wasn't bringing her to jail to see you, so what was the point? I told a few friends the truth about her but apart from that I just let everyone gossip and make their own stories up."

Johnny couldn't believe it, this was all too much to take in. "So, why now, why tell me now when I'm still the criminal you left behind. You don't want a life like that, you've just told me that."

Her heart was low and her lips trembled. "I still love you and nobody will ever come close to what we had together. You're my first love and my last love. I've tried to get over you Johnny but it's just not happened. I wish I could just switch off the feelings I have for you but it's not like that, is it?" She was after some kind of feedback from him. Did he still love her or had he really moved on?

Sandy coughed to make her presence felt, the pair of them hadn't seen her sneak up, she was as quiet as a mouse. "Sit down Sandy, I'll get you a drink" Johnny mumbled. He stood quickly, he couldn't wait to get away, his mind was working overtime, he didn't know what the hell to do.

Sandy glared at Natalie, she knew exactly who she was, she didn't need an introduction. There was an awkward silence and they were staring at one another. Natalie picked up her glass and finished her drink. She looked at Sandy and knew in her heart that this girl was more than she could ever be. She wore designer clothes, her hair was styled neatly and everything about her said class. She was no council estate bird. Natalie looked down at her black jeans and tried to wipe the blotches of chocolate from them. She was the underdog and realised now that she was better off walking away. Standing to her feet she placed her hand on Sandy's shoulder, she was getting emotional and any minute now she was would have burst into tears. "Look after him, he's a good lad really. Tell him I said good luck with his new life." Natalie left and Sandy didn't know what to make of her statement. Johnny was back now and his head was twisting one way then the other - where was Natalie? She couldn't have just upped and left. They needed to talk, he needed to see his child.

Sandy could see how agitated he was and wanted to make sure he hadn't changed his mind. "So, shall we set off tonight? I'm having tea with my mam and then I'm all yours. I'm surprised she's took it so well. I thought she would have tried to stop me leaving but she was all up for it. She told me to go and spread my wings." Johnny wasn't listening to a single word she said, he was in a world of his own and what Natalie had just told him had knocked him for six.

Johnny sat in June's front room watching the time tick by. His bags were packed and anytime now he would heading out into the big wild world away from Manchester to make a new life for himself. The thought of Natalie having his child had sent his head west. Perhaps, she'd done the best thing by not telling him. Even now his life was anything but stable and he questioned if he could ever be the father Natalie needed him to be. Johnny would always be a bad boy, trouble found him, it was just the way it was and all his life it was all he knew. Johnny was chain-smoking, if he was going to see his child he had to leave now, he had to go before Sandy came to pick him up. But, was it the right choice? He stood up, sat back down, paced the front room, he just didn't know what to do! Two paths were set before him and his head was fucked trying to work out which one to take. Sandy was ambitious, she would always do well. She would always have the best of everything. He could have that life with her instead of scrimping and scraping every day for money. She'd already said she was setting him up in business and with her help and the contacts she had they were set to rake in legitimate money on a business venture she had planned. But Natalie was the love of his life, more than that she was the mother of his child; maybe he'd get a proper job here, they could have a family…

June walked into the room and she was aware of his dilemma. All she wanted for him was happiness and to be away from the area. She sat down next to him and hugged him in her arms tightly. "I wish I could help you Johnny but it's got to be you who decides. Where is your heart at?"

Johnny didn't know anymore. Sandy was a lovely girl and she would bend over backwards for him. Where Natalie on the other hand was a different kettle of fish, she was feisty and never took any shit from him. She wanted just the basic things in life like a chip-muffin, a kebab every now and then, not fancy food like Sandy. He lifted his head up and gasped his breath. "I don't know anything anymore June. Love has got nothing to do with this. If I stay here my life will always just be me in and out of nick. I have a chance to change and I'll regret this for this rest of my life if I don't go and see for myself."

"So, you're going then?" Johnny nodded.

"Yes, I'm leaving with Sandy. I'm just going to see my mam and Annie though before I go. I've bought them a bunch of flowers each, I need to say goodbye."

June choked up and patted her hand on his knee.

"That's nice Johnny. Go on, you've not got long before you leave. Hurry up and I'll make us something nice to eat. I've got some spam in for you. I know you love it. I can throw some chips and an egg in with it too."

Johnny zipped his coat up and walked to the table to pick the flowers up. "I'll be back soon." Johnny was gone.

Johnny walked up Rochdale Road and he was taking in all the sights. In his heart he loved the place where he'd grown up and never thought he would ever move away. As he walked past Queen's Park he smiled to himself and remembered the days gone by. Every kid played in this park, especially in the summer time. He closed his eyes tightly and he could hear the screams and laughter from his youth. Brown sauce butties, mojo chews and bottles of cream soda that he'd nicked from the corner shop. They were the days, the time when he was happy. His feet quickened and before he knew it he was sat at his family's graveside. There was no headstone there yet, there were just piles and piles of flowers laid on top of their graves. They were buried next to each other, side by side. Johnny started to read some of the sympathy cards attached to the flowers and he smiled when he read the kind words from people who had loved them too. "Mam, if you can hear me, I'm leaving Manchester. I've got to go and try and make you all proud of me. I know you are looking after Annie now and my heart is calmer knowing that you are both together. This is my second chance to make it right but I need to know I'm doing the right thing. What if I could be happy with Natalie, what if she's the one?"

There was no reply to his question, no peace of mind. A blackbird hopped about not far from where he sat and he just sat watching it with a smirk on his face. "I don't suppose you've got the right answer have you, little bird?. It's all right for you, you can just fly away." The bird squawked and dug its beak deep in the ground. Johnny stood up and closed his eyes. He was praying. Before he left he made the sign of the cross across his body and smiled up at the sky.

Sandy and Johnny were heading for London. She had friends there who said they would put them up until they were sorted. Johnny was quiet and his head was resting on the car window. "Are you alright," she asked him. "Yes, it's just all so final isn't it? I'm a Manchester lad me and what if I don't fit in when we get there?"

Sandy started chuckling. "Stop thinking like that. You'll be fine. Honest, you won't look back once we get there." Her finger poked at the petrol dial. "Oh, bleeding hell. I need petrol. I need to pull over at the next service station. I'm starving anyway and we can grab a bite to eat." Johnny nodded and sat up straight in his seat. The next service station wasn't far away and he was dying for a wee.

Sandy sat in the café and started to eat her burger and chips. Johnny had been ages in the toilet and she was starting to worry about him. She picked up a chip and dipped it into her tomato ketchup. Licking her fingers slowly her eyes were fixed to the door, where on earth was he, he'd been ages. Sandy finished her food and gathered her belongings together. She stood up and left the café. The toilets were in front of her and she paced the floor outside still waiting on Johnny. He did say he had stomach ache but surely he must have finished by now. A middle-aged man was about to walk into the male's toilets and she stopped him. "Excuse me, my boyfriend went in there about ten minutes ago and he's still not come out. Can you check he's alright for me I'm starting to worry?" The man sighed and agreed. Sandy stood biting her fingernails as she waited for him to come back. Minutes later the man popped his head back through the door. "Nobody's in here love except me. I've checked every cubicle twice, he must have left."

Sandy's heart was in her mouth, she sprinted out to the car-park and checked for her car. Running at speed she twisted her head looking about the car-park. In the distance she could see it and relief was all over her face. Johnny had the keys in his pocket and for a short time she thought he'd actually got off and left her stranded. Maybe he'd got back into the car for a sleep, after all, he said he was knackered. Sandy stood at the driver's door and she could see the car keys dangling from the lock. Her head shot inside the vehicle looking for Johnny, he wasn't there. Sinking to her knees she knew now that he'd left her. She always knew that he never loved her. His heart was still with Natalie. Sandy bolted to her feet, her money, the stash. With shaking hands she opened the boot of the car. The bag was still there. Her jaw was swinging low and she blew a laboured breath. Slowly, she opened it and straight away she knew some of the money was missing. The bastard had her over. She quickly counted the bundles of money and shook her head slowly. He'd not taken a lot of cash but enough to make a difference to his life. Her eyes shot to a white folded piece of paper inside the bag. She picked it up and read her name on the front of it. It was Johnny's writing. The words "Sorry" was all it said. Sandy sobbed as she locked the boot of the car and climbed back into the driver's seat. Taking a few minutes she wiped her eyes and set off on the rest of her journey. It would never have worked anyway, she reasoned, they were from different walks of life and in reality he'd probably done her a favour. Taking a few deep breaths she smiled and mumbled. "Once a thief, always a thief," she sighed. Opening her window slowly she pulled the silver pistol from her jacket pocket and flung the firearm as far as she could into a nearby field. The gun would never be found and her secret would be safe forever more. She had done what she did for her mother and now the debt was paid in full she had no further use for it. Sandy would never come back to Manchester. This was her new life. A time for her to be happy. Sandy turned the music up and started to sing along to the radio.

Johnny arrived back in Manchester, he'd managed to get a lift with a lorry driver heading through town. Johnny had a bounce in his step now and he was smiling from ear to ear. He'd been shopping and his hands were weighed down with bags. This was the first time in ages that he had genuinely looked happy. As he walked down the street he was humming a song. Johnny walked down the garden path and placed his bags on the floor. He was rooting in his pocket and his expression changed. Here it was, the moment he'd planned in his head for years. He took a deep breath and rapped on the letterbox. Standing back from the door he prepared himself for what was about to happen next. He was anxious and forever licking at his dry lips. Natalie opened the door and it was obvious she'd been crying, her eyes were red raw. "Johnny, what are you doing here?"

Johnny was on a bended knee now and in his hands he held a small red box that was open slightly. Johnny swallowed hard and his emotions took over as he began to speak. "Natalie, I've always loved you and always will. Will you marry me?"

A small child walked into the hallway and gripped her mother's legs from behind. "Mummy, who is this, what is he doing?"

Natalie picked the girl up in her arms and kissed her. She turned to face Johnny and smiled. "This is your daddy Amy. I've told you so much about him and now he's come back from working away. We can be the happy family I told you we would be."

Johnny moved towards the child, he was blubbering and he struggled to talk. "Daddy's never leaving you again princess, not ever." The three of them shared a hug and each of their heads were touching. Johnny smiled and looked at Natalie. "So, is it a yes then, will you marry me?"

Natalie offered her hand out to him and he slid the white gold diamond ring on her finger. It was official, they were engaged. Natalie was gobsmacked when she looked at the ring, this was so expensive and the diamond was incredible. "Johnny, this must have cost a fortune where on earth did you get the money from?"

He smiled and tapped the side of his nose. "Ask no questions, I'll tell no lies, he smiled.

Some things never change do they?

THE END

Other books by this author

Broken Youth
Black Tears
Northern Girls Love Gravy
Bagheads
Teabags & Tears
The Visitors
Sleepless in Manchester
Covering Up
Riding Solo
The Pudding Club
Grow Wars
The Square
Team Handed